William Hilary Coston

The Spanish-American War Volunteer

Ninth United States volunteer infantry roster and muster - biographies - Cuban

sketches - Vol. 1

William Hilary Coston

The Spanish-American War Volunteer
Ninth United States volunteer infantry roster and muster - biographies - Cuban sketches - Vol.
1

ISBN/EAN: 9783337378455

Printed in Europe, USA, Canada, Australia, Japan

Cover: Foto ©Andreas Hilbeck / pixelio.de

More available books at **www.hansebooks.com**

THE
SPANISH-AMERICAN WAR VOLUNTEER

Ninth United States Volunteer Infantry
Roster and Muster
Biographies • Cuban Sketches

BY W. HILARY COSTON, B. D.

Chaplain Ninth United States Volunteer Infantry

Publisher of "Ringwood Home Magazine," and Author of "A Freeman and Yet a Slave"

SECOND EDITION

(Revised and Enlarged)

Camp Meade
MIDDLETOWN, PA.
PUBLISHED BY THE AUTHOR
1899

Dedication

The Spanish-American War Volunteer

is

Affectionately Dedicated

to

Major Duncan B. Harrison

the Efficient Officer and
Faithful Friend of the Private Soldier

REGIMENTAL COLORS.

Introduction.

THE compiler of the statistics of the Roster and Muster of the Ninth United States Volunteer Infantry acknowledges the incompleteness of his effort, but he is conscious that the statements made will be found accurate and reliable, so far as given, as to the formation of the several companies, and the record of the dates and places of enlistment of the men, and their initial illness. These are of primary importance to enlisted men, and will be found to be of increasing value to them. As the time of their service becomes more and more remote, the essentials will become less clear in their memories, and it will become proportionately difficult for them to establish their identity with the organization. Disease, which is ever faithfully engaged in the work of removing members of the family organization, will prove as active and diligent in taking from our regimental organization our companions, who, with us, severally suffered the fevers of possible death on San Juan Hill, at San Luis, at Camp Cheever, at El Cobre, at El Myria, at Palma, at Cristo, and at Songo, and in the hospital at Santiago. With these important truths in mind, the need of the Roster and Muster becomes plainly apparent to the reader.

The writer regrets that he has been unable to secure sketches and portraits of the entire staff, as well as those of all the line officers; but they are gentlemen of varying capacities, of keen instincts, of broad charity, and essentially excellent soldiers and efficient officers.

(7)

The Purchase of Opportunity.

THE ARMY A MEDIUM THROUGH WHICH THE
AFRO-AMERICAN MAY ACQUIRE A PLACE IN AMERICAN CIVILIZATION.

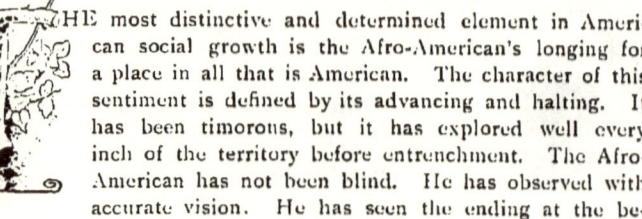 HE most distinctive and determined element in American social growth is the Afro-American's longing for a place in all that is American. The character of this sentiment is defined by its advancing and halting. It has been timorous, but it has explored well every inch of the territory before entrenchment. The Afro-American has not been blind. He has observed with accurate vision. He has seen the ending at the beginning of every American war, and has succeeded in placing his contribution prominently among the victorious achievements of the nation. Accused of cowardice, he has proved most courageous and reliable in battle. He is an object of friendly study. He has sought entrance here and there. He has been repelled, but he has lingered at the threshold of American thought, and has finally been admitted to a place in American consciousness. His presence in art and war has received respectful recognition, and in these he is assured of an increasing mental acreage for intellectual and industrial expansion, and for moral and religious development. The pessimism of despair will not deter him. He is optimistic, and will not be palsied by doubt.

Without the shedding of blood there is no salvation. The Afro-American has bled in all the wars by which our civilization has been established and perpetuated. The forces that seem to us spent are not lost to an ever-accumulating civilization. The expenditure is recompensed. New conditions are making, friendly influences are accumulating. Volcanic eruptions are not of spontaneous origin. Ages of gaseous accumulation have preceded and contributed to the eruption of today. Conditions, positive and negative, attend the progress of the race. They are confirmative and helpful; they are obstructive and violent. The latter have no permanent place in the illuminated consciousness of American desire, and hence, though they be repressive and violent, they will not survive. French history furnishes innumerable types of repressive influences, and still the people survive. The influences opposing the Protestant reformation in Germany were seemingly irresistible, yet the reforming spirit found place, passed into Switzerland, and into the Netherlands, and secured the ultimate right of people to live and to differ in religious faith and practice. The insane brutality of Russia, Germany and France has been arrested, and the Jew will find in each of these countries a sentiment of toleration sufficient to secure to him safety in life and property.

So, too, will the Afro-American find an increasing public sentiment favoring him, purchased by his beautiful gallantry and by the shedding of his blood at El Caney, Siboney, and San Juan, as well as on the bloody fields of the Civil War, that will eventually arrest, upon every inch of American territory, the most vehement hostility to him, and will expel it from every American institution. His mental equipment must be increasingly intelligent and alert; his habits increasingly industrious and reliable; his conduct increasingly moral and religious. Assiduously must he seek to remove every obstacle that would justify the most sensitive prejudice, or excite it into opposing his presence in the several branches of government service or of that of the several states.

As to the strength of our newly-acquired position in the military service of the government, I am pleased to quote from a history of the Spanish-American war, which is said by officers who commanded at Santiago to be the fairest history of the war put forth:

"While we talked, and the soldiers filled their canteens and drank deep and long, like camels who, after days of travel through the land of 'thirst and emptiness,' have reached the green oasis and the desert spring, a black corporal of the Twenty-fourth Infantry walked wearily up to the 'water hole.' He was muddy and bedraggled. He carried no cup or canteen, and stretched himself out over the stepping-stones in the stream, sipping up the water and mud together out of the shallow pool. A white cavalryman ran toward him shouting, 'Hold on, bunkie; here's my cup!' The negro looked dazed a moment, and not a few of the spectators showed amazement, for such a thing had rarely, if ever, happened in the army before. 'Thank you,' said the black corporal. 'Well, we are all fighting under the same flag now.' And so he drank out of the white man's cup. I was glad to see that I was not the only man who had come to recognize the justice of certain Constitutional Amendments, in the light of the gallant behavior of the colored troops throughout the battle, and, indeed, the campaign. The fortune of war had, of course, something to do with it, in presenting to the colored troops the opportunities for distinguished service, of which they invariably availed themselves to the fullest extent; but the confidence of the general officers in their superb gallantry, which the event proved to be not misplaced, had still more; and it is a fact that the services of no four white regiments can be compared with those rendered by the four colored regiments—the Ninth and Tenth Cavalry and the Twenty-fourth and Twenty-fifth Infantry. They were to the front at La Guasimas, at Caney, and at San Juan, and, what was the severest test of all, that which came later in the yellow fever hospital. I saw groups of the black soldiers of the Twenty-fourth Infantry carrying into their places the sick as they came, and carrying out the dead as they died, and burning the infected clothing, and scrubbing the place with chloride of lime and other disinfectants. Superb as was the behavior of the Twenty-fourth Infantry in the San Juan charge, the battle they fought for forty days in the yellow fever hospital here was a still more gallant fight, and one which cost more dearly in precious lives. And there is no name that more deserves to be inscribed in letters of gold upon the regimental flag than that of Siboney, to commemorate those who faced, in that slough of despair, that charnel-house of the wrecked army, a danger and a death more terrible than any they had to fear from the Spanish fire. * * * They sang as they came, and long before they reached the ford I knew it must be a column of the colored troops, as no other men in the army could sing as these men sang, as they came trudging along through the darkness and up to their knees in the mud:

> "'When through the deep waters I call thee to go,
> The rivers of woe shall not thee o'erflow.'

"They sang with their deep, rich voices, as they came up to the ford. I found it was the Twenty-fourth Infantry, which had been ordered back to Siboney to nurse and to guard the sick in the yellow fever hospital.* They were under orders to push on and assume their trying duties at daybreak in the morning, so I only had an opportunity to shake by the hand several of my friends in the gallant

---

*The Twenty-fourth Infantry was ordered down to Siboney simply to do guard duty. When the regiment reached the yellow fever hospital it was found to be in a deplorable condition. Men were dying there every hour for the lack of proper nursing. Major Markley, who had commanded the regiment since July 1, when Colonel Liscum was wounded, drew his regiment up in line, and Dr. La Garde, in charge of the hospital, explained the needs of the suffering, at the same time clearly setting forth the danger to men who were not immunes of nursing and attending yellow fever patients. Major Markley then said that any man who wished to volunteer to nurse in the yellow fever hospital could step forward. The whole regiment stepped forward. Sixty men were selected from the volunteers to nurse, and within forty-eight hours forty-two of these brave fellows were down, seriously ill with yellow or pernicious malarial fever. Again the regiment was drawn up in line, and again Major Markley said that nurses were needed, and that any man who wished to do so could volunteer. After the object lesson which the men had received in the last few days of the danger from contagion to which they would be exposed, it was now unnecessary for Dr. La Garde to again warn the brave blacks of the terrible contagion. When the request for volunteers to replace those who had already fallen in the performance of their dangerous and perfectly optional duty was again made, the regiment stepped forward as one man. When sent down from the trenches the regiment consisted of eight companies, averaging about forty men each. Of the officers and men who remained on duty during the forty days spent

regiment, and to wish them God-speed as they marched on through the night; but for a long time after the column had disappeared, swallowed up in the darkness, I could hear the deep, manly voices of these brave men, who shirked no duty, whether upon the battle-field or in the noisome pest-house, singing:

> "'I'll strengthen thee, help thee, and cause thee to stand,
> Upheld by My righteous, omnipotent hand.' "

The following Official Reports, extracts from the "Annual Report of the Major-General Commanding the Army," will serve to give an almost complete history of the gallant Ninth Regiment, as they cover many operations in which members of the regiment took part:

HEADQUARTERS SECOND SQUADRON,
NINTH UNITED STATES CAVALRY,
Intrenched before Santiago, June 8, 1898.

THE ACTING ADJUTANT-GENERAL, FIRST CAVALRY BRIGADE.

Sir: I have the honor to submit the following report of the part taken by my squadron of the Ninth Cavalry in the fight of July 1:

Shortly after the cannonading at Caney had begun, Dimmick's squadron of the Ninth Cavalry, under command of Lieutenant-Colonel Hamilton, Ninth Cavalry, received orders to move at the head of the brigade and follow the Cubans.

The squadron moved, in accordance with this order, along the road from El Poso toward Santiago about 300 yards, when Colonel Hamilton received orders to march on and pass the Cubans. This order was carried out, and Colonel Hamilton was ordered to throw out an advance guard. H Troop (Lieutenant McNamee) was the leading troop, and took up the advance, guard formation.

Lieutenant Hartwick, commanding the advance party, received orders to advance to the river (San Juan) and halt. This order was carried out. Shortly after this the shelling of the enemy's works by one battery at El Poso began. During this shelling the advance party was withdrawn about 100 yards, by order,

---

in Siboney, only twenty-four escaped without serious illness, and of this handful, not a few succumbed to fevers on the voyage home and after their arrival at Montauk.

The following is a complete list of those who died at Siboney:

Captain Charles Dodge.

Co A.—Privates (1) Humphrey Montgomery, (2) James R. Sidden, (3) Isaac A. Laster, (4) Grozier Appleby, (5) Budd Ashton, (6) Frank Carter, (7) W. M. M. Perry.

Co. B.—(1) Corporal Tom Robertson; privates, (2) Edward Penn, (3) Charles Diggs, (4) John Richards.

Co. C.—Privates (1) J. Nelson, (2) Robert Ramsey, (3) John Mealy.

Co D.—Privates (1) Henry Chubbs, (2) John Garrett.

Co. E.—Corporals (1) Charley Wamble, (2) James J. Buford; privates, (3) Abram Benson, (4) J. P. Phillips.

Co. F.—(1) Corporal Henry A. Shaw; privates (2) Charley Hicks, (3) Richard H. Brown.

Co. G.—Privates (1) Walter Reeves, (2) Effa J. Bassett, (3) Herman Rause.

Co. H.—(1) Corporal Lewis Johnston; musicians (2) Robert Brookes, (3) William Brent; privates (4) Carter Boggs, (5) Warren Green, (6) William Mosley, (7) Sandy Smith, (8) Mortimer Spencer, (9) William Griggs; or thirty-six deaths in all, including officers and enlisted men. Some forty men have been discharged from the regiment owing to disabilities resulting from illness which began in the yellow fever hospital.

and then ordered to again take up the advance, and to throw out flankers as soon as the river was crossed.

After crossing the river, Lieutenant Hartwick threw out skirmishers to the right, but could not do so to the left on account of the dense undergrowth.

The "point" advanced about 200 yards across the river, when three rifle shots were received from the enemy. The advance party halted; Lieutenant McNamee came forward with the support and took command. At this time General Hawkins and staff came up and reconnoitered the enemy's lines from this point. Then a party of the Sixth Cavalry came up and the advance guard, H Troop, was withdrawn about 100 yards, and moved to the right of the line, with the following formation:

The Ninth Cavalry on the right of the Sixth Cavalry, in two skirmish lines, E and C Troops in front, and H and D in rear. Shortly after this we were moved by the right flank and then forward a short distance. While lying in this position the enemy opened fire. At this fire Lieut. W. S. Wood, adjutant Ninth Cavalry, was wounded, and also two troopers of Troop D and one of Troop C. We then moved forward by rushes, but without firing. Owing to the dense undergrowth, H and E Troops overlapped the right troop of the Sixth Cavalry. This was soon remedied, and E Troop touched the Sixth Cavalry on our left, with H Troop on the right of E. C and D Troops were moved to the right and somewhat to the rear, to cover the open wheat field to our right. In the advance from this position the Sixth Cavalry moved slightly to the left and the Ninth swung to the right, each taking a different objective, ours being the San Juan house. This made a gap, which was filled by one squadron of the First Cavalry, under Captain Tutherly, who had been notified of the gap by Captain Kerr, of the Sixth Cavalry. Shortly after the First Cavalry came up and formed on our left. Colonel Roosevelt, of the First Volunteer Cavalry, rode up, followed by some of his men in skirmish order. Colonel Roosevelt said: "I understand the Ninth Cavalry is carrying this hill by rushes, and I am ordered to reënforce you. Where is your colonel?" Colonel Hamilton was then satisfying himself that the First Cavalry had formed on our left. At this point the order "forward" was given, and repeated to Colonel Roosevelt. The line, composed of Tutherly's squadron of the First Regular Cavalry, Dimmick's squadron of the Ninth Cavalry, and Roosevelt's command of the First Volunteer Cavalry, charged with a cheer and took the hill. Owing to the wire fences and dense undergrowth, the charge was one cheering, mixed mass of the commands above mentioned. Shortly after this Colonel Carroll directed Colonel Hamilton to send a detachment of men to protect the right flank. While Colonel Hamilton was leading a detachment for this purpose he was shot and instantly killed. At about this time Capt. C. W. Taylor was wounded, as were many of our men.

As soon as the death of Colonel Hamilton was reported to me by Lieutenant Hartwick, who was by his side when he fell, I assumed command, and ordered a forward movement of the Ninth Cavalry to support the First Volunteer Cavalry, advancing to the crest beyond. Captain McBlaine, Troop D, and Lieutenant Walker, Troop C, on the right, pushed promptly forward; Troop E, Captain Stedman, Troop H, Lieutenant McNamee, on the left. While this movement was taking place I was sent to have the First Cavalry, on our left, move forward with us. On returning, General Sumner directed me to hold what troops I had at that point till the hills in front had been taken. But D and C and detachments of the Tenth Cavalry had moved gallantly forward and taken the crest in their front; H and part of E, mixed with the First Volunteer Cavalry, the crest in their front.

The Ninth Cavalry was afterwards assembled and held the right of our line, which was reënforced by the Thirteenth Infantry coming up on our left.

The following-named officers took part in the engagement, and every one is deserving of the highest praise for his conspicuous conduct :

Lieut. Col. T. M. Hamilton, Ninth Cavalry, killed ; First Lieut. W. S. Wood, adjutant, wounded ; Capt. C. A. Stedman, commanding Troop E, and Capt. C. W. Taylor, commanding Troop C, wounded ; Capt. J. F. McBlaine, commanding Troop D ; First Lieut. C. W. Stevens, on duty with Troop E ; First Lieut. M. M. McNamee, commanding Troop H ; First Lieut. A. A. Barber, on duty with Troop D ; Second Lieut. K. W. Walker, squadron adjutant and commanding Troop C, and Second Lieut. E. E. Hartwick, on duty with Troop H, and acting regimental adjutant.

The bearing and conduct of the men in this fight was all that could be desired, and served to maintain the good record of the regiment.

General Chaffee relieved the Ninth Cavalry and Thirteenth Infantry about noon. I joined the cavalry division on the left of First Volunteer Cavalry.

The above is a true copy of my report made to General Sumner, commanding brigade July 8, 1898.

Respectfully submitted,

E. D. DIMMICK,
Captain, Ninth Cavalry, Commanding Squadron.

FORT SILL, OKLA., October 20, 1898.

THE ADJUTANT-GENERAL, U. S. A., Washington, D. C.
(Through troop and regimental commander Ninth Cavalry.)

Sir: Having made only a brief report as commanding officer Troop H, Ninth Cavalry, principally of casualties, after the battle of San Juan, July 1, 2 and 3, 1898, and understanding since that the reports, if any made by troop commanders, were not appended to regimental and brigade reports, I have the honor to submit a full report of the part taken by Troop H, Ninth Cavalry, in that engagement.

The troop arrived at El Poso about 12.30 a. m., July 1, with the squadron and lay down and slept until daylight. After a hasty breakfast we were soon prepared to march and waited some time for orders, the men sitting down in column of fours.

About 7 a. m. the squadron was ordered forward, and H Troop being in the lead that day, I was directed to follow the Cubans. The Cubans had filed by us about one-half hour before we started and had gone down the trail that led into the bottom toward the crossing of the rivers and the heights of San Juan. Having marched about 300 or 400 yards down this trail, we were halted on account of these men, who were standing still and who blocked up the road.

In a few minutes the brigade commander (Colonel Carroll) rode up, and we were ordered to precede the Cubans. They gave way for us, falling back in the brush and sides of the road, making an opening through the center of their column, through which we passed. When our column passed through I was ordered by Colonel Carroll, and also by our regimental commander, Lieutenant-Colonel Hamilton, to move forward my troop as advance guard till I reached the river, and there to halt and take up a position. I accordingly ordered Second Lieutenant Hartwick to move forward the first platoon as vanguard, with "point" advanced about 200 yards, and to push out flankers wherever openings in the dense brush would permit. I followed with the rest of the troop at a distance of about 300 yards, keeping up connecting files to the front and rear. I also sent out flankers from my reserve whenever a side path was crossed.

When we started to march, our batteries on the hill in our rear opened fire on the enemy at San Juan, and the guns of the enemy replied to this fire, the projectiles from both passing over us as we advanced along the road. We had advanced about a mile when Lieutenant Hartwick sent word back to me that he had reached the river (Acguadores Ford) and could see the enemy and their works distant about 700 yards. At the same time Colonel Carroll and Captain House rode up, and directed me to cross the river and reconnoiter a short distance beyond. The troop took up the march again. Lieutenant Hartwick crossed the ford and moved with the "point" cautiously up the main road and the trails leading therefrom for about 200 yards, when he received five or six shots from the enemy's small arms, the first that had been fired in this action. He then halted and deployed the men in groups along his front. I crossed over with the reserve, deployed it to the right, and moved forward in the brush and high grass till I had reached a point on a line with the advance party; ordered the men to lie down and not to fire without orders. Our line then covered the ford and stream a distance of about 300 yards.

Leaving the first sergeant with my part of the line, I moved over to the left, and sent a patrol from the advance party along a trail that led down the stream, I then went back to the ford to see if the other troops were coming up, and to receive further orders. I saw General Hawkins at this time, with some of his aids, examining the position of the enemy from the top of a tree near the ford. The squadron not appearing, I returned to my troop, and waited about half an hour. Lieutenant Wood, our adjutant, then came up from the right, and told me the squadron had crossed the stream higher up to my right, and directed me to move by the right flank and join it. The day was now extremely hot, and a heavy fire from the enemy had commenced. Lieutenant Wood was wounded, and, thinking the battle about to begin for us, I ordered the men, as they moved to the right in single file, to pile up their rolls and haversacks, and retain only arms and canteens. This was done, and I placed Saddler Lochman in charge of the property, telling him to seek cover close by. Subsequently, before daylight July 2, I had the rations brought up and later the blanket rolls, with little loss of either.

Colonel Hamilton formed the squadron in two lines, with intervals of 2 yards between troopers and a distance of about 100 yards between the lines. Troop H was placed on the left of the second line. In this manner we were moved still farther to the right, and then forward about 200 yards, made by rushes. All this time we were under a heavy fire, which seemed to fly high, however, and was probably directed against troops in our rear and still on the other side of the stream, as few men of our squadron were hit by it here. About noon we advanced about 100 yards farther, and both lines became one, Captains Taylor and McBlaine extending their troops to the right. Troop H was now the left center troop, with Captain Stedman's Troop E on my left. Meantime the troops in front had done considerable firing by volley against the position of the enemy on the first hill and house directly in our front; and while we could not see him on account of the trees, the fire from this point was severe. The whole line now continued to fire volleys by troops till about 1 p. m., when the word was given to charge. At this time the First Volunteer Cavalry that had been acting as reserve, came up from the rear and joined our line, and the two organizations charged over the remainder of the bottom, across the San Juan river, and up to the top of the hill. The loss of Troop H in this charge was: Trumpeter Lewis Fort and Private Johnson killed, and Corporal Mason, Privates Prince, Nelson, and Edward Davis wounded. On the crest of the hill the troop, like others, were intermingled with other troops, but all lined up and poured a rapid fire on the main works of the enemy on the ridge beyond. At this time our brigade commander, Colonel Carroll, was wounded, and Colonel Hamilton killed. I rallied H Troop, getting some thirty men together at the time, and moved forward with the general advance on the main position. There being no brush or wire in our front to contend with, I determined to advance now in good order. The other troops of the squadron had been called to the right. I ordered Lieutenant Hartwick to follow in rear, deployed the troop into line, and, placing myself in front of the center troop, passed over the hill, down the slope, forded the upper end of the lake, and moved quickly up the slope to the Spanish works, but the enemy had given way.

Colonel Wood, First Volunteer Cavalry, who had succeeded to the command of our brigade, came up and ordered me to move over to the right with my troop, and hold certain hills which he pointed out, at all hazards, till I was relieved. I accordingly moved over and occupied the ground indicated. I sent Lieutenant Hartwick to patrol still farther to the right, where he found C and D Troops of our squadron in position. Later the squadron was assembled on the ground occupied by me, and remained there till relieved, about 7 p. m., by the Thirteenth Infantry.

The next morning, July 2, the troop moved with the squadron to the left and rejoined the cavalry division near the center of the line. Here the troop continued digging and occupying intrenchments until the surrender of the Spanish army and the city of Santiago.

It will be seen, from the foregoing account, that my troop was the first organization to penetrate and reconnoiter the ground to the front the morning of July 1, and crossed the first river, the Acguadores, near its junction with the San Juan, several hundred yards in advance of other troops. The country is covered with a dense undergrowth, and great caution had to be exercised to avoid being ambushed by the enemy. In this connection, much credit is due Second Lieut. Edward E. Hartwick, Ninth Cavalry, who conducted the movements of the "point" and flankers in the advance. Lieutenant Hartwick pushed steadily on until he was fired on by the enemy, and directed by me to halt. This officer displayed great coolness in a very trying and dangerous position. During the assault and throughout the entire day, by his courage and prompt action, I was enabled to get the best results from the troop. I recommend him for consideration.

As to the enlisted men of the troop, they all did well and displayed patience, courage, and discipline of a high order. I wish to particularly mention Sergt. Elisha Jackson, now second lieutenant, Tenth United States Volunteers, who, during the movement in the morning, July 1, was in the extreme advance (the point), and during the whole day was ever in the front, and by his example encouraged all about him. Also Privates Bates and Pumphrey, who, while the troop was under a heavy fire, stood up and moved out from cover the better to see and fire on one of the enemy who, from a tree in front, was firing on us. Also of Sergt. John Mason and Private Nelson, who were badly wounded while charging up the hill near the head of their troop; and of Private Edward Davis, who, although suffering from a scalp wound, the blood streaming down his face, only waited to have his head bandaged when the first hill was taken, and then joined the troop in the next advance.

I feel that the record of the troop would be incomplete were this report not made, and respectfully request that it be appended to the regimental report now on file in the Adjutant-General's Office.

Very respectfully, your obedient servant,

M. M. McNamee,

First Lieutenant, Ninth Cavalry, Commanding Troop H while in Cuba.

— —

Camp A. G. Forse,

Huntsville, Ala., December 19, 1898.

The Adjutant-General, U. S. A., Washington, D. C.

(Through military channels.)

Sir: I have the honor to submit the following report of the part taken by Troop D, Tenth Cavalry, in the engagements before Santiago de Cuba, so far as it is known to me.

On the 30th of June the troop marched with the second squadron of the Tenth Cavalry, Major Wint's, from Sevilla, and encamped a few hundred yards beyond El Poso, on an eminence overlooking the basin of the San Juan river or creek. My troop served as support to Lieutenant Smith's, which was on picket about 100 yards to its front. In the morning it was placed on picket, relieving Lieutenant Smith's troop. Soon after my sentinels were posted I was ordered to withdraw my troop and prepare to march. Having done so, I took my place with my troop in the column, and, after waiting from half an hour to an hour for the column to move, marched with the column past El Poso and the division hospital in the direction of San Juan. The military balloon passed over our regiment from rear to front while we were at a halt. At a halt made soon afterwards, I was ordered to have my men strip themselves of everything but arms and ammunition. The rolls, haversacks, and canteens of my men were taken off and laid on the ground near the road, and two men detailed to remain with them as a guard. About this time our balloon commenced coming down near the head of our regiment. When about 100 feet from the ground it was fired at by the enemy's artillery. About the same time we received a volley of infantry fire coming down the road over our heads, too high to strike anyone. The troop ahead of mine started to the rear, but was soon checked. I understand that the impulse to break to the rear was imparted to it by the Seventy-first New York. My men were lying down in the road facing to the left, by order of the squadron commander, Major Wint. The enemy's fire, delivered in volleys, kept raking the road and riddling the dense foliage about us. I thought that the enemy had the range of our position, or at least the direction of this road, and that the situation demanded that the troops be moved off the road, either to the right or left, or formed so as to face in the direction from which the fire was coming. I looked around for the squadron commander, to get his permission to move my troop off the road, or make a change of front with it to the right. He was not anywhere in sight. I had seen him some time before going toward the right of our line, or head of our column. After waiting some time for him to return, I acted on my own responsibility by bringing my troop around at right angle to the road, its right resting on the road, its left lying in the wood. In this position I was free from the troop on my right, in case it should again break to the rear. I was under the impression that we were much nearer the enemy than afterwards proved to be the case, and expected the regiment to deploy across the road at any minute.

From my studying of tactics and the drill regulations, together with my limited experience in field exercises, I knew that in dismounted fighting, especially in a densely wooded country, the time comes when the direction of operations is necessarily left to the company commanders, and I judged that this time had come, or could not be far off. I did not know but that the squadron commander was disabled, and I was determined that my men should not be decimated without doing any execution through fear of responsibility or lack of initiative on my part. I felt that it would be erring on the right side to anticipate slightly the proper time for independent action on the part of company commanders. After waiting a minute or two in my new position, the enemy's fire not abating and no superior officer appearing, I faced my troop to the left and pushed into the wood far enough to clear the road by about 10 or 20 yards with the rear of my column, when I came upon a line of infantry skirmishers apparently without officers. I had my troop face to the right, or in the general direction in which the road ran, and prepared to advance. In anticipation of the difficulty of penetrating the dense undergrowth, I took immediate charge of one platoon, and gave my lieutenant, Second Lieut. J. F. Kennington, Tenth Cavalry, charge of the other, with instructions to keep his platoon in touch with mine. I then proceeded to advance in a direction generally parallel to the road which I had just left. I expected that by the time I arrived abreast of the head of my regiment I would find it deployed or deploying. Under the enemy's unaimed fire we pushed through the dense wood and undergrowth, waded a creek about knee deep, and a short distance beyond it came upon a line of troops lying in a road; but it was not our regiment. Here I received word from my lieutenant that he, with his platoon, was some distance to my right. He inquired whether he should join me. As there was a heavy fire coming down the road, and I did not wish him to expose his men unnecessarily, I answered in the negative. The bearer of the message to and from me was Sergt. George Dyals, of my troop, who was afterwards wounded so that he lost the sight of one eye. He has since been discharged for physical disability.

The wood terminated in a thin belt just beyond this road. After lying a few minutes in the road, I proceeded with my platoon through this belt of wood and came upon open ground, overgrown with tall grass reaching nearly to the waist. Here the enemy's fire seemed to come principally from our left. I accordingly faced my men to the left, and filed off in that direction. As a number of bullets dropped near us, Sergt. James Elliot, of my troop came up to me, and, pointing to a tree on our right, said that he saw something stirring in it; that it looked like a Spaniard, and that he would like my permission to fire at it. I looked at the tree, but it was so dense that I could not see into it. I had been cautioned by troops whom I had passed against firing, as there were troops of ours in front. Remarking that it might be a Cuban or one of our own men, I refused the permission. Soon afterwards, while we were lying down, Private George Stovall, of my troop, was shot throught the heart and killed; the same shot wounded Private Wade Bledsoe in the thigh. About 100 yards farther on we came upon a squad of infantrymen sitting under some trees on the edge of the aforementioned belt of wood, around an officer who was lying on his back bleeding from the face, and who died while we were there. I believe that this officer and Privates Stovall and Bledsoe were shot by the sharpshooter whom Sergeant Elliott wanted to fire at. The infantrymer stated that our men were falling back and the Spaniards advancing. We could not see any enemy. On our left was a stream, which I took to be the one which we had crossed. From the other side of it came sounds of voices and loud reports of firing. We could not tell whether they were Spanish or American, but I thought it was best to take our chances on their being American. We accordingly waded the stream, and, pushing into the wood on the opposite bank, found ourselves among the men of General Hawkins' brigade. They were lying in a road on the edge of the wood. Beyond them stretched a plain about 600 yards wide, overgrown with tall grass, like that through which we had just passed. At the farther edge of the plain was a hill about 150 feet high, now known to our troops as San Juan hill, or a part of it. On the top of this hill was a block-house and a structure that looked like a shed. Here and there a puff of light smoke indicated that the position was manned by infantry, who were firing at us. About 100 yards in front of the line which I joined was a thin line of infantry firing at the enemy on the hill. It seemed to be falling back on the main line. There was no firing in the latter. My men and myself lay down in this road with the infantry. Everybody whom I could then see was lying down except one officer of infantry, who was walking up and down the road in rear of the line, exposed to a fire which raked the road. From conversation with officers of the Sixteenth Infantry, I understand that this was Capt. George H. Palmer of that regiment. I asked him whether it was not about time to advance to the support of the line out in the plain, which seemed to me to be falling back. He replied that he supposed it would be pretty soon, and kept on walking as before.

Sergeant Elliott, of my troop, asked permission to go up to the fence and do some firing. I replied, "Go ahead, Sergeant, if you think that you can do any good." He accordingly stood up by the fence and fired seven shots, when, having attracted the enemy's fire, he fell back and lay down.

Immediately in front of us beyond the road ran a barbed-wire fence. There were no wire nippers in my troop. With a view to an advance through this fence, I dug with my hands at one of the fence posts, but soon concluded that I could not accomplish anything in that way. I then stood up and pulled and pushed at the post, but made no appreciable impression on it. So I lay down again and continued looking out on the plain for signs of an advance. After a while I observed near the edge of the open plain on our left a swarm of men breaking forward from the road. I went up to the top of the wire fence by step-ping from wire to wire near a post, and jumped off the top, calling to my men as I struck the ground to come on. Corporal John Walker, of my troop, got a bayonet and cut the wire. My men and a number of infantrymen went through the open-ing thus made. I struck out as fast as the tall grass would permit me toward the common objective of the mass of men which I now saw surging forward on my right and left — San Juan hill. The men kept up a steady double time, and com-menced firing of their own accord over one another's heads and the heads of the officers, who were well out in front of the men. I tried to stop the firing, as I thought it would seriously retard the advance, and other officers near me tried to stop it; but a constant stream of bullets went over our heads, the men halting in an erect position to fire. The men covered, I should say, about 50 yards from front to rear. They formed a swarm rather than a line. When they were not firing they seemed to be all cheering and yelling. Our firing, though wild, was not altogether ineffective, and retarded the advance less than I had thought it would. I could see the side of the hill dotted with little clouds of dust thrown up by our bullets. We evidently peppered it pretty hotly from top to bottom, and I have learned since then that many dead and wounded Spaniards were found in the trenches on the top of the hill. These casualties, however, were caused in part, perhaps mostly, by the fire of our small advance line prior to the assault.

This line was, I understand, composed mostly of classified marksmen and sharp-shooters.

As we approached the foot of the hill, our artillery commenced firing over our heads at the enemy on top of it. This caused a slowing up in the general advance. When I was about half way up the hill I was disabled by three bullet wounds, received simultaneously. I had already received one, but did not know it. What took place subsequent to my disablement, in the direction of the enemy, is known to me only through the statements of my men and others, substantiated by the deposition inclosed herewith. My platoon went to the top of the hill with the infantry, and was soon afterwards conducted by Lieut. J. J. Pershing, regimental quartermaster, Tenth Cavalry, to the line of the Tenth Cavalry, a short distance to the right.

The following men of the platoon especially distinguished themselves: Sergt. James Elliott, Corpl. John Walker, and Private (now Corporal) Luchious Smith. Sergeant Elliott and Private Smith were, during the ascent of the hill, constantly among the bolder few who voluntarily made themselves ground scouts, drawing the attention of the enemy from the main line upon themselves. Corporal Walker was with the handful of fearless spirits who accompanied Lieut J. G. Ord, of the Sixth United States Infantry, forming with that splendid young soldier the point of General Hawkins' gallant brigade, the head and front of the assault, and it was Corporal Walker who avenged the death of Lieutenant Ord.

First Sergt. William H. Givens was with the platoon which I commanded. Whenever I observed him he was at his post exercising a steadying or encour-aging influence upon the men, and conducting himself like the thorough sol-dier which I have long known him to be. I understand, to my great satisfaction, that he has been rewarded by an appointment to a lieutenancy in an immune regiment.

I think it due to the other men of my troop to say that, with one exception, they proved themselves ready to follow me wherever I would lead them. Their conduct made me prouder than ever of being an officer in the American army, and of wearing the insignia of the Tenth United States Cavalry.

The movements of the platoon commanded by Lieutenant Kennington have, I believe, been reported to you by that officer.

I took into action, including Lieutenant Kennington's platoon, but not includ-ing the 2 men left to guard the packs, 2 officers and 48 men. My losses were as follows:

Killed, Private George Stovall. Wounded, Capt. John Bigelow Jr.; Sergt. George Dyals, Sergt. Willis Hatcher, Private J. H. Campbell, Private Henry Fearn, Private Fred Shockley, Private Harry Sturgis, and Private James F. Taylor. Missing, Private James Clay.

The accompanying map, marked D, is intended to show roughly the course taken by my troop after it left the regiment, and the general direction of the attack made by the regiment.

Very respectfully,

JOHN BIGELOW Jr.,
Captain, Tenth Cavalry, Commanding Troop D.

TROOP C, TENTH CAVALRY,
In Camp in Front of Santiago de Cuba, July 5, 1898.

THE ADJUTANT, TENTH CAVALRY.

Sir: Pursuant to instructions, I have the honor to report the part taken by Troop C, Tenth Cavalry, in the engagement in front of Santiago on July 1 and 2, 1898.

The troop, with 1 officer and 51 men, left its camp (with the regiment) at 4.30 p. m. June 30, and bivouacked that night on the road about 400 yards south of the sugar mill, and after the artillery engagement on July 1, left at 9.20 a. m. for the line of blockhouses held by the enemy.

About 10.30 a. m., while on the road, the enemy opened fire. Packs were dropped nd left under guard, and the troop ordered into the river bottom, where it remained about half an hour, for protection from fire until it could deploy. While here a shell burst over the troop, and I was struck by a small fragment in the left side above the point of the hip, and received a slight flesh wound. My troop cut the wire fence to the right of the creek and deployed into the woods in the rear of the front line of the regiment, and lay under cover in support on the right of the second squadron until the command to advance was given.

While advancing, and near the road, Colonel Wood, the brigade commander, came by and told me to move my troop to the right and toward the blockhouse. I had 1 man killed and 7 wounded in reaching the top of the hill. Captain Jones came up with Troop F, Tenth Cavalry, soon after I reached the blockhouse, and I reported my troop to him, and formed, with his, a skirmish line, and moved to the blockhouses and intrenchments on the next hill. Here my troop got separated from Captain Jones's, but with 18 men of my own and several from other organizations, moved forward about 400 yards, when the fire became very severe and I had 2 men wounded, and halted.

After passing the intrenchments on the second hill my line joined that of Lieutenants Fleming and Miller, of Troop I, Tenth Cavalry, which was on my right, and from then our line was continuous. Shortly, Colonel Roosevelt and part of his regiment joined our right, and I reported to him with my troop. His command took position behind the crest which we now occupy, and that night my troop and Troop I intrenched and held the trenches during July 2 and 3, and joined the regiment July 4.

Casualties: Killed, 1 man; wounded, 1 officer, 9 men.

Very respectfully,

EDWARD D. ANDERSON,
First Lieutenant, Tenth Cavalry, Commanding Troop.

CAMP FIRST SQUADRON, TENTH CAVALRY,
June 27, 1898.

THE ASSISTANT ADJUTANT-GENERAL, YOUNG'S BRIGADE.
(Through Squadron Commander.)

Sir: I have the honor to report that on the 24th instant 2 commissioned officers and 53 enlisted men of Troop E, Tenth Cavalry, went into action, with other troops of the brigade, against the regular Spanish infantry, and were placed by General Young in person in support of Capt. J. W. Watson's (Tenth Cavalry) 2 Hotchkiss guns, and also to support the troops in our front should they need it. The position of the troop was in plain view of the Spaniards, who occupied a high ridge and had the exact range; but pursuant to their instructions, they held their position one hour and a quarter without firing a shot, for fear of firing upon our own men. Their coolness and fine discipline were superb.

In connection herewith, it gives me great pleasure to call attention to the great gallantry of Second Lieut. George Vidmer, Tenth Calvary, and Privates Burr Neal, W. R. Nelson, Augustus Wally, and A. C. White, who, under a very heavy fire, came to my assistance in carrying Major Bell, First Cavalry, to a place of safety, he being shot through the leg below the knee and his leg broken.

CHARLES G. AYERS,
Captain Tenth Cavalry, Commanding Troop E.

One corporal, W. S. White, killed, and Trumpeter W. H. Johnson slightly wounded.

Very respectfully, your obedient servant,

C. G. AYERS,
Captain Tenth Cavalry.

HEADQUARTERS TENTH UNITED STATES CAVALRY,
Camp Hamilton, Santiago de Cuba, July 20, 1898.

THE ADJUTANT-GENERAL, SECOND BRIGADE, CAVALRY DIVISION.

Sir: In obedience to instructions from your office 19th instant, I have the honor to submit report covering the operations of the regiment from July 1 to 17, 1898:

July 1.—Took part in general engagement around Santiago City, beginning at 6.30 a. m.

Killed : Troop A, John H. Smoot ; Troop B, Corpl. William F. Johnson ; Troop C, Private John H. Dodson ; Troop D, Private George Stroal ; Troop F, First Lieut. W. E Shipp (brigade quartermaster); Troop G, First Lieut. W. H. Smith and Private William H. Slaughter.

Wounded : Maj. T. J. Wint. Troop A, First Lieut. R. L. Livermore and Second Lieut. F. R. McCoy, Sergt. Smith Johnson, Corpl. Joseph G. Mitchell, Privates William A. Cooper, Benjamin Franklin, Wiley Hipsher, Richard James, Robert E. Lee, and Trumpeter Nathan Wyatt ; Troop B, Private John Chinn and William Gregorey and Peter Saunderson, on duty with Hotchkiss guns ; Troop C, First Lieut. E. D. Anderson, First Sergt. Adam Houston, Sergts. Edward Lane and Walker Johnson, Privates John Brown, William Matthews, Lewis Marshall, Benjamin F. Gaskins, and Frank Ridgely ; Troop D, Captain John Bigelow Jr.; Sergts. George Dyres and Willis Hatcher, Privates J. H. Campbell, Fred Shockley, Wade Bledsoe, William Tyler, Harry D. Sturgis, and Henry Fearn, on duty with Hotchkiss guns ; Troop E, Sergt. John L. Taylor, on duty with Hotchkiss guns, and Q. M. Sergt. William Payne, Blacksmith Lewis L. Anderson, Privates Henry McCormack, Gilmore Givens, Hillery Brown and Allen C. White ; Troop F, Second Lieut. H. C. Whitehead, Sergts. Amos Elliston and Frank Rankin, Corpl. Allen Jones, Blacksmith Charles Robertson, Privates Isom Taylor, John Watson, and Benjamin West ; Troop G, Second Lieut. T. A. Roberts, Sergt. E. S. Washington, Corpl. Marcellus Wright, Privates Charles Arthur, John Brooks, Charles Hopkins, Joseph Williams, and Samuel T. Minar ; Troop I, First Sergt. Robert Milbrown, Sergt. U. G. Gunter, Privates Frank D. Bennett, Thornton Burkley, Thomas H. Hardy, Wesley Jones, and Houston Riddill.

Firing ceased about 7.30 p. m., the regiment then occupying a part of the most advanced intrenched position. Troops on guard and extending intrenchments during the night.

July 2.—Firing commenced at 3 a. m., and became general and very heavy at 5.30

a. m. Remained in trenches during the day. Firing ceased by 7.20 p. m.; changed position about dark, 800 yards to the right, occupying and extending some works. An attack by the enemy 10 to 10.35 p. m. Very heavy fire, artillery and musketry. Wounded : First Lieut. M. H. Barnum, regimental adjutant. Troop A, Private Luther D. Gould ; Troop C, Private Benjamin F. Tyler ; Troop D, Trumpeter Sprague Lewis and Private John F. Taylor and Second Lieut. H. O. Willard. Work on intrenchments continuing during night, heavily guarded.

July 3.—Heavy firing 5.46 a. m., musketry fire, shells from artillery. Heavy firing from navy heard about 9 a. m., off Santiago City. Flag of truce 12 m. All firing to cease at 12 m. until further orders, by order of General Shafter. 1 p. m., work on bombproof inaugurated ; also drainage to intrenchments looked after, sinks for refuse about camp, and latrines for the regiment. Wounded : Troop A, Private W. H. Brown and Private John Arnold, Troop G.

July 4.—Flag of truce all day ; extending works, sand-bag revetments constructed. Heavy firing by navy heard about noon. Command assembled at 12 m.; General Miles' telegram concerning battle of 1st read ; bands playing national airs.

July 5.—All quiet ; flag of truce. News of Admiral Cervera's fleet reached camp.

July 6.—Work on fortifications and bombproof continuing. Truce off at 5 p. m. No firing. Two batteries of Second United States Artillery, with mortars, arrived ; work on intrenchments resumed.

July 7.—Flag of truce at 5 a. m. All quiet ; armistice ; General Shafter passes through camp. More work given to occupy.

July 8.—Flag of truce 5 a. m.; work on bombproofs and intrenchments continued ; all quiet.

July 9.—Flag of truce. Strengthening of position continued.

July 10.—Firing commenced at 4.30, small arms and artillery. Spanish very slow in replying ; ceased about 7.15 p. m.

July 11.—Pickets firing 5 30 a. m.; firing more general about 6 a. m. New troops arriving ; cease firing sounded 1.05 p. m. Firing heard until 1.45 p. m. Terrific rain and thunder storm during night.

July 12.—All quiet ; General Miles passes through camp. Truce.

July 13.—Truce ; all quiet ; strengthening works.

July 14.—Three flags of truce ; early a. m. notice of attack to commence at 12 m.; news of surrender received in camp ; work of strengthening position suspended.

July 15.—All quiet ; truce. Gathering loose ammunition from about intrenchments.

July 16.—Truce.

July 17.—Command put in line of trenches to witness formal surrender of General Toral, commanding Spanish forces, from 9 to 9.30 a. m., and again at 12 m. to greet the ascent of the American flag over the Province of Santiago de Cuba.

Very respectfully,

T. A. BALDWIN,
Lieutenant-Colonel Tenth Cavalry, Commanding Regiment.

- - - - -

HEADQUARTERS SECOND BRIGADE, CAVALRY DIVISION,
Camp Hamilton, Cuba, July 22, 1898.

ADJUTANT-GENERAL, CAVALRY DIVISION,

Sir : In compliance with your letter of July 19, I have the honor to submit the following report, covering the operations of this brigade from July 1 to and including the surrender, July 17 :

On the night of June 30 the brigade camped at El Poso, about 3 miles east of Santiago. Camp was broken at 5 a. m. July 1, and at about 6.30 a. m. Captain Grimes' battery opened fire on the blockhouse on the San Juan hill, about a mile east of Santiago. This fire was promptly replied to by the Spaniards. This brigade, with the rest of the army, was soon put in march toward San Juan, the leading regiment of the brigade being the First Volunteer Cavalry. After proceeding about half way to the San Juan hill, the leading regiment was directed to change the direction to the right, and by moving up the creek to effect a junction with General Lawton's division, which was then engaged at Caney, about 1½ miles toward the right, but was supposed to be working toward our right flank. After proceeding in this direction about half a mile, this effort to connect with General Lawton was given up, and the First and Tenth Cavalry were formed for attack on the East Hill, with the First Volunteer Cavalry as support. During this attack on the East Hill, and as a continuation of it the attack and capture of the next range of hills by assault, the entire brigade became involved. Due to the rank vegetation, more or less mixing of commands took place at this time, but no confusion resulted, as each soldier acted with such organization as he found himself with until the action was over, when he joined his proper command. Firing ceased at about 7 30 p. m., and our men threw up such intrenchments as were possible during the night, our position being on the commanding crest on which is located the San Juan blockhouse, and extending to the westward and around the city of Santiago. This crest commanded the remaining Spanish intrenchments and also the city. Early on the morning of July 2 firing began, and by half past 5 it was general. The position of the two armies remained the same. Firing ceased at 7.20 p. m. During the early night several changes in the position of regiments were made, which left this brigade as follows : First Cavalry connecting with General Chaffee's brigade on the right ; Tenth Cavalry connecting with First Cavalry, and First Volunteer Cavalry connecting with Tenth Cavalry, with First Brigade, Cavalry Division, on left of First Volunteer Cavalry. During the night the trenches were extended and improved. A determined attack on our lines was made from 10 to 10.30 p. m., but was repulsed. Firing began at 5.45 a. m. on the 3d and continued until 12 a. m., when it was stopped by order of General Shafter and flag of truce sent out. Work on splinter proofs began at 1 p. m. and continued until men were well protected in this respect. Sand bags also distributed and utilized on trenches and approaches. Flag of truce in effect on July 4 and 5, and until 5 p. m. July 6. No firing between this hour and 5 a. m. July 7, when another flag was out. Until 4.30 p. m., July 10, there was no firing, but intrenchments were improved and extended. At 4.30 p. m., July 10, small-arms and artillery firing was resumed by our forces, and continued until 7.15 p. m. Reply of Spaniards slow and ineffective. On July 11 picket firing began about 5.30 a. m. At 6 o'clock it was more general and continued until 1.05 p. m., when "cease firing" was sounded. Truce in effect July 12, 13, and until 12 m. July 14, when attack was to begin. News of surrender received before hour for attack, and work of improving intrenchments suspended. July 15 and 16 quiet. Command formed on July 17 at trenches, to witness formal surrender of General Toral's forces.

Very respectfully,

T. A. BALDWIN,

Lieutenant-Colonel, Tenth Cavalry, Commanding.

HEADQUARTERS TENTH UNITED STATES CAVALRY,
Before Santiago de Cuba, July —, 1898.

ADJUTANT-GENERAL, SECOND BRIGADE, CAVALRY DIVISION.

Sir: I have the honor to submit the following report of the part taken by the Tenth Cavalry in the battle of July 1, 2, and 3, 1898, before Santiago de Cuba:

On the morning of July 1 the regiment, consisting of Troops A, B, C, D, E, F, G, and I, field and staff, occupied a position on the left of the Second Brigade, Cavalry Division, the line extending nearly north and south on a ridge some 3 or 4 miles from Santiago. At about 6.30 a. m. a battery of artillery, posted a short distance from our right, opened fire upon the works of Santiago, the regiment being exposed to much of the return fire of the enemy's batteries. After the artillery firing had ceased the regiment moved to the right, passed the sugar mill, and proceeded in rear of the brigade down the road leading toward Santiago. The movement was delayed as we approached the San Juan river, and the regiment came within the range of fire about one-half a mile from the crossing. Upon reaching the river I found that the Seventy-first New York Volunteers were at the crossing, and that the regiment preceding mine had gone to the right. The Tenth Cavalry was here subjected to a converging artillery and infantry fire from the three blockhouses and intrenchments in front and the works further to the left and nearer to Santiago. This fire was probably drawn by a balloon, which preceded the regiment to a point near the ford, where it was held. I was directed to take a position to the right, behind the river bank, for protection. While moving to this position and while there the regiment suffered considerable loss. After an interval of twenty or thirty minutes I was directed to form line of battle in a partially open field, facing toward the blockhouses and strong intrenchments to the north occupied by the enemy. Much difficulty was found on account of the dense undergrowth, crossed in several directions by wire fences. As a part of the cavalry division under General Sumner, the regiment was formed in two lines, the first squadron, under Maj. S. T. Norvell, consisting of Troops A, B, E, and I, leading; the second line, under Maj. T. J. Wint, consisting of Troops C, F and G. Troop D, having crossed further down the river, attached itself to a command of infantry, and moved with that command on the second blockhouse. The regiment advanced in this formation in a heavy converging fire from the enemy's position, proceeding but a short distance, when the two lines were united into one. The advance was rapidly continued in an irregular line toward the blockhouses and intrenchments to the right front. During this advance the line passed some troops of the First Cavalry, which I think had previously been formed on our right. Several losses occurred before reaching the top of the hill, First Lieut. Willam H. Smith being killed as he arrived on its crest. The enemy having retreated toward the northwest to the second and third blockhouses, new lines were formed and a rapid advance was made upon these new positions. The regiment assisted in capturing these works from the enemy, and with the exception of Troops C and I, who in the meantime joined the First Volunteer Cavalry, then took up a position to the north of the second blockhouse, remaining there during the night.

With some changes in the position of troops, they held this line on the 2d and 3d under a very heavy and continuous fire from the enemy's intrenchments in front, and the regiment now occupies a part of the most advanced intrenched position. Some troops lost their relative positions in line during the first day of the battle, but attached themselves to others and continued to move forward.

During the entire engagement the regiment acted with extraordinary coolness and bravery. It held its position at the ford and moved forward unflinchingly, after deployment through the dense brush under the heavy fire from the enemy's works. The officers and men in general throughout exhibited great bravery, obeying orders with unflinching alacrity while attacking with small arms an enemy strongly posted in intrenchments and blockhouses and supported by artillery.

Per cent. of officers killed and wounded, 50; of enlisted men, 16½; for whole regiment, 18.

Very respectfully,

T. A. BALDWIN,
Lieutenant-Colonel, Tenth United States Cavalry, Commanding.

TROOP A, TENTH CAVALRY,
Near Santiago, July 5, 1898.

ADJUTANT TENTH CAVALRY.

Sir: I have the honor to report, in accordance with instructions from your office of this date, the following relative to the part taken by Troop A, Tenth Cavalry, in the actions against the Spaniards of July 1, 2, and 3, 1898:

On the morning of July 1 the troop formed part of the support to a battery of artillery on the extreme front of the line of troops. After the battery removed from the action the troop was ordered out on the road leading toward Santiago, and in the direction of the intrenchments and blockhouse occupied by the Spaniards. The troop was on the right of the First Squadron of the Tenth Cavalry. After proceeding for probably a mile and a half, the latter part of which march was under heavy fire from the enemy, the troop was directed to take its place in line on the left of the First United States Cavalry. In accomplishing this the troop passed under a heavy fire of shell and of musketry. Shortly after this formation the troop, in connection with the others on its right and left, was ordered to change its front and move in line against the Spanish blockhouses. The fire from the enemy at this time was very heavy. I had lost two men wounded in forming line upon the creek bank, and in this movement forward the troop was much impeded by heavy thickets and dense chaparral. The rush forward was continued without intermission. A portion of the right platoon, under Lieutenant Livermore, became separated in one of the thickets, and under instructions received personally from the brigadier-general commanding, continued up the slope toward his right and toward the first blockhouse. The balance of the troop, with Lieutenant McCoy and myself, also moved in that direction, but, observing that a large number of troops had succeeded in reaching the slope on account of their shorter line, I continued my march at a rapid gait to a point nearer the second blockhouse, swinging the troop in a diagonal direction and advancing, firing and receiving fire, until I reached the summit of the hills between the second and third blockhouses. Upon this crest I was directed by an aid of the brigadier-general commanding to hold the ridge. At this juncture Lieutenant Livermore arrived, having come by way of Blockhouse No. 1. During his march he had been subjected to a heavy fire, losing several men wounded.

The troop held the crest referred to for about an hour, at times being subjected to an extremely heavy fire from about 150 Spaniards, who were in line in front of their barracks, and others in the timber who had retreated from the blockhouses and were continuing the fight. The fire at one time became so heavy and the line of the Spaniards appeared so regular that I was apprehensive that my force might be too small to hold the ridge. Lieut. H. G. Lyon, Twenty-fourth Infantry, appeared at this juncture and offered to submit himself to my orders. I had just previously discovered Lieut. J. B. Hughes' Hotchkiss mountain battery approaching the position. I requested him to place one of his guns in action, which he promptly did, Lieutenant Lyons forming on the left of the gun and opening fire, A troop being on the right of the gun. I held the position until the arrival of a light battery and other troops, among them the Seventy-first New York, when I placed my men parallel to the position on the opposite side of the road, and in contact with the squadron of the Tenth Cavalry, to which I belonged, which had in the meantime arrived at that point. During this time Lieut. F. R. McCoy was severely wounded while actively directing the fire of this platoon. I had lost up to this time 1 enlisted man killed and several wounded. While in the position above referred to, and in contact with the squadron, the troop lying below the ridge, Major Wint directed that the crest be occupied, as the enemy had increased his fire upon our lines. Troop A was immediately moved forward and opened fire, having 1 man wounded at this point, and 1 man killed in the line, a straggler from the infantry. The fire ceased about dark and the troop lay under arms in its place under the hill. A detail from the troop assisted in building earthworks during the night.

On the morning of July 2 the troop moved with the squadron up into the rifle pits, a short distance to the right of the previous position, where details from the troop engaged the enemy during the entire day, one man of the troop being wounded while in the rifle pit. On the evening of the 2d the troop moved to a point still farther to the right, assisted in digging rifle pits within 500 yards of the advanced works of the enemy. During the 3d the firing between the lines of rifle pits was continuous until about noon. The troop is now occupying this position.

During the series of close fights on the 1st, and in the engagements in the rifle pits up to the 3d at noon, the troop lost 1 officer wounded, 1 enlisted man killed, and 11 enlisted men wounded.

I respectfully invite the attention of the regimental commander to the fact that, in my judgment, the conduct of the officers of Troop A, First Lieut. R. L. Livermore and Second Lieut. F. R. McCoy, could not be surpassed for coolness and the skillful performance of duty under heavy fire, and I recommend that proper recognition of their gallant service be bestowed by proper authority. The behavior of the enlisted men was magnificent, paying studious attention to orders while on the firing line, and generally exhibiting an intrepidity which marks the first-class soldier.

Very respectfully, your obedient servant,

WM. H. BECK,
Captain, Tenth Cavalry, Commanding Troop A.

—

IN THE FIELD, NEAR SANTIAGO DE CUBA,
June 27, 1898.

THE ADJUTANT, TENTH CAVALRY.

Sir: In obedience to verbal instructions of this date I report as follows relative to the affair of June 24 with the Spaniards at La Guasimas:

Shortly after the Hotchkiss guns, under Captain Watson's direction, opened fire upon the Spanish position, and the squadron of the First United States Cavalry had been deployed in front of the works occupied by them, I was directed to take my troop (A, Tenth Cavalry) and proceed to the left of Captain Galbraith's troop of the First Cavalry, which was on the left of the First Cavalry squadron, and support him. This I immediately proceeded to do. I found Captain Galbraith's troop, and after a short consultation with him, extended his line with my troop and pushed the line parallel to the hill upon which the Spaniards were located. The First Cavalry squadron was pushing its line forward in their front. I judged this by their firing. My line was at a right angle, approximately, to that of the First Cavalry as I proceeded on the extension of Galbraith's line.

Finding that the hill to the south of that upon which the Spaniards were located was, in my judgment, too far for effective carbine firing, I moved steadily on, deflecting to the right, and proceeded on the southern slope of the hill upon which the Spaniards were intrenched, nearly reaching the summit, when I discovered the First United States Volunteers on my left and communicated with them, stating what troop I commanded. This made the line continuous from the right of the First United States Cavalry squadron to the left of the First United States Volunteers. I continued my line of march until I reached the summit of the hill upon which the Spaniards were intrenched, to the south and west of their works. I sent Lieutenant McCoy, of my troop, along the ridge to discover if the Spaniards still occupied their works. He returned, reporting that they had left.

While I was proceeding, as above stated, I heard heavy firing in the direction in which I was pushing, which I ascertained afterwards was the firing occasioned by the attack of the First United States Volunteers upon the Spaniards in their front.

During my entire march I received the fire from the enemy at times, but could not see him, and reached the point at which I was aiming to intercept the Spaniards on their retreat but a few moments after they had fled.

The side of the hill was extremely rough, covered with Spanish daggers, dense chaparral of all kinds, and rocky, making it impossible to see for any distance.

After receiving Mr. McCoy's report I crossed the summit of the hill and marched down the north side, thus completely covering the ground occupied by the Spaniards in our immediate front.

I found toward the eastern part of the summit a wounded man of B Troop, Tenth Cavalry, and a number of stragglers from the First Cavalry, and troops of the Tenth Cavalry, whom I brought in.

I will add that the enlisted men of A Troop, Tenth Cavalry, behaved well, silently and alertly obeying orders, and without becoming excited when the fire of the enemy reached them.

I am, sir, very respectfully, your obedient servant,

WM. H. BECK,

Captain, Tenth Cavalry, Commanding Troop A.

Report of Operations of Troop I, Tenth Cavalry, on July 1, 2 and 3, 1898.

July 5, 1898.

ADJUTANT-GENERAL, SECOND BRIGADE, CAVALRY DIVISION,

About 3.30 p. m., June 30, 1898, troop received orders to move. About 4 p. m. troop started with regiment, but owing to delay did not get into position until after dark. Troop bivouacked alongside of road with regiment. Remained there during bombardment of next morning. Returned with regiment; left packs alongside of road under charge of guard, and lay down under such cover as possible. Two men in troop were wounded here while troop was marching along road. Troop remained here about five minutes, when I received orders to move to right of road.

We moved to the right, crossed creek, and moved alongside of creek to fairly good cover. Remained here for about half an hour, exposed to a pretty heavy artillery fire. Then received orders to move forward and form skirmish line on edge of creek, perpendicular to last position. Troop moved forward from this position by successive movements until the second creek was reached, when troop moved to right and crossed creek. The left of troop, under command of Lieut. A. M. Miller, moved directly up the hill and participated in attack on blockhouse on right of enemy's position. This part, under Lieutenant Miller, afterwards crossed the valley between the blockhouses, and was in the attack on the blockhouse on left of enemy's position. It then moved forward with the First Regular Cavalry and First Volunteer Cavalry until it reached the position now held by First Volunteer Cavalry, the latter being on left and Regular cavalry on right. The right of troop, under my command, passed creek, bore to right, crossed fence into road, moved down road about 30 yards, crossed through fence to right of road, and took position behind ridge, a short distance to right of fence ; from this position advanced through swampy ground to right of pond directly on trench between two blockhouses. In this charge the troop had caught up with preceding troops and was well up to the front. Troop occupied ground in front of this trench, and fired volleys at enemy's next line of intrenchments, while the enemy was manning them. Troop then advanced through wire fence, and advanced to extreme edge of hill, now occupied by intrenchments of First Volunteer Cavalry. There were First Volunteer Cavalry and Tenth Cavalry in this position— in all, about 100 men. Lieutenant Anderson, of the Tenth, here joined me. Remained here about an hour, when was informed line was being formed in the rear. Went back and formed on left of First Volunteer Cavalry. Troop assisted in digging trenches that night.

July 2.—Part of troop in trenches ; remainder about 20 yards in rear until about 2 p. m., when it was ordered down to base of hill. Men in trenches relieved at 6 p. m. At night attack troop formed line, under orders, near crest of hill, near position in camp.

July 3.—Remained in camp until 3 p. m., when troop was ordered to right, and joined rest of regiment.

Losses.—Wounded : First Sergt. Robert Millbrown, Sergeant Gunter, Private Bennett, Private Burkley, Private Hardy, Private Wesley Jones, Private Riddell. Missing : Private J F. Chinn Jr.

The entire troop behaved with great gallantry. I have no special recommendation to make. One recruit, Private Elsie Jones, particularly distinguished himself. I have recommended him before. in fight of June 2.

Lieutenant Miller conducted himself with great coolness, and used good judgment in giving orders.

Very respectfully,

R. J. FLEMING,
First Lieutenant, Tenth Cavalry, Commanding Troop I.

ASSISTANT ADJUTANT-GENERAL, SECOND BRIGADE, CAVALRY DIVISION.
(Through military channels.)

Sir: I have the honor to submit the following report of the operations of Troop I, Tenth Cavalry, under my command, in the action of the 24th of June:

Strength of troop: Officers—First Lieut. R. J. Fleming, Tenth Cavalry, commanding Troop I; Second Lieut. A. M. Miller, Tenth Cavalry. Enlisted men— Sergeants, 7 ; corporals, 6 ; privates, 37 ; total, 50. Aggregate, 52.

The troop was on road leading out into open space where action commenced, and was the third troop in the Tenth Cavalry squadron. In this position the troop was well protected by high banks on either side of road. I heard an order from the brigade commander to the squadron commander, Major Norvell, to send forward two troops of the Tenth. Not knowing that Captain Beck's troop had already gone forward, I did not immediately move out, until Troop B, in my front had gone about 30 yards. Then the squadron commander informed me that I should also go forward. I moved out, with troop inclined to the right, into the thick underbrush on right of road, then moved forward until left of my troop rested against old fence where the hospital was afterwards placed. In this movement to the right I passed beyond B Troop, which I found posted just as I entered woods on right of road. This troop, as we moved forward, inclined to the right, and during the remainder of action was on my right. Up to this time I had no knowledge of the position of the enemy.

While the troop was in this position, with left against wooden fence, I moved out into the open space on the left and met Major Bell, First Cavalry, who informed me that the First Cavalry was in front of my left, and cautioned me not to fire to the front. By this time I discovered that the enemy was posted on the high ridge immediately in front and to the right. I moved back to the troop, moved them to the right so as to uncover the First Cavalry as much as possible, and then moved directly for the hill, seeking cover wherever possible, and advancing on the run across open spaces. On account of not knowing the position of First Cavalry, my men were cautioned not to fire unless by order of an officer. After arriving at the steep part of ridge the ascent was very difficult. The underbrush was impenetrable in most places, the side of the ridge being covered, in addition, by a thick, prickly weed, through which paths had always to be cut with knives and sabers.

In only two cases did I see any of the enemy, when I allowed part of my men to halt and fire ; but with these two exceptions we advanced steadily, as the cover was perfect. The advance, however, was very slow, owing to the difficulty of getting through. Just before we struck the first fortification of the Spaniards, the left of my line caught up with the right of Captain Wainright's troop, of the First, under command of Lieutenant Witman, who reached the top of the hill immediately before my troop. I passed along the top of the ridge until I reached the descent on the other end. The detachment of First Cavalry passed down and joined the troop, and I posted outposts on the ridge in order to protect the right of our line in the valley below.

Shortly after Colonel Wood, of the First Volunteer Cavalry, came to my position and ordered me to establish outposts. When he learned I had already done so he told me to remain until relieved. I was relieved shortly after, but remained in position until 3.30 p. m., when I marched back to camp.

Three men (privates) were wounded in troop, all while in position near wooden fence at commencement of advance.

Wounded—Kelley Mayberry, Amos B. Reed, sent to hospital ship ; Wesley Jones, shot in hand, but remained during the fight ; slight wound.

The entire troop behaved with great coolness and obeyed every order. Owing to the underbrush it was impossible for me to see but very few men at a time, but as they all arrived on the crest about the time I did, or shortly after, they certainly advanced steadily.

I would especially like to mention the conduct of three men who were under my personal observation: Farrier Sherman Harris, for unusual coolness and gallantry. He kept constantly in advance and picked out the best cover for the men in his immediate rear. Wagoner John Boland, for coolness in action. I think he killed the

Spaniard found on crest, as we could see one man standing behind tree, about 400 yards from us, and Boland coolly fixed his sight and took careful aim and fired, although the bullets were falling very thickly around us, as the enemy had apparently discovered our position. Immediately after he fired the Spaniard either jumped or fell, but he looked as though he fell. Boland remained there until the firing ceased. Private Elsie Jones, for unusual coolness and gallantry. He has been only two months in the service, but behaved like a veteran. I would also like to mention the conduct of Second Lieut. A. M. Miller, of my troop. He displayed great coolness and gallantry, and used the best judgment in directing the movements of the men under his command.

Very respectfully, your obedient servant,

R. J. Fleming,
First Lieutenant, Tenth Cavalry, Commanding Troop.

Report of Gun Detachment, Second Cavalry Brigade, composed of Tenth Cavalrymen, on July 1.

Before Santiago de Cuba, July 1, 1898.

Adjutant-General, Second Cavalry Brigade.

Sir: I have the honor to report that on July 1, 1898, this detachment went into action on the road about 100 yards beyond the first crossing of the San Juan creek and opened up on the blockhouse and intrenchment about 600 yards to the right of the road and did some effective work with 8 or 10 shots, and, not having any cover, was forced to retire, having 2 men wounded in a very few moments—Sergt. J. G. L. Taylor, Troop E, Tenth Cavalry, and Private Peter Saunders, Troop B, Tenth Cavalry. I later opened fire with one gun on hill at second blockhouse nearest the town, on an intrenchment occupied by Spanish troops, and forced them to leave the same. After a few shots I was relieved by a light battery and retired. Shortly after, with two Hotchkiss guns and a machine gun, I took position on crest occupied by a troop of the First United States Cavalry (Captain Galbraith's), and with the Hotchkiss guns did some effective work on a blockhouse in our immediate front, about 800 or 900 yards distant. The machine gun did good work on an intrenchment.

I wish to mention as particularly meritorious and gallant, Sergeant Watson and Private Saunders, both of Troop B, Tenth Cavalry, in aiding a wounded corporal of the Third Cavalry to a hospital under a heavy artillery fire, he being deserted by everyone else. The same men deserve special mention for their magnificent behavior during the entire time they were in action. Private Saunders was wounded in the first action and taken to the rear. I also want to mention Private Daniels, of Troop F, for gallant behavior in the first action.

Very respectfully,

James B. Hughes,
First Lieutenant, Tenth Cavalry, Commanding Detachment.

Palo Alto, Puerto Principe Province, Cuba, July 8, 1898.

Adjutant-General, U. S. Army, in the field.

Sir: In compliance with instructions from the commanding general, I proceeded rom Port Tampa, Fla., June 21, 1898, with 50 men of M Troop, Tenth Cavalry (mounted), and Daly's pack train of 65 animals, aboard the steamship Florida, and with the steamship Fanita, both loaded heavily with cargo of ammunition, provisions and clothing, General Nunez and staff, and 375 armed Cubans, to the south coast of Cuba, and attempted a landing at San Juan river, June 29, the point first chosen by General Nunez. The point was guarded by Spaniards, who fired upon landing party without effect. I spent the night in small boats in futile attempts to land, the difficulty being due to a coral reef which lined the entire coast, and prevented the boats from touching shore. Hence we were unable to engage the land forces, and decided to seek another landing place. This would have been an ideal point to land had the coast been of sand and the cargo less bulky.

June 30, sailed down the coast to Tunas, and in afternoon attacked the blockhouse at Tayabacoa, which was defended by about 100 regular soldiers, intrenched. The blockhouse was shelled by my convoy, the gunboat Peoria, under Captain Ryan, while a small force of Cubans and Rough Riders, under Mr. Winthrop Chandler, attacked by land. I cannot speak too highly of the gallantry of Mr. Chandler's men, who fought overwhelming numbers until dark, when they withdrew under cover of darkness with the loss of 1 killed (General Nunez's brother) and 7 wounded out of a party of 28 men. The Florida, while moving nearer land with reënforcements, ran aground, and for twenty hours was completely at the mercy of a land battery of even small caliber.

July 1 the situation had not changed for the better. The Spaniards were being rapidly reënforced; a regiment of cavalry and over 500 infantry and several batteries of artillery arrived in plain sight and began to throw up heavy intrenchments on shore. Our gunboat was too small to hope to cope with the land forces, and after making every effort to haul the Florida afloat I was compelled to lighten cargo by transferring to Fanita, and throwing overboard some of the heaviest articles. About noon, however, the gunboat Helena came unexpectedly to our assistance, shelled the blockhouse, and hauled the Florida afloat.

Captain Swineburne deserved and received my sincere thanks for his timely assistance. The Spaniards were completely deceived by the formidable display, and a waterman, captured by the Peoria during the night, having informed me that the nature of the expedition was unknown on shore, and that the belief existed that United States troops intended landing in force at Tunas, I decided to adopt a ruse in order to concentrate all the Spaniards in and around Tunas while I effected a landing elsewhere. I therefore called upon Captain Swineburne early on the morning of the 2d, and laid my plans before him. He readily consented to aid me, and at 9 a. m., in company with the Peoria, opened a terrible fire upon the Spanish blockhouse and intrenchments in and around the town of Tunas. The Spanish replied with great spirit, and kept up their fire until their guns were all completely silenced by the fire from the gunboats. The fort and adjacent houses and some shipping were destroyed, and report says many men killed and the railroad depot destroyed. The effect of this bombardment was as was calculated. The troops were rapidly concentrated at Tunas, while we steamed 40 miles down the coast to Palo Alto, leaving the Helena to keep up the deception.

Arriving at Palo Alto, I found a good landing in a swampy and unfrequented district; made connection with General Gomez, and since July 3 have been steadily unloading within 12 miles of the trocha and of the strongly garrisoned town of Jucaro. The Spaniards are concentrating within a few leagues, and at this writing it is difficult to say whether I shall be able to get the entire cargo off before the attack. I have placed my troop in the camp of Gomez, and will remain in the island, sending the ships back by First Lieut. G. P. Ahearn, Twenty-fifth Infantry,

who came with me as a volunteer, and who has been very useful and efficient
during the entire trip.   In this connection I wish to call attention to a very gallant act of his, displayed the night of the attack upon the blockhouse at Tayabacon.
Several wounded men were left ashore under the guns of the fort, and Lieutenant
Ahearn volunteered to go after them.   The night was a bright moonlight one, and
several boats sent out had returned, not daring to go close to land, when Lieutenant Ahearn took a water-logged boat and crew of regulars, landed and brought
away the wounded men.   It was considered, and deservedly so, a very gallant deed.
I have placed Lieutenant Ahearn in charge of the next expedition, which I hope will
be approved by the commanding general.   I can do more good here in securing the
landing for him.   There are 500 horses yet to come and some ammunition.   I have
instructed Lieutenant Ahearn to report in person to the commanding general, in
order to give him information of importance, which I think can be done better by
him than through written report.   I shall hang around the coast and await the next
expedition.

I would request that the balance of my troop, M, Tenth Cavalry, be sent to me
by Lieutenant Ahearn upon his return trip.   The Cubans are greatly encouraged
by the timely assistance, as they were in a starving condition.   The suffering is fearful, they tell me, throughout the land.   It is very necessary to have a good naval
escort.   Captain Ryan, of the Peoria, has done splendid work for the success of the
present trip, and, if possible, I should like to see him detailed for the next trip.

Very respectfully,

C. P. JOHNSON,
First Lieutenant, Tenth Cavalry, Commanding Cuban Expedition.

———

NEAR SANTIAGO, CUBA, July 5, 1898.

ADJUTANT TENTH CAVALRY.

Sir: I have the honor to submit the following report of the action which took
place on this field July 1, 2 and 3, 1898:

Troop F, Tenth Cavalry, which I commanded, was in column of twos in the road,
as a halt, awaiting the passage of a column of infantry, when fire from the Spanish
intrenchments opened.   The troop came under a very severe fire—musketry and
artillery—at once, with no means of determining from whence the fire came, as all
view was entirely cut off by the densest underbrush which lined the road, and
no effective cover to get to.   After something like half an hour of this fire the
squadron was put in the attacking line as support and moved forward.   In the brush
and amid the roar of guns all sight of the firing line and touch of adjoining troops
was lost.   Lieutenant Whitehead, and a part of the second platoon, were also
separated from the troop, and I think passed in front of the troop from left to right
during the advance.   Lieutenant Whitehead joined his detachment to the first command he met and advanced with it.   The troop advanced at double time on the
enemy's works as soon as out of the brush and in sight of the works.   On arriving
on the hill on which the works stood, it was found that the works were carried and
the Spaniards were retreating to the next crest.   The troops had become mixed up
in a crowd of disorganized soldiers at the works.   It was at once assembled, line of
skirmish was formed, the advance taken up in the direction of the retreat of the
enemy.   While at the first works Lieutenant Anderson, with a part of Troop C, reported to me as the senior officer of the regiment present, and was put on the skirmish
line on the right of my troop.   We advanced together over the next ridge and down

it to within about 500 yards of the works at present occupied by the enemy. Here we remained for some time, exchanging fire with the enemy in the works. My left was on the road. There were troops on my left, and a little less advanced, and troops on my right a little more advanced, but their firing was not strong. Being, so so far as I knew, unsupported, I sent word back to the squadron commander describing my position, and was ordered to return to the crest of the hill which our troops now occupy, on the road. Here I received word that the hill was to be held at all hazards. The troop occupied the crest, exchanging fire with the enemy, until dark. During the night a trench was dug and occupied at daylight, the morning of the 2d. The troop remained in the trench until late in the afternoon, every exposure at the trench drawing fire from the enemy. The fire was returned only when several of the enemy exposed themselves at once. On the night of the 2d the troop was joined with the regiment and moved further to the right on the general line, where it again intrenched, and has remained in the trenches to the present time.

Lieutenant Whitehead, who was separated from the troop at the commencement of the advance, returned to it soon after it reached its most advanced position, bringing his detachment with him.

I wish to mention both Lieutenant Anderson, who was with me from the termination of the first assault, and Lieutenant Whitehead, for their coolness and bravery. I could only do justice to the troop by mentioning by name all who were engaged, not only for their bravery, but for their splendid discipline under the most demoralizing fire.

Killed—First Lieut. W. E. Shipp, on temporary staff duty.

Wounded—Second Lieut. H. C. Whitehead, slightly, and continued in action; Sergt. Amos Elliston, Sergt. Frank Rankin, Corpl. Allen Jones, Blacksmith Charles Robertson, Private Isom Taylor, Private Benjamin West.

Very respectfully,

T. W. JONES,
Captain, Tenth Cavalry, Commanding Troop F.

BEFORE SANTIAGO DE CUBA, July 5, 1898.

THE ADJUTANT, TENTH UNITED STATES CAVALRY.

Sir: In compliance with instructions from your office, I have the honor to submit the following report concerning the part taken by Troop D, Tenth United States Cavalry, while in action against the Spaniards July 1, 2 and 3:

On the morning of July 1 Troop D, under command of Capt. John Bigelow Jr., occupied the line of outposts, and performed this duty until withdrawn preparatory to the forward movement. While advancing along the road, and in close proximity to the balloon, the troop was subjected to a very severe artillery and small-arms fire, but remained orderly and unshaken. Sergeant Hatcher was wounded at this time. The fire becoming more severe, the troop was ordered to take cover, which they retained only for a few minutes. The deployment was made to the left and occupied considerable time, owing to the great difficulty met with in getting through the dense underbrush and chaparral. The line being formed, Troop D, occupying the extreme left, crossed creek and moved toward blockhouse on left of road leading to Santiago. Two wire fences were met with, which, owing to the absence of wire nippers, held the troop unnecessarily long under a well-directed and deadly fire. At the first fence one private is believed to have been killed; at the second, one was severely wounded. Beyond the fence the troop advanced under a heavy fire and charged the blockhouse on the hill. When at a distance of about 75 yards from the blockhouse, Captain Bigelow received three wounds, and was removed to the rear by Privates Henderson and Boarman, Troop D. This removal took place under heavy fire.

Corpl. J. Walker was probably the first soldier to reach the top of the hill, and is believed to have shot the Spaniard who killed Lieutenant Ord. The troop remained in the vicinity of the blockhouse until ordered to join the regiment to the right of blockhouse, and were under fire, then under command of Major Wint. A portion of the troop under my command became separated during some turning movement, and as soon as I learned that contact with the troop was lost I moved on blockhouse near ford. From this point I marched my detachment under heavy fire, at double time, across field between two blockhouses, intending to connect with what appeared to be troops of the Tenth Cavalry, who were to my left and front. When part way across, I was halted by General Sumner and ordered to place my men in position and to act as a part of his reserve. On July 2 and 3 the troop took up position in the line of investment.

Very respectfully,

A. E. KENNINGTON,
Lieutenant, Tenth Cavalry, Commanding Troop D.

BEFORE SANTIAGO DE CUBA, July 5, 1898.

ADJUTANT TENTH UNITED STATES CAVALRY.

Sir: The following is a report of the part taken by the First Squadron of the Tenth Cavalry, consisting of Troops A, B, E and I, in action with the Spaniards on the 1st, 2d and 3d instants:

On the evening of June 30 the regiment, as part of the Second Brigade, Cavalry Division, took position on the extreme left of the line, about 5 miles from Santiago.

On the morning of the 1st, after an artillery duel of short duration between Grimes' battery and the artillery of the enemy, the regiment moved forward toward the town to the crossing of the San Juan river, when it immediately became engaged. The regiment took position in a wood, and here suffered considerable loss, due to the fact that the whole of the enemy's fire appeared to be directed to this point. In a short time we moved out of the wood by the right flank and then deployed to the left, being then directly in front of the enemy and about 1 mile distant from his works, marked by three houses about half a mile from one another. The enemy were strongly intrenched in front of these houses. The line, consisting of the Cavalry Division, under direction of Brigadier-General Sumner, moved forward in double time, under a terrific fire of the enemy. We had a very heavy jungle to march through, besides the river (San Juan) to cross, and during our progress many men were killed and wounded. The troops became separated from one another, though the general line was pretty well preserved. The works of the enemy were carried in succession by the troops, and the Spaniards were steadily driven back toward the town to their last ditches. We now found ourselves about half a mile from the city, but the troops, being by this time nearly exhausted, here intrenched themselves for the night under a heavy fire. By dark this line was occupied by all the troops engaged during the day.

July 2 we changed our position to about 600 yards to the right, and were under a heavy fire during the whole day until dark, when we were again changed to about half a mile to the right and a little nearer to the works of the enemy.

July 3, and until noon, we were engaged with the enemy. At noon firing was suspended on both sides by reason of a flag of truce being sent forward, presumably to give notice of the bombardment of the city.

The conduct of the officers and enlisted men of my squadron was simply superb.

The following is a list of the killed and wounded: Killed—Troop A, Private John H. Smart; Troop B, Corpl. William F. Johnson. Wounded—Troop A, First Lieut. R. L. Livermore, Second Lieut. F. R. McCoy, Sergt. Smith Johnson, Corpl. Joseph G. Mitchell, Trumpeter Nathan Wyatt, Privates William A. Cooper, Benjamin Franklin, Wiley Hipsher, Richard James, Daniel Blue. All July 1. July 2, Private Luther D. Gould. July 3, William H. Brown. Troop B, July 1, Privates John Prim and William Gregory; July 2, Second Lieut. Harry O. Williard. Missing—Saddler John H. Ubanks, George Berry and William Jackson. Troop E, July 1, Sergt. William Payne, Blacksmith Lewis L. Anderson; Privates, Henry McCormick, Gilmore Givens, Hilly Brown. Troop I, July 1, First Sergt. Robert Millbrown, Sergt. W. G. Gunter, Privates Frank D. Bennett, Thornton Berkley, Thomas H. Hardy, Wesley Jones, Houston Riddle. Missing—Private John F. Chinn.

Respectfully submitted,

S. T. NORVELL,
Major, Tenth Cavalry, Commanding First Squadron.

TROOP B, TENTH CAVALRY,
One Mile from Santiago de Cuba, July 5, 1898.

ADJUTANT TENTH CAVALRY.

Sir: I have the honor to report the part taken by B Troop in actions of the 1st, 2d and 3d instants.

B Troop was on the right and advanced as skirmishers, guide center. Being informed by General Sumner that the objective was the house ahead, I advanced by two rushes and then double time. The country advanced over was covered with thick brush, and on emerging in the open near the house I could find only 7 men of the troop. With these I advanced to the house, arriving at the rear of and along with Colonel Victor's line, which I found deployed in front of mine on beginning the advance. Without stopping, I followed with the 7 men of my troop the retreating enemy to the most advanced position occupied at this present time. After helping to hold this position an hour or so, I went back as soon as it was reënforced, to find my troop. On the 2d and 3d my troop, with others, held the position gained. Casualties : One officer wounded, 1 corporal killed, 2 privates wounded.

Very respectfully,

J. W. WATSON,
Captain, Tenth Cavalry, Commanding Troop.

TROOP B, TENTH CAVALRY,
Six miles from Santiago, Cuba, June 27, 1898.

ADJUTANT TENTH CAVALRY.

Sir: I have the honor to submit the following report of part taken in the engagement on the 24th instant by the Tenth Cavalry detachment temporarily in charge of four Hotchkiss mountain guns.

I put the guns in position under the personal direction of the brigade commander.

The distance was estimated at 1,000 yards. This being found a little high, the sights were lowered to 900 yards and kept at that range during the engagement. Great difficulty was experienced in observing the effect of the shots, owing to the smoke which hung in front of them, and the brush on each side, but two of the first at 900 yards were seen to go to the right spot, and it was presumed the others were going right. The shells were used sparingly, as I could bring only one box (50 rounds) of ammunition. Twenty-two shots were fired. The fire was directed mainly at a rock fortification held by the Spaniards, but sometimes at a thick clump of bushes on a high point near the fortification. In looking over this part of the field after the fight I found where three shells had struck ; one had struck the center of the rock fort, another had cut off a small tree 18 inches above the top of the fort, and a third had exploded 20 feet in front of a line of 10 or 12 Spaniards (as shown by the line of empty cartridge shells which they had used). Nearly all the others undoubtedly struck in the near vicinity of these three, and it is hoped contributed to the success of the day.

Casualties : Corporal Love, B Troop, left arm grazed by bullet ; Private Gaines, same troop, shot in finger left hand.

Corpl. W. F. Johnson, B Troop, deserves special mention for his efficiency and perfect coolness under fire. He was non-commissioned officer in charge, and the Hotchkiss battery was apparently, on account of the smoke from it, a special target for the enemy's fire.

Respectfully submitted,
J. W. WATSON,
Captain, Tenth Cavalry, Temporarily Commanding Battery.

SEVILLA, SANTIAGO DE CUBA, June 27, 1898.

THE ADJUTANT, TENTH UNITED STATES CAVALRY,

Headquarters of Regiment in Field.

Sir: I have the honor to submit the following report:

At about 7:15 to 7.20 a. m., June 24, 1898, Troop B, Tenth Cavalry, was marching along the road or trail leading from Altares to Santiago de Cuba. A few minutes after I heard several shots, and directly the squadron of the Tenth Cavalry was halted, my troop being about 20 yards from a little creek directly in front and thick brush on the left, the right being slightly more open. About this time a volley from the Spanish was fired ; the first I heard at about 7:30 a. m., I should judge. I cautioned the men to lie down on the left side of the road and keep in shelter as much as possible. A few minutes after this Troop A, Tenth Cavalry, was ordered to the left of the line, and I was ordered by Major Norvell, Tenth Cavalry, to report to Brigadier-General Young, U. S. Volunteers, for instructions. I did so immediately. The General was standing in a most exposed position, about 30 or 40 yards beyond the creek already spoken of, slightly in rear of the Hotchkiss gun battery. The General ordered me to move my troop out on the extreme right at once, prolonging the line of the First United States Cavalry, already there. I ordered the troop forward at once, telling them to take advantage of all cover available. In the meantime the volleys from the Spanish were coming in quite frequently and striking the ground on all sides near where we were. I found it very difficult to move the men forward after having found cover, and ran back to a portion of the troop near an old brick wall, and ordered them forward at once. They then made a dash forward, and in doing so three or four men were wounded, Private Russel severely. Who the others were I do not know. We encountered a severe fire directly after this move forward, and Private Wheeler was wounded in the left leg. There was a wire fence on our right, and such thick underbrush that we were unable to get through right there, so had to follow along the fence for some distance before being able to penetrate. Finally was able to get the greater portion of my men through, and about this time I met Lieutenants Fleming and Miller, Tenth Cavalry, moving through the thicket on my left. I there heard the order passed on "not to fire ahead," as there was danger of firing into our own forces. In the meantime there was shouting from the First Cavalry in our front, "Don't fire on us in rear." My troop had not fired a shot to my knowledge, nor the knowledge of any non-commissioned officers in the troop. About this time I found I was unable to keep the troop deployed, as they would huddle up behind one rock or tree, so I gave all sergeants orders to move out on the extreme right and to keep in touch with those on their left. Then, with a squad of about 5 men, I moved to the right front, and lost the troop; i. e., I could see nothing of them except the men with me.

But as I had given explicit instructions to my sergeants, in case I was lost from them, to continue to advance until halted by some one in authority, I moved ahead myself, hoping to find them later on. In making a rush forward 3 men of my squad were lost from me in some way. I still had 2 men with me, Privates Combs and Jackson, and in the next advance made I picked up a First Cavalry sergeant who had fallen out from exhaustion. After a terrific climb up the ridge in front of me, and a very regular though ineffective fire from the enemy, kept up until we were about 60 yards from the summit of hill, we reached the advance line of the First United States Cavalry, under command of Captain Wainright. I then reported to him for orders, and moved forward when he next advanced. The firing had ceased, and no more shots were fired, to my knowledge, after this time. With the First Cavalry, Troop G, we followed along the right of the ridge and down to the right front, encountering no opposition or fire from the enemy, but finding the enemy's breastworks in confusion, ammunition and articles of clothing scattered around; also one dead Spaniard and two Mauser rifles. At the foot of the ridge we met some of the First Volunteer Cavalry, and being utterly exhausted, I was obliged to lie down. Soon after, Captain Mills, adjutant-general of Second Brigade, Cavalry Division, came up to where I was and placed me in command of Troop K, First United States Cavalry, whose officers were wounded. I then marched them forward in the road to where General Wheeler was sitting, and received orders from Colonel Wood, First Volunteer Cavalry, to remain until further orders, and to make no further advance. Directly afterwards, learning the action was over, I reported back to General Young, and received orders to remain camped with the First Cavalry Squadron, where the action had closed. In the meantime, I should have stated that I had found the principal part of my troop and collected them and left them under the first sergeant, when I went back to receive orders. So far as I know, and to the best of my knowledge, the men of my troop acted with the greatest bravery, advancing on an enemy who could not be seen, and subjected to a severe and heavy fire at each step, which was only rendered ineffective to a great degree by the poor marksmanship of the enemy, as many times we were in sight of them (I discovered this by observation after the engagement), while we could see nothing. We were also subjected to a severe reverse fire from the hills in our right rear, several men being wounded by this fire. Throughout the fight the men acted with exceptional coolness, in my judgment.

The casualties were: Privates Russel, Braxton and Morris, severely wounded; Privates F. A. Miller, Grice, Wheeler, and Gaines, slightly wounded; i. e., less severely. None killed.

Very respectfully,

HARRY O. WILLIARD,
Second Lieutenant, Tenth United States Cavalry, Commanding Troop B.
Tenth Cavalry, during action near Las Guasimas, June 24, 1898.

FORT DOUGLAS, UTAH, October 4, 1898.

THE ADJUTANT-GENERAL, U. S. A.
      (Through military channels.)

General: Hearing that my previous report of the operations of the Twenty-fourth Infantry, during that part of the battle of San Juan that I had the honor to command the regiment, may have been lost owing to the unavoidable circumstances incident to the campaign, or (it having been written in pencil on any paper I could obtain) some portions erased, I have the honor to submit the following supplementary report, which I respectfully request be filed with the first one, if in your office, or in default, taken as the original.

On the morning of July 1 I had command of the Second Battalion of the regiment. consisting of Companies B, C, D, and H, the regiment being commanded by Lieut.-Col. E. H. Liscum, Twenty-fourth Infantry, from whom I had received the order to conform to the movements of the leading battalion. Proceeding along the road which followed the course of the Acguadores river, the regiment arrived at a point where the Seventy-first New York was lying down, when orders were received for us to lie down to escape the fire of musketry then coming from our right flank. Some few moments having elapsed, and hearing heavy fire in our front, I went to the head of the rear company of the first battalion to ascertain if the remainder of this battalion had gone on. I found that it had, and through some misunderstanding this company had remained behind. I hastened back and ordered my battalion forward. We crossed the Acguadores river at what is known as the "bloody bend," under an increased and more effective fire from the intrenchments on San Juan hill, and proceeded over the river bottom to a point where I could see out toward San Juan hill. In this bottom I could not see the rest of the regiment ; but reaching a place where the undergrowth was not so thick, I saw Lieutenant-Colonel Liscum with some of the first battalion behind a slight rise on my right. Ordering my battalion to follow me, I went to him and reported. The leading company of my battalion, however, had missed me and proceeded on down the river. I rejoined it at once and conducted it out of the river and on to the plain in front of the hill.

There was a strong wire fence just on the bank of the river at this point, which was completely swept by the enemy's fire and impeded the advance. The wires, however, were cut in places, the fence pulled down in others. by men and officers working together, and the battalion was formed on the plain, ready for the charge.

The behavior of both officers and men at this place was noticeably brave and heroic, Capt. Charles Dodge Jr., Twenty-fourth Infantry (who had thoughtfully provided himself with wire cutters) and his company doing especial service ; Captain Dodge repeatedly expressing himself while aiding and encouraging his men cutting the fence. The companies up to about this time had been together. Company D, under command of Capt. A. C. Ducat, however, had debouched from the column while the fence was being cut and pulled down at the head of the battalion, and, forming on the bank, had gone ahead some distance — I should judge about 150 yards — and I believe that this company was the first of the regiment to reach the top of the hill. There were with me at this time Company H, commanded by Capt. A. A. Augur, Twenty-fourth Infantry ; Company B, commanded by First Lieut. J. D. Leitch, Twenty-fourth Infantry ; Company C, commanded by Capt. Charles Dodge Jr., Twenty-fourth Infantry ; part of Company A, Twenty-fourth Infantry, under command of Second Lieut. A. R. Kerwin, Twenty-fourth Infantry, and parts of other companies which had joined me while in the river bottom, noticeably some men of the Seventy-first New York, some six or seven in number. Lieutenant-Colonel Liscum having been wounded, and Maj. A. C. Markley, Twenty-fourth Infantry, the next in rank, not being present at this juncture, by virtue of my rank I was in command of the regiment. The order to charge was given as soon as the line was formed, and the command rushed across the open meadow and up the hill until another wire fence was encountered. This was at once cut and pulled down, and we arrived at the crest. While crossing this meadow we were under a severe fire, and many were killed and wounded.

Arriving at the crest, I saw Captain Ducat with his company engaged in firing upon the retreating enemy, Captain Ducat using a musket, rendering himself conspicuous for his bravery and exposure to the enemy's fire. He was wounded severely while standing at full height, and taken off the field. In forming the men for and during the charge, I desire to especially mention Capt. A. A. Augur and First Lieut. J. D. Leitch, who came under my immediate observation, for coolness and bravery under such destructive fire. By this time the greater parts of all the companies of the regiment were on the hill. Being informed by the acting adjutant-general of the Third Brigade, Lieut. W. L. Simpson, Ninth Infantry, that Lieutenant-Colonel Liscum had been wounded, and that Major Markley, the next in rank, could not be found, that I was in command of the regiment, and should assemble and form it, I immediately did so, and under orders from Brigadier-General Hawkins, I disposed the companies to hold the hill, or that part of it in our front to the left of the blockhouse. All this time the fire from the enemy's intrenchments near Santiago was severe, as was the artillery fire from their battery, which commanded the hill. In disposing his men in accordance with my orders, Capt. J. J. Brereton, while bravely exposing himself, was wounded in the leg, and after his wound had been dressed insisted upon remaining on the hill for some time, though suffering much from it. The regiment having been placed along the crest, G, H, and C constituted the firing line, and the other companies reserve. This disposition held until Maj. A. C. Markley, Twenty-fourth Infantry, made his appearance, about two hours later, and assumed command.

Corpl. Richard Williams, Company B, Twenty-fourth Infantry, who was under my observation during the whole time we were exposed to fire, is worthy of especial mention for bravery and fidelity to his commanding officer.

The bravery of First Lieut. Albert Laws and Second Lieut. A. R. Kerwin, Twenty-fourth Infantry, in dressing the wound of Captain Ducat on the crest of the hill under heavy fire, was also noticeable.

I am, very respectfully, your obedient servant,

HENRY WYGANT,
Captain, Twenty-fourth Infantry.

CAMP BEFORE SANTIAGO, CUBA, July 13, 1898.

ADJUTANT TWENTY-FOURTH UNITED STATES INFANTRY.

Sir: I have the honor to submit the following report, as directed, relating to the part taken by Company C, Twenty-fourth Infantry, in the assault on Fort San Juan, before Santiago, Cuba, on July 1, 1898:

The company left camp about 7.30 a. m. July 1, 1898, and marched with the regiment to the front, being the fourth company in the Second Battalion, which was commanded by Capt. Henry Wygant, Twenty-fourth Infantry. There were 2 officers and 59 enlisted men who marched with the company.

Just before reaching the San Juan river the battalion was ordered to lie down in the road under cover of the brush and jungle, to escape the terrific fire that was being poured in from the right flank. This road was occupied by a great number of the Seventy-first New York Volunteers, who, I presume, like ourselves, were await- ing orders to move to the front. One man of my company (Private Augustus Snoten) was wounded here, and I sent him to the rear under the care of Sergeant Staff. This sergeant subsequently joined the company and participated in the fight. The shoot- ing from our right, while in the road, was said to be from sharpshooters, who were firing on the Thirteenth Infantry, immediately on our right and front ; consequently my company was not allowed to fire, and at this time it was well in hand. The rapidity of the firing increasing in our immediate front, and believing that the services of my company — the last in column in the regiment — were needed, and not knowing the whereabouts of the regiment or battalion commander, I assumed the responsibility of ordering my Company (C) to the front in double time, and passed on the road a portion of Company H, Twenty-fourth Infantry, under command of Second Lieut. C. H. Miller, who asked me what he should do, and I told him to fol- low along. My company soon reached the crossing in the San Juan river, and find- ing it much crowded by the intermixing of troops, I pushed it to the left down the stream for about 100 yards, and here we found a barbed wire fence, which cut us off from the field over which we had to advance. The fence was cut, however, by the cutters the company had been provided with, and the men passed in, taking position on the right of a line of infantrymen — I think the Ninth Infantry — under a bench of ground found at this point. Company B, Twenty-fourth Infantry, com- manded by First Lieut. J. D. Leitch, Twenty-fourth Infantry, followed the com- pany out of the river. All this time the company was under a very severe fire, and the men behaved splendidly.

On emerging from the San Juan river and after taking position in the open field, I met Captain Wygant, who ordered me to withdraw my company and follow him. This I did by passing again to the stream with my company and marching down it to a point that brought the battalion led by Captain Wygant to a point in the open field about 200 yards farther on the left flank of the firing line. Here Captain Wygant led the advance and commanded the movement in person. In this march to the extreme left a second wire fence was encountered, but this also we were able to cut. I mention the cutting of the wire fences, because I believe that each com- pany should be provided by the Government with a suitable number of cutters, as in this instance, at least, they were found invaluable.

In the charge across the open field parts of Companies C, B and H participated, but the intermixing of all troops rendered it impossible for me to keep all of my company as an organization together. I have, however, the names of 20 men who actually reached the trenches at Fort San Juan, and who took part in the firing.

The company was assembled, by order of Captain Wygant, the battalion com- mander, just in rear of the crest of the hill (San Juan), and Brigadier-General Hawkins ordered me to occupy the crest of the hill with my company, C, and this I did at a point just south of the blockhouse, which was still under fire. I was subse- quently relieved from this duty by order of Captain Wygant, the battalion com- mander, and replaced by Company B, Twenty-fourth, under command of Lieutenant Leitch.

In this engagement the company lost among the enlisted men 1 killed, 6 wounded, and 1 missing in action.

Very respectfully, your obedient servant,

CHAS. DODGE,

Captain, Twenty-fourth Infantry, Commanding Company C.

Report of D Company, Twenty-fourth United States Infantry, engagement July 1, 1898.

The regiment marched down road toward Santiago and entered part of road surrounded by brush (very thick). Company D was in second battalion of regiment. The regiment had not marched very far along this narrow road (11 a. m.) when it was subjected to fire, which apparently came from all sides. Men lay down in road, none being wounded here. Shortly afterwards an order came to move across a small stream (San Juan river). Captain Ducat led his company across, Second Lieutenant Gurney keeping them closed up. The fire here was terrific from Fort San Juan on right, and from sharpshooters (Spanish), whom we found afterwards in trees.

The company, after advancing about 10 yards beyond stream, went through barbed wire fence to right and advanced to a small embankment in open field 20 yards to right of stream, all company well in hand at this point. Captain Ducat here gave command to advance, and the whole company, in good order in line of skirmishers, followed the brave example of its captain and second lieutenant. The company advanced rapidly over open ground toward Fort San Juan, a high hill in front of them, and arrived at bottom, the fire killing or wounding men on all sides.

Second Lieut. John A. Gurney, shot in breast, advancing across open, died shortly afterwards. He fought with extreme bravery, and fell due to exposure in keeping men in order and encouraging them on.

First Sergt. Merriman H. Ellis, shot in foot, in open.

Corpl. Pat Keyes, shot both legs, in open.

Privates Mason Robinson, shot in open, back; and William Johnson, shot in open, arm.

The company was almost exhausted when it arrived at the bottom of the hill, but it continued to follow the courageous and determined example of its brave commander, and advanced rapidly up the hill. The Spaniards broke and fled from trenches. Firing continued from sharpshooters (Spanish) in trees. The top of hill was reached at 12 o'clock, noon, and fired on fleeing Spaniards, the captain himself taking a gun, and after firing two shots was hit by, supposedly, a Spanish sharpshooter in tree. The brave company commander was carried from field with wound in hip. Company assembled by battalion commander. Company D was first company of regiment to arrive on hill (Fort San Juan), and was led by its company commander.

After fleeing Spaniards had gotten clear of hill, firing commenced from Spanish trenches in front and about 800 yards away. This was kept up all rest of day, but company lay down under cover of hill, and suffered no loss. After dark trenches were dug.

The whole company fought bravely.

Casualties, July 1.—Capt. Arthur C. Ducat Jr., hip; Second Lieut. John A. Gurney, breast, died in twenty minutes; First Sergt. Merriman H. Ellis, foot; Corpl. Pat Keyes, legs; Private Mason Robinson, back; Private William Johnson, arm.

This report is made in the absence of D Company's officers—Capt. A. C. Ducat, wounded, and Second Lieut. John A. Gurney, dead—from close inquiries and from my personal observation.

Very respectfully,

ARTHUR R. KERWIN,
Second Lieutenant, Twenty-fourth United States Infantry, Commanding Company D.

The Adjutant, Twenty-fourth Infantry.

Sir: With reference to the fighting of July 1 and 2, I have the honor to make the following report relative to my company:

At about 12 o'clock noon on the 1st instant, my company, with the entire regiment, was halted in the road on the near side of the San Juan river, and lay there for some fifteen or twenty minutes under the galling fire of a lot of expert sharpshooters. Our orders forbade any reply, although the sharpshooters were in the trees near us across the river. Under this fire Corpl. Aaron Black was mortally wounded—shot in the head—and Privates Samuel Bridgewater and Pearl Bonnselor were shot in the foot and leg, respectively. There is a bend in the road to the front of where my company lay. No orders reached me here except that to not reply to any of the enemy's fire.

Lieutenant Keene, commanding Company E, came back and reported to me for orders as the senior officer with the battalion. The fire had affected him as it had me, and he wanted to put his men where they could either get cover or reply to the fire. I thus discovered that part of the regiment was gone, and went to the ford and called across to the brigade adjutant-general, asking for orders to advance. He directed me to move forward across the stream.

I gave this instruction to Lieutenant Keene, who, under my advice and instruction, took a left-hand trail under cover. Seeing that this trail would likely become congested if I tried to follow, I decided to push directly across at the ford, which I did.

I was here instructed that my company was to take its place on the left of Company E, so I moved down the creek under cover of the bank toward my place in line. I was moved back and forth in the stream several times, and finally was ordered to move on to the left and try to get the enemy in flank.

In the movements across the stream and back and forth in its bed most of my company became separated from me. I went through two wire fences (across the stream) and went up on the bank, to the left of the company commanded by Lieutenant Noyes, Ninth Infantry, through a wire fence diagonally across the field, through two more wire fences (all this under heavy fire), then through two more fences (at the foot of the hill), and up to the crest of the hill on the extreme left.

I did not discover the smallness of my command until after I debouched into the first field. When I went up the hill my idea was to get a flanking fire on the enemy. When I reached the top he had retired. My command (of 14 men) was under fire from two houses to our right and front and from small parties of the enemy across on the hill beyond our line. My men reported seeing Spaniards in these two houses, so I fired three volleys at them, which caused a decided commotion among them. Firing was then begun upon them from the blockhouse, now in our possession.

Major Boyle, Ninth Infantry, here came up and I reported to him for orders. He directed me to have my men, in connection with his own, throw up temporary fortifications (hasty intrenchments), which I did. During all this time every time one of our men showed himself he was greeted by shots from the enemy.

The Ninth Infantry having taken position, I went to get permission from the brigade commander to return to my regiment and report for duty.

The following named men were killed: Corpl. Aaron Black, Private Richard Bissell. Wounded—Corpl. William Tate, Privates George Baylor, Charles Pope, Frank Hill, Samuel Bridgewater, Harry Moore, Henry Miller, and Pearl Bonnselor.

On the the night of the 1st the company worked under my supervision, throwing up intrenchments until 3 a. m. Much of the work was done with bayonets, the company tools having been taken away from us. The company lay in the trenches all day and was relieved by the Seventy-first New York. At 10.30 the alarm was given and we moved into the trenches among the Seventy-first New York, under heavy fire from the enemy. Sergt. Frank Banks was shot at my side (and has since died) as we were moving to the trenches. We poured a heavy fire upon the enemy until the "cease firing" was sounded, and then lay in the trenches until (half an hour later) the enemy's fire stopped, when we returned to our places.

During the whole of the two days my only officer, Lieut Kerwin, behaved himself with coolness, courage, and energy, which entitle him to the greatest credit.

It would be hard to particularize in reporting upon the men of the company. All — non-commissioned officers, privates, even newly joined recruits — showed a desire to do their duty, yea, more than their duty, which would have done credit to seasoned veterans. Too much can not be said of their courage, willingness, and endurance.

Very respectfully, your obedient servant,

BEN. W. LEAVELL,
Captain. Twenty-fourth Infantry, Commanding Company A.

HEADQUARTERS TWENTY-FOURTH INFANTRY,
Fort San Juan, Cuba, July 5, 1898.

THE ADJUTANT-GENERAL,
Third Brigade, First Division, Fifth Army Corps.

Sir: I have the honor to report that this regiment, under command of Lieut. Col. E. A. Liscum, Twenty-fourth Infantry, went into action about 10 a. m., July 1, 1898, assisting in the capture of this fort, marching westerly in column of twos past division headquarters, turning to the right and crossing a creek in a woods (about one-fourth mile) near the tile factory, taking position and opening fire behind a wire fence. The leading company, G (Captain Brereton), formed on left into line under a severe fire from in front and a fire in the rear, which was not noticed at first. I commanded the leading battalion.

When the company was about two-thirds on the line the men began to come over the creek in ones and twos, some companies being delayed for some reason. At the same time Captain Brereton called my attention to a man shot in the back, when I first noticed the reports of rifles, showing quite a heavy fire in the rear. There was a great deal of other noise and confusion by other regiments. I reported this to Colonel Liscum, and he sent an officer to stop it and to bring up the other companies (also orderlies). I returned to my place, when Captain Brereton reported that another man had been killed by a ball from the rear. I reported this to Colonel Liscum, and he ordered me to go back and send up the other companies and to stop the firing in the rear, supposed to be by our own troops. I found the companies, which were delayed by no fault of their own, and telling the officers to hurry up, hastened to find the troops who were firing on us, supposing they must be on a parallel road in the chaparral; but have since found it was the enemy's soldiers hidden in tree tops in a thicket of thorns, and finally gave up, after calling to them until I was hoarse, and returned to my regiment, which in the meantime had changed places with other troops, which I joined and went forward with until I found the adjutant, Lieutenant Tayman, with whom I went to the top of the hill;

but seeing some of my regiment on the right, went around to them and joined with Lieutenants Lyon and Murphy, and thus got separated from the regiment, which had charged up the hill to the left, and, being requested by Colonel Wood, U. S. Volunteers, to hold a place in his line, did not return to my regiment (because none of the officers knew where it was), until about an hour after the action. The part of the regiment with me were engaged also.

In this action 2 officers were killed (Lieutenants Gurney and Augustin), and 4 wounded (Lieutenant-Colonel Liscum, Captains Brereton and Ducat, and Lieutenant Brett), and 7 men killed and 74 wounded, 3 of whom have since died.

Very respectfully,

A. C. MARKLEY,
Captain, Twenty-fourth Infantry, **Commanding Regiment.**

HEADQUARTERS TWENTY-FOURTH INFANTRY,
Fort San Juan, Cuba, July 7, 1898.

THE ADJUTANT-GENERAL,
Third Brigade, First Division, Fifth Army Corps.

Sir: I have the honor to make the following addition to the report of the part taken by this regiment in the battle of July 1, 1898 :

A brief statement of the part this regiment took in the battle, with all the essentials, and of what it would like to be credited with, is this :

On the march to the front this regiment was the rear one of the three in its brigade. After coming under fire, it was ordered to take position on the left, and marched about one mile by the flank, under fire, to its place ; advanced over the flat, the same as other regiments, assisting in the capture of Fort San Juan, getting on top of the hill among the first, with a creditable number of men of its small companies, and in time to get men killed, and to silence one gun by volley fire.

Very respectfully,

A. C. MARKLEY,
Captain, Twenty-fourth Infantry, **Commanding Regiment.**

HEADQUARTERS TWENTY-FOURTH INFANTRY,
Camp Wikoff, N. Y., September 18, 1898.

ADJUTANT-GENERAL U. S. ARMY, Washington, D. C.

Sir: I have the honor to make the following report of a tour of duty of the Twenty-fourth Infantry at Siboney, Cuba, believing that a report is justified by the unusual nature of the service performed and the qualities shown by the officers and men in performing it :

I beg to say first that after my attempts to write this report in usual official form I find from the nature of what ought to be said that I can not do it. I will therefore ask the indulgence of the department and do the best I can, simply desiring to do justice to the regiment, particularly to the enlisted men, for the nobility of character displayed by them.

The regiment had participated in the campaign before Santiago, Cuba, and in the capture of Fort San Juan, which it had the honor of holding after capture until July 9, when moved to the trenches on the left.

On July 15, hostilities having ceased, the regiment was ordered out of the trenches, and put its camp in order for sleep and rest. On that day was first heard the startling news that yellow fever had broken out in the army, and that Siboney was a great hospital, with a pest camp in addition. This had a visibly depressing effect upon officers and men, run down and weakened physically and mentally, all regiments alike, by the unavoidable hardships of a campaign in Cuba in its hottest and most unhealthy season.

About 4 p. m. an order was received directing me to proceed at once with the regiment and report for duty to Colonel Greenleaf, Medical Department, at Siboney, reporting hour of departure. The regiment marched at 5.30 p. m., by which time all had regained their composure, and were in better spirits to face the 14-mile night march over that bad road and the serious business at the end of it.

In darkness the tired troops toiled in single file through the mud puddles, unbridged streams, and thorny thickets, arriving on the hill at Siboney at 3.30 a. m. with 8 companies, 15 officers and 456 enlisted men. At daylight I went down into the camp to get an idea of the situation, finding some 600 patients packed closely, with insufficient protection and attendance, unavoidable and the fault of no one at that time, there being also the large pest camp about a mile out on the railroad. The state of affairs was very plain.

Some time later I met Colonel Greenleaf, and informed him that I had arrived at Siboney with the Twenty-fourth Infantry. Colonel Greenleaf, who left Siboney that day, most courteously told me the needs of the place, which I had by that time plainly seen myself, and referred me to his successor, Major La Garde, Medical Department, who showed the delight he felt at seeing, in the assistance sent him, his old friends, the Twenty-fourth Infantry.

The sight of such misery as I had never before seen impressed me deeply. I told Major La Garde that I had but one idea, and that was to help him take care of the sick, sinking every other consideration, and that I believed the regiment would feel the same way, in which I was not disappointed.

Returning to the regiment, officers' call was sounded and consultation held, great liberty of action being offered the officers. What occurred need not be stated ; but it did not take the officers of the Twenty-fourth Infantry long to decide what they would do, which was to camp with the sick. The courage and cheerfulness of Major La Garde had a good effect.

Here it should be said that camping space is restricted at Siboney to a small strip of rocky ground between the cliffs and sea, and much of this is made untenable by the presence of a reeking lagoon and by infected ground. Each company had to clear away and pile the debris of burned buildings for its camp, while subsequently, with new arrivals, officers, men, surgeons, civilian nurses, and sick were all huddled together.

The regiment then, on Sunday, July 16, went into camp, and the details required were then announced.

First, the rather staggering demand for 65 nurses for the pest camp, the others being for nurses, cooks, burial parties, attendants, etc., for the hospital proper— about 70 men. Volunteers for the service were then called for.

This was the crucial test of the mettle of the men, and an anxious moment indeed. In preparation for it, an interview had been had with Capt. A. A. Augur, commanding Company H, a man of high and strong character, and a course of action decided on. Captain Augur then explained matters to his men, and called for volunteers for the pest camp. Fifteen gallant fellows responded from his company, and this fine example soon produced more than were needed for all purposes.

It is now well to give an account of Siboney.

The troops at Siboney at this time were mostly volunteers—the Thirty-fourth

Michigan, twelve companies; a battalion each of two other regiments, and of the Signal Corps and United States Engineers, together with detachments, large or small, from most of the regiments "at the front," in charge of stores and baggage left behind, about 3,000 in all; the two supply depots—quartermaster and commissary— of the army at Santiago; over 200 Spanish prisoners of war, and the two hospitals already named, with corps of attendants.

The Juragua Railroad to Santiago was part of the command.

This important place was a separate command under Brigadier-General Duffield, U. S. Volunteers, then present sick, whom I practically succeeded, governing by tacit consent, until the major-general commanding ordered the Thirty-fourth Michigan a few miles out, leaving me the important separate command of Siboney, an honor conferred by Major-General Shafter.

My staff consisted of one officer, who also commanded a company, and was sometimes sick.

The camp was so crowded, so full of rubbish, and in such filthy condition from previous occupancy by Spanish, Cubans, volunteers, and by other hospitals, that large fatigue details were necessary. But large details for loading and unloading transports in the harbor and the railroad were also made, and the sick list of the troops began to be large. The volunteers were unskilled, needing the presence of a regular officer, who could not be spared. The officers of my regiment were rapidly falling sick from disease contracted in the trenches, and the other battalions were wisely ordered away. It was found best—in fact necessary—to command all fatigue parties, big and little, myself, this labor being an important feature, too long to explain why. Besides, there were not enough officers to command companies and do the regimental work. As the cooks, etc., were mostly from my regiment, with Major La Garde's approval, I took charge of the kitchens, laundry, etc., and of all disciplinary matters, in hospital and out.

With the depletion of the working force came daily increase of patients from the front and from our own men, until it seemed hopeless to try to make any headway. The troops at Santiago being in a distressing condition, the general commanding giving me all assistance in his power, I endeavored to avoid adding to his burdens.

No report of the nature of a reproach or accusation against anyone, as stated in a recent newspaper article, was ever made by me.

By the end of July yellow fever had overrun all the hospitals, including a new one established in a large railroad shed. All was pest camp; even separation of cases was impossible. All wards had it. Surgeons, nurses and hospital stewards were now among the patients; and so it continued to about August 20, when determined steps were taken to break up the place.

Of this regiment, Captain Dodge had died; 2 officers were expected to die; 3 were dangerously ill, and 5 more or less so. Out of 16 present, 10 were in hospital, 3 well, 3 sick, but doing well; sick and well living mostly within a radius of 50 feet Officers kept up when they should have gone into hospital, making it worse for them when they did give up.

Not a jar occurred. The officers of this regiment were a unit, as usual.

Of the 65 enlisted men sent as nurses to the pest camp July 16, most had succumbed, their places being filled by others. When these went down, the gaps were filled, and the same was the case in all the hospitals and the whole camp the whole time.

Day and night would come appeals to me from the surgeons and others for men to replace those stricken down, which was met by my appeal in turn to the companies, which would be answered by some who had been sick and not yet well coming forward and offering to fill the places "till you can get somebody else." Often out of the whole regiment it would be impossible to get 12 men for fatigue duty, and those who reported were not really fit to work, but would rarely avail themselves of the permission, always given, to be excused if not able, but would keep at it until they had to give up. A trouble was that those who recovered did not get strong. All worked in some way, regardless of rank.

The labor required was taking down and putting up tents, changing to new ground, ditching tents, moving the sick, unloading stores, digging graves, cleaning up filth for the multitude of sick, and innumerable other things. Working convalescents was tried until unexpected deaths warned us to stop. Major La Garde and myself worked together as one man.

Out of the 456 men who marched to Siboney only 24 men escaped sickness. All were not down at one time, of course, but on one day 241 were on sick report, although death and "sending North" had reduced the regiment in numbers.

It is a notable fact that in these forty days not even a murmur was heard from a soldier of the Twenty-fourth Infantry (or officer either), I am sure. Though discipline was enforced with strictness, not an infraction worth noticing occurred.

These men are usually light-hearted and noisily merry in camp in a pleasant way, but this camp was silent; no amusements—nothing to lighten the dead weight on their minds day and night—during this long and dreary time. Having no proper cooking utensils, their meals were not even a pleasure and a distraction. But they bore all bravely and patiently, faithfully doing what they could, showing in these colored soldiers unexpected qualities of the highest order.

About August 8 Major La Garde himself, broken down and worn out, was attacked with yellow fever.

A detachment of over 200 men of the First Illinois Volunteers was on duty at Siboney all of this time, camped first out on the railroad near the pest camp, then a mile northeast of Siboney. The officers were Captain Whygam, commanding; Captain ———, soon taken sick and sent North, and Lieutenant Pollock—able, fearless and zealous officers, deserving great credit. This command did valuable service loading bridge timbers and handling stores, the men being faithful and willing, but its enormous sick list of 190 men soon made it cease to be a factor.

This command went North with the Twenty-fourth Infantry.

By August 22 such progress had been made in breaking up the hospitals that the welcome order was received for the regiment to prepare to go North.

Six officers were in the hospital, 4 of whom were sent home on the hospital ship Berkshire, and two were left behind by the regiment, being too ill for removal. Eleven officers and 289 men were able to go with the regiment on the transport, but many were too sick to attempt to march in ranks, so on August 26, its forty-first day at Siboney, the regiment marched to the train, band playing and colors flying, with 9 officers and 198 men.

Proceeding by rail to Santiago, the regiment, with the battalion of the First Illinois before named, embarked on the transport Nueces, and sailed the same day, August 26, arriving at Montauk Point, N. Y., September 2, with considerable sick, including 2 officers, but no deaths, and one of the cleanest ships that came to that place.

The regiment went into Camp Wikoff, the finest camp in every respect that I have ever seen, and with the most excellent hospitals possible, in my opinion. Yet notwithstanding all this and the fine weather, the men began to fall sick in great numbers, several dying.

One officer became sick, but the sick officers improved, one getting well.

The regiment lost in this service 1 officer (so far) and about 30 men, and effectually showed that colored soldiers were not more immune from Cuban fever than white.

Very respectfully, your obedient servant,

A. C. MARKLEY,
Major, Twenty-fourth Infantry, Commanding Regiment.

FORT SAN JUAN, CUBA, July 9, 1898.

THE ADJUTANT-GENERAL,
   Third Brigade, First Division, Fifth Army Corps.

Sir: In compliance with your instructions, I have the honor to report that on July 1, 1898, having reported to you from Lieutenant-Colonel Liscum, you directed me to proceed to the division commander for reënforcements, at the same time telling me to hurry up all troops in rear. I cleared the road for some little distance from the ford and proceeded up the path along the stream for about a mile and a quarter. I met Major Reade, of General Kent's staff, to whom I delivered the message, and who directed me to return, ordering all troops I might find on the way to the front, and engage the enemy. On my return, I directed, by General Kent's order, a field officer, of the Second Infantry, to move down the path with his command, rapidly, which he did. I then directed the column of the Seventy-first New York Volunteers to do the same, but on reaching the head of the regiment I found the road blocked by other troops, and the regiment turning up the hill to the left. I again directed the colonel of this regiment to move down the path, and he replied that he would as soon as the regiment could be moved. At this time and point there was great confusion, the road being completely blocked—the troops, seemingly, not knowing where to go. The congestion of the road, and the very severe fire of the enemy, from the hill, and the sharpshooters, in the trees, added to this panicky condition ; in fact, they were at this place, turning out of the main road into a side space, leading up the hill to the left.

After some difficulty, I succeeded in getting troops to move, and in speaking to the Seventy-first New York Volunteers, several captains, notably Captain Rafferty, volunteered to move forward if I would show the way, which I did, leaving the command (three companies, I believe) with Captain Rafferty, in the stream, directly in front of the blockhouse on the hill, from which they emerged into the second line, moving toward the hill. I then proceeded to join my regiment, but noticing a great many men under the bank, in the stream, just opposite the brickyard, I went back into the stream and succeeded in getting them out, and started across the field, after which I joined my regiment.

Very respectfully,

CHAS. E. TAYMAN,
First Lieutenant and Adjutant, Twenty-fourth Infantry.

FORT SAN JUAN, July 5, 1898.

THE ASSISTANT ADJUTANT-GENERAL,
   Third Brigade, First Division, Fifth Army Corps.
      (Through Adjutant Twenty-fourth Infantry.)

Sir: In compliance with instructions from your office, I have the honor to submit the following report :

On the morning of July 1 the regiment (Twenty-fourth United States Infantry) left camp at about 7.30 a. m. under command of Lieut. Col. E. H. Liscum, Twenty-fourth Infantry, for the front. I had command of the Second Battalion, composed of Companies H, D, B, and C. On reaching a point in a sunken road running westward on the river, the regiment encountered a number of troops lying alongside of the road, under a heavy fire from a blockhouse and intrenchment on the north, where it was halted, and instructed to lie down for shelter. My orders were to conform to the movements of the First Battalion, which had also halted and sought shelter.

The company immediately in my front of the leading battalion was still in the road (which was full of troops in confusion), when, hearing the heavy firing in my front increasing, I concluded to move my battalion in that direction. Passing this company of the other battalion, I discovered that the rest of that battalion had gone on. I crossed the ford of the river which was struck soon after, resuming the forward under a destructive fire, and was unable to see the rest of my regiment. Ordering my battalion to follow me, I turned through a gap in a wire fence, where I saw some companies of the regiment under a slight rise, sheltered from the direct fire from the blockhouse and intrenchments on the hill to their right. I reported to Lieutenant-Colonel Liscum, who was with these troops, and informed him that my battalion was behind me.

I waited for a few moments for the head of the battalion to appear. Finding that they were not yet visible, I went back to the creek, where I found that they had passed the place where I had turned off, and had gone too far to join with the First Battalion, and, seeing other troops forming for the charge, I formed on the west bank.

As the battalion emerged from the creek the fire was exceedingly severe, and men were dropping on all sides from its effects. As soon as a line was formed I gave the order to charge.

The advance was made across an open meadow, subjected to heavy and effective fire from the enemy. There were with the battalion at this time the greater part of Companies H, B, and C, commanded by Capt. A. A. Augur, First Lieut. J. D. Leitch, and Capt. Charles Dodge, respectively, D company, commanded by Capt. A. C. Ducat, having left the column and charged on my right, as they recrossed the stream before the rest of the battalion. There was some delay in getting up on the bank of the creek, which was quite steep, on account of a wire fence at the top.

Captain Dodge, who commanded Company C, had provided his company with some wire-cutters, which were very useful at this time, and as this work was done by him and his company under this fire, it was an extremely hazardous task.

The battalion reformed under the shelter of the hill after crossing the meadow, and then charged the intrenchments on the hill, tearing down wire fences and springing over obstructions as they went. When crossing the meadow I was some distance ahead of my battalion, but was unable to keep up with them going up the hill; so that part of the battalion arrived at the crest before me. Those who had arrived were engaged in firing upon the retreating Spaniards, and in this firing each company of my battalion was represented. Captain Ducat was wounded while standing on the crest. Upon finding that I was the ranking officer of my regiment upon the ground, I assumed command of the same and assembled it, assigning each company to its place.

The brigade commander ordered me to dispose my regiment so as to hold this crest, ordering C and G companies to the firing line. Capt. J J. Brereton was wounded while on this dangerous duty.

About an hour after, an officer senior to me having arrived, I relinquished command.

The gallantry and bearing shown by the officers and soldiers of the regiment under this trying ordeal was such that it has every reason to be proud of its record. The losses of the regiment, which are shown by the official records, show the fire they were subjected to. The casualties were greater among the officers than the men, which is accounted for by the fact that the enemy had posted in the trees sharpshooters, whose principal business was to pick them off.

Very respectfully, your obedient servant,

HENRY WYGANT,
Captain, Twenty-fourth United States Infantry, Commanding Second Battalion.

INTRENCHMENTS, TWENTY-FOURTH UNITED STATES INFANTRY,
July 5, 1898.

ADJUTANT-GENERAL,
Second Brigade, Second Division, Fifth Corps.

Sir: I have the honor to submit the following report of the part taken by the Twenty-fifth Infantry in the 1st inst.:

The regiment formed firing line on the right of the Fourth Infantry, facing a Spanish fort or blockhouse about half a mile distant. On moving forward, the battalion, composed of Companies C, D, E, G and H, and commanded by Capt. W. S. Scott, received the fire of the enemy, and after advancing about 400 yards, was subjected to a galling fire on their left. Finding cover, the battalion prepared for an advance up the hill to the fort. This advance was made rapidly and conducted with great skill by company officers.

On arriving within a short distance of the fort the white flag was waved to our companies, but a cross fire prevented the enemy from advancing with it, or our officers from receiving it. About twenty minutes later a battalion of some other regiment advanced to the rear of the fort, completely covered from fire, and received the flag, but the men of the Twenty-fifth Infantry entered the fort at the same time. All officers and men behaved gallantly. One officer was killed and 3 wounded ; 8 men were killed and 20 wounded.

About 200 men and 10 officers were in the firing line. I attribute the comparatively small losses to the skill and bravery of the company officers ; viz., First Lieutenant Caldwell and Second Lieutenant Moss and Hunt. Second Lieutenant French, adjutant of the battalion, was among those who gallantly entered the fort.

The battle lasted about two hours, and was a hotly contested combat.

Very respectfully,

A. S. DAGGETT,
Lieutenant-Colonel, Twenty-fifth Infantry, Commanding.

HEADQUARTERS, TWENTY-FIFTH INFANTRY,
Near Santiago, Cuba, July 16, 1898.

THE ADJUTANT-GENERAL,
Second Division, Fifth Corps, near Santiago, Cuba.

Sir: Feeling that the Twenty-fifth Infantry has not received credit for the part it took in the battle of El Caney, on the 1st instant, I have the honor to submit the following facts :

I was ordered by the brigade commander to put two companies (H, Lieutenant Caldwell, and G, Lieutenant McCorkle) on the firing line in extended order. The right being uncovered and exposed to the enemy, I ordered D company (Captain Edwards), to deploy as flankers. The battalion was commanded by Capt. W. S. Scott. The battalion advanced about 300 yards under fire, the Fourth Infantry on its left, where the line found cover, halted, and opened fire on the blockhouse and intrenchments in front of it. After the line had been steadied and had delivered an effective fire, I ordered a further advance, which was promptly made. As the Fourth Infantry did not advance, my left was exposed to a very severe fire from the village on the left. I immediately ordered Company C (Lieutenant Murdock), which was in support, to the front, and E company (Lieutenant Kinnison), from regimental reserve to take its place. Thus strengthened, the four companies moved up the hill rapidly, being skillfully handled by company officers. On arriving near the fort the white flag was waved toward our men, but the fire from the village on our left was so severe that neither our officers nor Spanish could pass over the intervening ground. After about twenty minutes some of the Twelfth Infantry arrived in rear of the fort, completely sheltered from the fire from the village, and received the white flag; but Privates J. H. Jones, of Company D, and T. C. Butler, H Company, Twenty-fifth Infantry, entered the fort at the same time and took possession of the Spanish flag. They were ordered to give it up by an officer of the Twelfth United States Infantry, but before doing so, they each tore a piece from it, which they now have. So much for the facts.

I attribute the success attained by our line largely to the bravery and skill of the company officer who conducted the line to the fort. These officers are: First Lieuts. V. A. Caldwell and J. A. Moss, and Second Lieut. J. E. Hunt. It is my opinion that the two companies first deployed could not have reached the fort alone, and that it was the two companies I ordered to their support that gave them the power to reach it. I further believe that had we failed to move beyond the Fourth Infantry, the fort would not have been taken that night.

The Twenty-fifth Infantry lost 1 officer killed* and 3 wounded, and 7 men killed and 28 wounded.

Second Lieut. H. W. French, adjutant of Captain Scott's battalion, arrived at the fort near the same time as the other officers.

I request that this report be forwarded to corps headquarters.

Very respectfully,

A. S. DAGGETT,
Lieutenant-Colonel, Twenty-fifth Infantry, Commanding.

---

*First Lieutenant McCorkle, killed; Captain Edwards and First Lieutenants Kinnison and Murdock, wounded.

SPECIAL ORDER No. 78.

Headquarters
9th U. S. V. Infantry,

S. S. MEADE, *April 27, 1899.*

The following letter is published for the information of the regiment :

HEADQRS. DEPT. OF SANTIAGO,
ADJT. GENL.'S OFFICE, CIVIL DEPT.,
SANTIAGO DE CUBA, *April 25, 1899.*

COLONEL CRANE, 9th U. S. V. I.

Sir— Your regiment having been relieved from duty in this department, it gives me great pleasure to assure you that I have always found your regiment to be efficient, well instructed and well disciplined, and that its services, taken as a whole, have been excellent and creditable.

The work done by the officers of the regiment in the suppression of bandits during the last two months has been especially worthy of commendation. I desire to express my appreciation of your own constant and untiring efforts to improve the condition and efficiency of your men, and to look after their welfare, in which endeavors you have been very successful.

Very respectfully,

LEONARD WOOD,
Major Gen. U. S. V., Commanding Dept. of Santiago.

By order of Colonel Crane.

(*Signed*) *JAMES LONGSTREET,*
First Lieut. 9th U. S. V. I., Adjt.

The Bandit Chasers.

⚜

I N connection with the foregoing letter of General Wood, the following extract from the *Telegraph*, of Harrisburg, Pa., will be read
with interest:

"When the Ninth Immunes marched through the streets of this city, in
the parade following the unveiling of the statue of General Hartranft, last
Friday, the thousands who witnessed the procession gazed upon a lot of
fine, sturdy black warriors. Their marching was regular, and the solid
martial column which they formed presented a magnificent showing. Their
drilling and maneuvers were correct in every detail, the execution of which
throws great credit on the boys and their commanders as well. They all
showed that riding a horse was as easy as keeping in step with the music of
the bands. Possibly all these good qualifications were noticed; but how
many people know the full story of their prowess, and what they have done
and gone through during their stay in the sunny isle of Cuba? These boys
have suffered privations and gone through many hardships.

"The Ninth Immunes were sent to the Santiago province for the sole purpose of clearing that state and the surrounding country of the numerous
tribes of bandits which infested the island of Cuba at that time, and were a
menace to both life and property. On landing, they immediately became
entangled with these desperadoes, and their troubles began at once. Like
everything else, it became a common occurrence for a squad to have a skirmish with the bandits four or five times a day. In a comparatively short
time, that section of the island was entirely cleared, and now the province of
Santiago is entirely free from the plague of bandits.

"The desperadoes almost completely overran the island, and murder and
rapine were daily occurrences. The rural guard failed time and again to
wipe out the evils of their work and effect the capture of the leaders; but a
company of the Ninth Immunes tracked these marauders to their lair, did
them battle in a hot fight, captured several of the leaders, and took them,
bound and gagged, to the authorities, in less than a month. The clean-up,
which was done with marked dispatch, took just about three weeks.

"Accompanying this regiment to Camp Meade is a letter of recommendation written by the governor of the island, in which he says that this
regiment drove out the banditti with more promptitude and dispatch than any
other regiment of regulars or volunteers on the island. The men of Company
I all highly appreciate Governor Wood's letter, and take great pleasure in
speaking about it.

"Lieutenant Wakefield, a popular young officer of Company I, when asked
about Cuba, always finds time to relate several interesting stories incident to
their campaign. He says many of his comrades, like himself, have com-

pletely fallen in love with the Pearl of the Antilles, and express their fond desire to live the rest of their days among the mountains of that sunny isle."

The full story of the experiences of Company I, in which they earned the title of "Bandit Chasers," is embodied in the following description of the events, which has been furnished by Lieutenant Wakefield:

"Company I was organized at Houston, Texas, the day following President McKinley's first call for volunteers, but did not, owing to the refusal of the Governor of Texas to recognize the colored man as a soldier, get into the service until July 2, 1898. On that date, in command of Capt. C. A. Windus, it left Houston for New Orleans, La., to join the Ninth U. S. Volunteer Infantry, one of the ten immune regiments provided for by act of Congress. It was one of the companies selected from the Ninth U. S. V. for the mounted service, and received horses and equipments February 24, 1899.

"On the 20th of March, 1899, Troop I, commanded by Lieut. A. J. Wakefield, left Songo, where it was stationed after being detached from the regiment, December 27, 1898, for Mayari, Cuba, and was joined at San Luis, Cuba, by Capt. C. A. Windus, March 22, 1899. The troop, under command of Captain Windus, left San Luis March 23, at 10 A. M., with two government wagons of provisions, for Mayari, and a detachment under Lieutenant Wakefield left at 1 P. M. When within four miles from Santa Ana sugar plantation, the road diminished to a rocky trail leading over the mountains, which was impassable for the wagons, necessitating their unloading and being sent back to San Luis, a guard being placed over the provisions. They then proceeded toward Mayari. Twelve miles from where the provisions were left, they were overtaken by Sergt. Thomas Cohen, who made a desperate ride over a trail that was unsafe to ride faster than a walk. He had been left in charge of the guard left with the provisions. He informed Captain Windus that one of the teamsters had returned and reported the murder of his comrade by a party of armed men.

"Troop I's mission to Mayari was to rid that section of the bandits who infested it, and were a menace to both life and property. Its troubles then began. The island was almost completely overrun by desperadoes, and murder and rapine were daily occurrences. The rural guard failed time and again to wipe out the evils of their work and effect the capture of the leaders, but Troop I tracked these marauders to their lair, captured several leaders and took them, bound and gagged, to the authorities in less than a month. The clean-up was done with marked dispatch, being accomplished in just about three weeks. Among the many hardships was that of riding for ninety-six hours, only dismounting to take hasty meals. This was when, scouring the country on the sharp lookout for bandits after the regiment's teamster (Godchau) had been found murdered. About sunset on the fourth day their search was at an end, as they had apprehended the gang that killed the teamster and effected their capture, not without hard fighting.

"Their work is finished; the dark cloud of terror has been swept away, and the clear and burning sun of peace casts its rays on the prisons filled with those bandits and cut-throats, of Santiago de Cuba province, who escaped the bullets of the Immunes. These merciless wretches, probably have been shot ere this as a penalty for their numerous and atrocious crimes."

Negro Troops, and Their Effect.

O show that the subject of negro troops is commanding great attention, I take the liberty of printing *in toto* the following editorial
which appeared in the New Orleans *Times-Democrat* of March
19, 1899:

"Gov. Allen D. Candler of Georgia, while in no way defending or
excusing the lynching of negroes at Palmetto, in that state—for he has
offered a reward for the capture of the men engaged in it—rightly places
the responsibility for the crime upon those who organized negro troops and
placed arms in their hands. Mr. McKinley and those who instigated him
into adopting this dangerous policy must bear the full responsibility for the
Palmetto slaughter. The President cannot escape it, or plead ignorance of
what his act in mustering negro troops would lead to. He was warned
again and again that the arming of negroes meant race war; that the negro
with a gun on his shoulder becomes a menace to the community, a brigand
and a bully, who insults and outrages all, who is filled with the passion of
race hatred and murder. We had experiences of this during the awful
period of reconstruction, when thousands of lives were sacrificed to the
mad attempt to confer power on the negro over the whites. The President
knew this well; and, now that he is in Georgia, knows it better. He had
heard the subject of race riots discussed in Congress a score of times; he
knew that the negro soldier is a danger to the community; and he was warned
by those who understood the South best that the raising of negro regiments
would unsettle the black race throughout the country, fill them with false ideas
of what they could demand, and lead to lynchings like that at Palmetto.
Yet to reward the small-fry negro politician who had worked under Hanna
to "fix" the southern delegations, and whose assistance he wants in 1900,
the President was willing to stir up all this trouble.

"The experience with negro troops has been exactly what the President
was warned of. Wherever they went riots and murder followed in their foot-
steps. Their camps were constant sources of danger to the surrounding
country; and it took almost as many white men to keep the negro soldiers in
order as there were negroes in our army. From the very beginning of the
enlistment they proved a curse. At Tampa their outrages aroused such
indignation that the white soldiers were called out to suppress them, but not
until a score or more of the insolent and lawless black brigands had been
killed. At Chickamauga, Griffin, and, indeed, all points where they were
stationed, there was riot and bloodshed. In Cuba it was the same story,
and the arrival of the negro troops there was attended with violence and

murder. We have already lost in these riots and lynchings more lives than the navy lost in all its gallant victories of the war. The negro troops have caused more bloodshed in this country than the Spanish army and navy caused in Cuba and the Philippines.

"These riots at the negro camps and at the various points through which the negro troops were moved during the war are but an item in the indictment. The trouble was not confined to the blacks who entered the service; but the "bad element" everywhere, all those who cherish in their hearts hatred of the white man, who believe in social equality, who would like to restore the rule of reconstruction, encouraged by the President's action, seeing their race recognized as the equal of the white man in courage, have been stirred up to that wild frenzy which the negro evinces on many occasions, and which has characterized the risings in Hayti, Martinique, Jamaica, and other islands, where the black man has conceived the idea that he is the equal of the white,— risings that have ended in the extermination of one or the other race.

"Governor Candler calls attention to the fact that there has been no racial animosity in Georgia for many years, and very little at any time. The two races seemed to get along well together. The negroes were satisfied with the position they occupied; and the whites were friendly toward them and gave them every encouragement. But ever since the enlistment of negro troops began, the race prejudice has been nursed into intensity. There were, unfortunately, several negro camps in Georgia, and many black regiments marched through the state. Wherever this occurred the negroes of the neighborhood became ugly and snarlish and dangerous. The inevitable result has followed at Palmetto, and we greatly fear that the lynching there is not the only one that we will have as the result of the President's mischief-making policy. There are the negro regiments stationed in Cuba—the Ninth Immunes, for instance, from Louisiana. These regiments have been enjoying social equality in the island, where a large proportion of the population is of negro or of mixed blood, and where that race line which the Anglo-Saxon insists on does not exist. Every one of these men will come back filled with the idea that he can play this social equality racket here, as well as at Santiago; that the theaters, hotels, restaurants and all places shall be open to him on the same terms as to the whites. We need not tell any of our readers who are southern, or who know aught of southern ideas, that this means many more Palmettoes.

"The man who starts a servile war, who arouses the lower race against the governing one, who stirs up negro passion and frenzy, must assume the responsibility for every drop of blood shed in race riots in the South, for every negro lynched by whites whose patience has been exhausted.

"Like Governor Candler, we have naught to say in defense of the mob that killed the negroes at Palmetto, but we know, and have always known, that this is an inevitable consequence of stirring up the negroes by placing arms in their hands. Every negro regiment raised means riots, and so many negroes killed or lynched. The country will have paid a big price in blood to enable McKinley and Hanna to buy black delegates to the Republican convention from the South."

A Call to Sleepy Justice.

T is difficult to understand the status of our Afro-American citizens. Are they citizens in the same sense as are white citizens of our country? The letter of the Governor of Georgia, as embodied in the article quoted from the New Orleans *Times-Democrat*, would imply that they are not. It further suggests that it is not intended that they shall ever become such. It is expressive of their being a servile class' and of a desire that they remain in such relationship to the government. It is not the expression only of the individual who happened to be the representative of a Commonwealth. It is the deliberate expression of an aggressive people; of a people who assiduously press their views, when morally right or when iniquitously wrong, until the people of the entire country will have acquiesced in them, and the general government has adopted them as its principle of polity. The very different superior, intellectual, moral, industrial and mercantile culture of the people upon whom these peculiar views are impressed are incompetent to withstand, as they are incompetent to understand, their insidious attacks upon the principles fundamental of free institutions.

The common and exclusive industrial trend, the silence of the press as to the vital interests embodied in this increasingly aggressive purpose and desire, warrant the inquiry as to whether this desire is not the national expectation of the people? It is foreign to the accredited American desire, and far too much out of harmony with its free institutions to be realized. How shall the institutions of Paine, of Lincoln, and of Grant produce at once and the same time a servile, slave class and a free man? How shall they, by repression of and injustice to a class of its citizens, make or expect them to become, patriots?

How shall the government expect their hearts to beat more rapidly when it shall have again become involved with a foreign power? How shall it expect them to volunteer and take the oath its soldiers are required to take to defend it at home and abroad?

Would our government avoid a possible calamity? Would it make it impossible for three or more millions of able-bodied men to become available as its defenders? Would it have them love it? And to be willing to die, if need be, for it?

The letters from the mayors of various cities and the governors of several northern states, where the Afro-American volunteers were encamped, as well as the reports of the commissioned officers who commanded regiments of infantry and cavalry during the Spanish-American War, make it plain that the "dissatisfaction" alleged against the Afro-American volunteers was not owing to their military inefficiency. They make it equally plain that it was of other origin than inefficiency.

But the term "unsatisfactory" is delusive, ambiguous and indefinite. Were the colored volunteers a disappointment in their mental and moral make-up? Had the staff officers of Afro-American immune regiments or the War Department expected them to be as were their fathers? Had they expected the free institutions of the country to have produced a monstrosity or a paradox in the colored youth who sat by the side of the white youth in the colleges of the north, or had they expected an alleged native servility in Afro-American officers that would cause them to accept other treatment in kind and degree than was accorded other men of similar rank? Have they mistaken the nature and trend of American institutions?

Is man the same? Will the same institutions, working upon the same mental and soul power, produce like men? Are the vassal grounds of Georgia and southern civilization class distinctions and caste prejudices?

Are there two distinct civilizations growing under our common "Old Glory?" Or has the desire for a black thing, more than a dog and less than a man, become the desire of all America,—of New York, of Massachusetts, of Kansas, of Illinois, of Ohio? Has this desire destroyed the required equipoise of the government? Let the leopard change its spots, let the wolf forget its cunning; but these institutions will never reproduce the negro of yore. To reproduce him, the cherished and lamented southern institution of the past must be resurrected and again equipped with its barbarisms. The white South, and not all of it, for a part of it is morally incapable, must resuscitate it, with its elements of brutality unknown to even Spanish colonial rule, from its own unique civilization. What uniqueness, what distinction it has in oppression, in false accusation, in barbarous executions, and the like.

If to the people, or that part of them to whom the Afro-American officer in the army is "unsatisfactory," as is an Afro-American gentleman at all times and in all places, justice is to go for its regulating principle as to him, then will our government have a dangerous class of citizens, so-called, at home, and the peculiar oath of allegiance, suggesting possible enemies at home, is well required of its soldiers.

A war with Germany is not an impossibility. In such an emergency, would all German-Americans remain loyal? In a war with England, would all Anglo-Americans remain loyal? In a war with France, would all Franco-Americans remain loyal? In a war with Russia, would all Russian-Americans remain loyal? In a war with Italy, would all Italo-Americans remain loyal? These questions are not intended to imply a probability of treasonable action on the part of these peoples. But as they may be considered assurances of permanent peace and comity between this and their native land, they are intended to suggest that Afro-Americans have no ties binding them to other than the government of the fathers of growing liberty. Having no ties binding them to a foreign government, shall they have none in this, their native land, making them increasingly more loyal? Shall this desire for and expectation of a servile class cause justice to condone its savagery and inhuman proclivities, and thereby make traitors of those who would have been of the most patriotic? But no power will ever prostitute the institutions now lifting Afro-Americans into national consciousness of the freedom of liberty.

If the "dissatisfaction" were based upon the inefficiency of colored army officers, it would be removable by and through the military and naval academies of the government. In fine, if the nation would have Afro-American affectionate allegiance, let it be to them as it is to all of its native-born and adopted citizens. No less than absolute equality of opportunity will secure it.

Italy may have accepted a half million dollars for the lives of its subjects that were slaughtered ruthlessly and without warrant in justice, and, in violation of its treaty right of asylum for them in this country. I, may again show its avaricious greed of money, and accept another gratuity for the lives of its subjects which have been again sacrificed, in abhorrence to human nature. And thus Louisiana may continue to disgrace our common nation.

At some time and in some place, the "best citizens,"—bankers, merchants, teachers, preachers and generals of the highly civilized South,—will murder, yes cruelly murder, by their favorite method, some Englishman, or Frenchman, or Russian, when it will be unfortunately learned, I fear, that not all Anglo-Americans, not all Franco-Americans, and not all Russian-Americans, will remain loyal to "Old Glory," upon which there would not be one dark spot if it were not for the section where oppression, robbery, and murder are tolerated, and fastened upon the weak and unlettered, who are weak and unlettered because of its desire for a servile people. I urge, not alone for the Afro-American, an "open door" of opportunity, but a "securing door" of sentiment and justice that will secure to citizens, or at least to foreigners, a right of trial, and security in life by American justice.

Is this alleged dissatisfaction with Afro-American volunteers who served in the Spanish-American war a candid deliverance of a justifiable dissatisfaction, or is it a diplomatic cover under which lies an unwarranted, cruel suspicion imputing probable treason to the only class of American citizens that has never produced a traitor?

I have said unwarranted suspicion. May it be qualified? If so, may it not be by the fact that the only ground existing for it exists, not in any experience this government has had with Afro-Americans, but alone in the injustice of those who desire him to remain forever the servant of servants?

NINTH REGIMENT U. S. V. I. BAND.
(From a photograph taken at Camp Meade, Pa.)

A PHILIPPINO HARP GIRL.

The Race Question in the Philippines.

THE lady harpist in the accompanying illustration represents a people who are acquainted with a race question very similar to the one now before the American people.

A recent writer says of them: The colored people of this colony would always be inclined to struggle for independence because the rule of the mother, or governing country, of the colony makes their access to the highest positions in the state impossible. In the Philippine Islands, the contempt manifested toward the colored tribes by the Spanish press had contributed very much toward making the gulf between rulers and ruled progressively deeper and harder to bridge. The pressure of colored people to the higher studies and the special schools far exceeds the percentage which one would anticipate from their proportion to the whole population. This intellectual aptitude made more perilous to the Spaniards their tenure of peaceable possession, and because of the Spanish press ever treating them with the most abject scorn, calling them anthropoids, and devoid of any capacity to attain European civilization, this gulf grew to vast proportions. The educated full-blooded Philippinos foamed with increasing rage at the attacks upon the capacity of their race and color. "The color of our skin," they said, "is a stigma with the Spanish lords and with all Europe, too; why thus insult us, and in so cowardly a manner, when the censorship at Manila makes it impossible for us to defend ourselves?"

But these insults, and the abuses to which they were continuously subjected for three hundred years, could only outwardly disturb them. It could not disturb their self-esteem and respect. Their leading spirits had critically studied the white race, and confirmed the opinion that the whites were made of the same earth as they, and that the whites could, under equal conditions, have been and done no more than what they were and had done. Only, the whites have adopted a lordly code of morals which, like the flag with contraband goods, covers the grossest treachery of right and other outrages which a white gentleman would not venture, indeed, to commit upon his peers; but which, in the treatment of colored men, belong, so to speak, to good tone and European smartness.

Our citizens, barring the colonial feature, will hardly recognize the monstrous features of color prejudice, and will probably inquire where in His realm is the gospel of the fatherhood of God and the brotherhood of man realized between the black and white races? It is a beautiful ideal, and may be obtainable. But in this country of Anglo-Americans, it is probably much further distant than in the island where the instrument of our harpist in the above illustration makes music to encourage the dream that sometime and somewhere the Philippino and the white American will find peace in the beneficence of His fatherhood and country in the love of His son.

Officers, 9th United States Volunteer Infantry.

REGIMENTAL STAFF OFFICERS.

CHAS. J. CRANE. *Colonel.*

DAVID M. SELLS, *Lieutenant-Colonel.*

DUNCAN B. HARRISON. *Major.*   ARMAND G. ROMAIN, *Major.*

1st LIEUT. JAMES LONGSTREET, *Adjutant.*

1st LIEUT. J. LEON JONES, *Quartermaster.*   1st LIEUT. JAMES T. ORD, *Quartermaster.**

MAJOR JAMES MITCHELL. *Surgeon.*

1st LIEUT. ALLEN J. BLACK. *Asst. Surgeon.*   1st LIEUT. W. EDSON APPLE, *Asst. Surgeon.*

CAPTAIN W. HILARY COSTON. *Chaplain.*

NON-COMMISSIONED STAFF OFFICERS.

Name	Rank	Date of Enrollment	Place of Enrollment	Remarks	Date of first Muster
HALL, POOLE S.	Sergeant Major	July 1, '98	Houston, Texas	Appointed 2nd Lieut. of Co. I, by A. G. O., May 22, '99.	
MINOR, JOHN S.	Q. M. Sergeant	June 10, '98	New Orleans, La.	Appointed Q. M. Sergeant June 10. '98. Transferred to Co I.	
DIBBLE, JOSEPH E.	Hospital Steward	July 1, '98	Houston, Texas	Appointed Hospital Steward July 1, '98	
BEVERLY, JAMES M.	Hospital Steward	July 1, '98	Houston, Texas	Appointed Hospital Steward July 1, '98	

*Detached service.

(62)

FABRE, FERDINAND . . . Hospital Steward . June 13, '98 . . . New Orleans, La. . . Appointed Hospital Steward July 18, '98 . . . .

ROBINSON, DAVID F. . . Hospital Steward . July . . '98 . . . New Orleans, La. . . Appointed Hospital Steward April, '99 . . . .

PATERSON, G. W. . . . Hospital Steward . June 20, '98 . . . New Orleans, La. . . . .

HALL, WILLIS . . . . . . Drum-major . . . June 10, '98 . . . New Orleans, La. . . Transferred to Band Aug. 1, '93, Co. B.
Discharged.

MacNEAL, JAMES W. . . Chief Musician . . June 24, '98 . . . New Orleans, La. . . Appointed Chief Musician July 18, '98. Appointed 2d Lt. by A. G. O, May 22, '99 . . . Oct. 26, '98

DUCONGE, OSCAR . . . Prin. Musician . . July 18, '98 . . . New Orleans, La. . . Appointed Prin. Musician July 18, '98 . . Sept. 8, '98

CASTRY, FRANÇOIS . . . Prin. Musician . . July 18, '98 . . . New Orleans, La. . . Appointed Prin. Musician July 18, '98 . . .

MUSTERING OFFICERS FROM THE UNITED STATES ARMY.

CAPTAIN F. H. EDMUNDS, U. S. A., *Mustering-in Officer.*   DR. DUNCHIE, U. S. A., *Medical Examiner.*

MUSTERING-OUT OFFICERS.

COL. S. P. JOCELYN, 25th Infantry (Colored), U. S. A.   CAPT. S. W. MILLER, 5th Infantry, U. S. A.

LIEUT. JOHN ROBERTSON, 6th Infantry, U. S. A.   LIEUT. H. J. PRICE, 24th Infantry, U. S. A.

MAJOR W. R. HALL, Surgeon, U. S. A., *Medical Officer.*   LIEUT. W. EDSON APPLE, 9th Regt. U. S. V. I.
Asst. Surgeon.

NOTE. — The 9th Regiment United States Volunteer Infantry was mustered into the service of the Government on June 28, 1898, for service during the Spanish-American War. It was mustered out of the service May 25, 1899.

Band, 9th United States Volunteer Infantry.

Name	Rank	Date of Enrollment	Place of Enrollment	Remarks	Date of first illness
Bryant, Joseph A.	Private	June 11, '98	New Orleans, La.	Transferred to Band from Co. A Aug. 1, '98	Nov. 7, '98
Castry, Charles	Private	Aug. 13, '98	New Orleans, La.	Transferred to Band from Co. G Aug. 13, '98	Nov. 3, '98
Conway, Charles B.	Private	June 20, '98	New Orleans, La.	Transferred to Band from Co. D Aug. 1, '98	Oct. 26, '98
Davis, George E.	Private	July 1, '98	Houston, Texas	Discharged Aug. 1, '98	Aug. 1, '98
Delisle, John B.	Private	Aug. 8, '98	New Orleans, La.	Assigned to Band Aug. 18, '98	Dec. 8, '98
Drayton, Louis	Private	June 21, '98	New Orleans, La.	Transferred to Band from Co. D Aug. 1, '98	Sept. 15, '98
Ellis, Arthur	Private	June 18, '98	New Orleans, La.	Transferred to Band from Co. C Aug. 1, '98	Dec. 8, '98
Gaspard, Etienne	Private	June 17, '98	New Orleans, La.	Transferred to Band from Co. C Aug. 1, '98	Nov. 3, '98
Irvin, Daniel	Private	June 25, '98	Galveston, Texas	Transferred to Band from Co. G Aug. 1, '98. Died April 14, '99, at San Luis, Cuba.	Nov. 12, '98
Jones, Edward D.	Private	Aug. 8, '98	New Orleans, La.	Assigned to Band Aug. 8, '98.	Oct. 31, '98
Lecouq, Octave	Private	July 28, '98	New Orleans, La.	Transferred to Band from Co. D Aug. 1, '98	Dec. 11, '98
Mayfield, Joseph A.	Private	June 11, '98	New Orleans, La.	Transferred to Band from Co. A Aug. 1, '98	Oct. 1, '98
Moseley, William	Private	July 13, '98	New Orleans, La.	Transferred to Band from Co. L	
Palao, Edgar J.	Private	July 6, '98	New Orleans, La.	Transferred to Band from Co. K Aug. 1, '98	Mar. 5, '98
Patterson, Dennis	Private	June 29, '98	New Orleans, La.	Transferred to Band from Co. I Aug. 1, '98	Nov. 12, '98
Richardson, Samuel	Private	June 28, '98	Galveston, Texas	Transferred to Band from Co. G Aug. 1, '98	
Ridgley, Emanuel	Private	June 20, '98	New Orleans, La.	Transferred to Band from Co. D Aug. 1, '98	Nov. 27, '98
Ridgeley, Usan	Private	June 27, '98	Donaldsonville, La.	Transferred to Band from Co. F Aug. 1, '98	Oct. 27, '98
Senegal, Achilles	Private	July 8, '98	New Orleans, La.	Transferred to Band from Co. L Aug. 1, '98	Sept. 24, '98
Wilson, John T.	Private	July 28, '98	New Orleans, La.	Transferred to Band from Co. F Aug. 1, '98	Oct. 27, '98

SURRENDER TREE, UNDER WHICH TERMS OF SURRENDER OF THE
ISLAND OF CUBA WERE MADE.

COLONEL. CHAS. J. CRANE.

Colonel Chas. J. Crane.

.. .. ..

THE organization of the 9th United States Volunteer Infantry was not accomplished without great difficulty and labor. From the inception of the movement to raise this regiment to the hour of its embarkation for Cuba it was opposed, and the most malignant attacks were made upon its patriotic and intrepid organizer. His knowledge of his own excellent military equipment, and his long experience with and confidence in the dormant ability of colored men to make ideal soldiers, gave to him mental and physical endurance which inspired his men and won the admiring personal loyalty of his officers. During the short period of not quite two months the regiment was organized, with 1,100 men, and sufficiently disciplined and drilled to meet the approval of and to be accepted by the Inspector General of the United States Army, and to convert the virulence of those who had opposed its organization into the highest laudation. With an appreciative knowledge of the facility with which men were enlisted and mustered for the Spanish-American war, the opinion is amply justified that the subject of this sketch made a record as an organizer and disciplinarian that could hardly be duplicated by an investigation which would embrace the entire organizing service of our army. The organization of the regiment went forward by his touch as if inspired by a magician's wand. Its organization, attended, as it was, by the discipline almost of a martinet, gave at once protection and military training to the men who desired to "avenge the Maine."

It was the fortune of the regiment to do service upon the Island of Cuba at the point where it disembarked on August 23.

Of the many experiences of the regiment, the saddest and most sudden was the death of Mrs. Chas. J. Crane, the wife of Colonel Crane. Her death was shocking and paralyzing in its unexpectedness. She was ever active in showing, in many ways, her interest in and care for the soldiers of the entire regiment. The men loved her, and sympathized with their beloved colonel in his and their bereavement.

The service of Colonel Crane has revealed to the government an emergency power of which our government was probably uninformed. It has done much for the Afro-American. It has discovered to him the value of discipline and the power of trained organization. Colonel Crane has given the Afro-American of the South probably his first lesson of liberty under law, and taught him how to secure in the fullest measure the satisfaction found in obedience to orders. The chaplain of the regiment acknowledges his personal indebtedness to Colonel Crane, and indulges the hope that the Captain of the Armies of Right will vouchsafe to him a continued career of usefulness and prosperity in the exalted service of our common country.

MAJOR DUNCAN B. HARRISON.

Major Duncan B. Harrison.

. . . . . .

MAJOR DUNCAN B. HARRISON has probably paid a larger price for the service he has been pleased to render to the men of his regiment than any of his fellow officers. He is characterized by the finest sensibilities, which have moved him to assume the interests of his men when they most needed protection and vindication.

On the 14th of November, 1898, a number of the soldiers of the 9th regiment became involved in a difficulty in a Cuban restaurant. A Cuban policeman, wantonly and without the semblance of justification, shot one of the men. This murderous act caused the loss of probably six innocent lives. Six Cubans and one Spaniard were mercilessly shot by enraged and unknown persons. For this crime two men, whose connection with the affair in the slightest degree was an absolute impossibility, were arrested and, after three months' confinement in prison at Santiago, were tried and vindicated by a military court, the personnel of which was of southern origin. Major Harrison was their principal attorney, and for having proved their innocence he has been most scandalously assailed. This has been done especially by papers which accept an accusation against an Afro-American as proof of his guilt.

Major Harrison is a gentleman and a soldier, and his devotion to the interests of his men won for him their affection to an immeasurable degree. The Cuban sun, during the months of their service in that island, was never too hot nor the rain too severe to interfere with the exercise of his watchful care over his men. Nor was the possibility of contagion of the many dangerous fevers too great to deter him from interesting himself in the cause of a needy soldier, or to take him, when he had fallen upon the march or drill, or been seized with one of those deadly fevers, in his strong arms to the hospital, there to minister to his needs as gently as if he were of his own kith and kin. He is free to a remarkable degree from racial bias, and while he is kind and sympathetic, he is still the disciplinarian and soldier, who wins the confidence and love, and commands the respect and absolute obedience, of his men.

The heroism displayed by Major Harrison has made the people of the United States his debtor to a large degree. It saved a large part of the regiment from almost certain death and the nation from a calamity which would have had a demoralizing effect upon our arms everywhere. Almost the entire regiment was prostrated upon San Juan hill by that deadly disease, yellow fever. In the tents and company streets men lay ill, suffering keenly. Though ill himself, and nearly exhausted by a vigil of many hours, he walked through the streets as though immune from death, directed his line officers to a faithful discharge of duties new to military experience, and by his example and hopeful words quickened the spirits and stimulated the courage of the sufferers for the struggle with disease which brought many from the valley and shadow of death to a new lease of life and usefulness.

LIEUTENANT J. LEON JONES.

J. Leon Jones.

.. .. ..

THE subject of this sketch, Lieut. J. Leon Jones,* regimental quartermaster
of the 9th United States Volunteer Infantry, was born in Houston, Texas,
August 3, 1874. When it was announced that several immune regiments
of volunteers would be organized in the south to take part in the Spanish-American
war, Lieutenant Jones, on account of prior military teaching, as an officer of the
"Cocke" Rifles, of the state militia, and a special desire to go to war to do his
duty in defense of his country's flag, assisted very materially in organizing Co.
I, 9th United States Volunteer Infantry, whose home name was given in
honor of Hon. Henry C. Ferguson, and known as the "Ferguson Rifles."
Colonel Crane, commanding the 9th regiment, had been ordered to New Orleans,
La., by the War Department, to organize and mobilize the regiment at that point.
The "Ferguson Rifles" having been accepted as one of the companies of the
regiment, Lieutenant Jones went with it as first sergeant. Shortly afterwards the
the regiment left for Cuba, and in three months after its organization he was one
of the non-commissioned staff officers, having been appointed regimental quartermaster sergeant, October 1, 1898. He served in that capacity with great
credit until the 12th day of April, 1899, when he was notified by the Adjutant
General of the army of his appointment that day as a second lieutenant in the
regiment. He was at the time acting as district commissary of subsistence
of Mayari, Cuba, and was continued in that capacity until the 24th of the same
month, when Colonel Crane appointed him regimental quartermaster and commissary of subsistence, relieving First Lieutenant James T. Ord (white). The
position is one of honor, he being on the colonel's personal staff. Aside from
the regimental chaplain, he is the only colored officer to fill a similar position in
any of the regiments having a white staff and colored officers of the line. Lieutenant Jones, though young, in the short space of ten months worked up from the
position of an enlisted man to one of the most highly responsible positions in
the regiment. He enjoyed the confidence and esteem of all his brother officers
and of the men in the regiment. His is a worthy example for others to follow.
As yet he is not fully decided on his future, though he is thinking very seriously of
continuing in the service. We predict for him a brilliant future as a military man.

*Promoted First Lieutenant by special order War Department, May 17 1899.

CAPT. W. HILARY COSTON AND FAMILY.
(Late Chaplain of Ninth U. S. Volunteer Infantry.)

W. Hilary Coston.

.. .. ..

W. HILARY COSTON was born at Providence, R. I. He attended the public schools of that city until he was seven years of age, when his parents removed to New Haven, Conn. Here he was again entered in the public schools. At the age of sixteen, by a fortunate circumstance, he secured the janitorship of Hopkins Grammar School, Yale Preparatory, which he attended for several years, when he was sent to Wilberforce University, from which he entered Yale Divinity School. He graduated in the class of '84, and immediately entered the ministry of the A. M. E. Church. He has had the varying fortunes of the ministry, and considers himself favored in having been privileged to contribute to the educational, moral and Christian influences which are lifting the American people into a higher appreciation of the Fatherhood of God and the brotherhood of man. He was appointed by President McKinley to the chaplaincy of the 9th United States Volunteer Infantry, which office was vacated by Rev. W. T. Walker, D.D., who had resigned it, to the deep regret of the men of the regiment, by whom he was highly appreciated and sincerely loved. The Reverend Mr. Walker is of pleasing appearance, easy of approach, and of tender sympathies. He has the reputation of being one, of the most eloquent members of the Afro-American ministry.

Chaplain Coston keenly appreciated his opportunity for exceptional service, and while he was not privileged to preach at regular intervals, he in a commendable measure adapted himself to army life, and tried to so come in contact with the men of the regiment as to impress them with the fact that Christ's life and work are being perpetuated and accomplished by a ministry which "goes about doing good."

Dr. Jos. E. Dibble, Hospital Steward.

JOSEPH E. DIBBLE.

·· ·· ··

DR. JOSEPH E. DIBBLE, whose portrait appears above, was a most valuable addition to the regiment from the time of his joining until the final muster-out. Within a short time after the first call for volunteers, the doctor offered his services to the government, and on July 1, 1898, at Houston, Texas, he was enrolled and immediately appointed to the position he so acceptably filled. He will always be held in grateful memory by those who were the beneficiaries of his kindly offices, and the fact that almost the entire regiment was at one time or other down with illness, amply demonstrates the hard work the doctor had to perform.

D. F. Robinson, Hospital Steward.

D. F. ROBINSON.

•• •• ••

HOSPITAL STEWARD D. F. ROBINSON was born in the state of Mississippi in 1862, and enlisted for the war with Spain June 16, 1898, joining the 9th Regiment U. S. V. I. at New Orleans, La. At the time he joined the regiment it was without a chaplain, and, by consent of Colonel Crane, he officiated in that capacity with signal ability and conscientiousness until the position was filled by a regular appointment by the President. He was appointed to his present position in April, 1899, and all his work has been marked with a sincere devotion to duty, and in his position as hospital steward he has been the means of adding much to the comfort of those who came under his ministrations.

LIEUT. COL. DAVID M. SELLS.

First Battalion

GEORGE H. NELSON.

.. .. ..

GEORGE H. NELSON was born in New Orleans, La., Oct. 12, 1870. His father having died when a small boy, he was adopted by a Congregational minister named Rev. Isaac H. Hall, who educated and cared for him as one of his own children. Lieutenant Nelson graduated from Straight University, New Orleans, class of '90, with the degree of B.S. Three years later he graduated from the Medical Department of the New Orleans University with the degree of M.D. For two sessions he was instructor in analytical chemistry. He was also organist of the Morris Brown Congregational church for more than fifteen years.

When the call for volunteers was made by President McKinley, Lieutenant Nelson was the captain of an independent military company called the "Faith Cadets," whose motto was "Courage and Faith." This company was organized in August, 1887. On May 30, 1890, this company, with others, participated in the memorial services of the colored G. A. R. of Mississippi and Louisiana, at the National Cemetery "Chalmette," when Lieutenant Nelson's company fired the first volley over the nation's dead in that cemetery. But soon a bill was passed in Louisiana making it a crime for an independent military company to exist without a special permission from the Governor. This permit could never be secured, and the company was allowed to sleep quietly on until the call was made. Then, like a flash, the men were brought together. Circulars were issued calling upon them to assemble at the old headquarters. This they did, officers were elected, and they with patience waited for developments. When the 9th regiment was organized, the "Faith Cadets" offered their services in a body, which were accepted by Col. C. J. Crane, and the men were mustered into service as Co. A, June 20, 1898, at Camp Corbin, New Orleans, La., with James C. Simpson captain, Geo. H. Nelson first lieutenant, and E. H. Phillips second lieutenant. Lieutenant Nelson was commissioned June 25, 1898.

E. H. PHILLIPS.

.. .. ..

LIEUTENANT E. H. PHILLIPS was born Dec. 26, 1867, in New Orleans, La. He attended the public schools until eleven years old, when the death of his father compelled him to leave school and assist in the support of his five younger brothers. He has been a bootblack, newsboy, peddler, farmer and book agent, and is now a wholesale and retail dealer in coal. In 1887 he became a member of the Faith Cadets, a military organization of New Orleans, and rose from the ranks to first lieutenant, the position he held when the body was disbanded by an act of the Legislature.

On April 21, 1898, he telegraphed to the governor of the state for permission to organize a company (it being a misdemeanor punishable by six months' imprisonment to do so without that official's consent), and without waiting for an answer hoisted a flag over his place of business, drew up a call for volunteers, and began to enroll names. This organization, the First Louisana Colored Volunteers, was the first volunteer organization in the state, and, as Co. A, became the nucleus of Col. C. J. Crane's regiment, the 9th U. S. Volunteer Infantry (Immunes), in which

W. H. FRANKLIN, First Lieutenant Co. E.

he was commissioned second lieutenant. He was appointed adjutant of the first battalion by Lieut. Col. D. M. Sells, and held that position until his company and Co. C were ordered on detached service at El Cobre, Cuba, where he was appointed quartermaster, which he remained until his regiment was ordered home. On account of his small stature he is known in the regiment as "Little Regular." What is thought of him by his superiors is best shown by the following:

"As your captain I take great pleasure in recognizing your worth and ability, and the great assistance you have rendered me in bringing my company up to its present standard of efficiency."   JAMES C. SIMPSON,
                                               Capt. 9th U. S. V. I., Com'd'g Co. A.

                                               "EL COBRE, CUBA, April 10, '99.
"I appointed you quartermaster of this detachment, knowing you to be honest and trustworthy."   E. J. SHEARMAN,
                                               Capt. 9th U. S. V. I., Com'd'g Detachment.

W. H. FRANKLIN.

WILLIAM H. FRANKLIN, first lieutenant, appointed August 16, 1898. Born in Gallatin, Sumner county, Tenn., March 25, 1857. Enlisted in 24th Infantry, April 16, 1876, and served continuously as private, corporal, sergeant and first sergeant in Cos. J and E, 24th Infantry, to August 17, 1898. Was in the engagements before Santiago, Cuba, from July 1, 1898. Appointed first lieutenant August 16, 1898, while serving as first sergeant Co. E, 24th Infantry at Siboney, Cuba. He accepted his commission August 18, 1898.

★ ★ ★

JOHN W. BROWN.

JOHN W. BROWN, second lieutenant, appointed October 24, 1898. He was born at Falmouth, Stafford county, Va., May 5, 1856. He enlisted April 24, 1876, in the United States army, was assigned to Co. D, 24th Infantry, July 12, 1876, and was discharged as a sergeant April 23, 1881. He reënlisted May 20 of the same year, was assigned to Troop C, 9th United States Cavalry, and served as a private, corporal, sergeant, first sergeant and saddler sergeant. He was appointed second lieutenant in the 9th United States Volunteer Infantry, accepted the commission on October 26, 1898, and joined the regiment at San Luis, Cuba, on December 6, 1898.

★ ★ ★

HENRY O. FRANKLIN.

HENRY O. FRANKLIN, second lieutenant, 9th United States Volunteer Infantry, was born in the town of Thibodeaux, parish of Lafourche, state of Louisiana, March 25, 1874. He attended the Thibodeaux public schools and Straight University, the A. M. A. school at New Orleans, and also Meilley's commercial night school in New Orleans. He has had continuous employment with different commercial firms in New Orleans ever since he left Straight University, ten years ago, and was employed at the Citizens' Bank of Louisiana for six years previous to his appointment in the 9th United States Volunteer Infantry, June 25, 1898, which position is still open to him when the regiment is mustered out. But Lieutenant Franklin intends to quit the south and seek a home in some of the new possessions of the United States as soon as he is discharged from the service.

Lieutenant Franklin is a member of Central church, and for three years was president of its board of trustees. He was also president of the Y. P. S. C. E., and for some time superintendent of the Sabbath school of Central church. This is one of the largest Congregational churches in the south. He was the secretary of the local Christian Endeavor Union of New Orleans, which organization sent him as their representative to the Boston C. E. convention in 1895.

Up until 1888, Lieutenant Franklin's father was considered one of the wealthiest and most prosperous colored men in Louisiana. He was, however, forced to leave

Henry O. Franklin, Second Lieutenant Co. C.

his home, Thibodeaux, by the "regulators," at the time aforesaid, and since then has been a resident of New Orleans.

Lieutenant Franklin's first duty in Cuba was guarding the Spanish prisoners taken on San Juan hill, August 25, 1898. He was in command of roads that led from the hill (San Juan) when the Spanish soldiers saw the last of San Juan, and passed out to embark for Spain. He was a member of the first general court martial for the military district of Mayari, and adjutant of the El Cobre detachment of the 9th United States Volunteer Infantry, consisting of Companies A and C. He hoisted the first American flag that floated over the town of El Cobre.

The following poem, by Miss Stella A. E. Brazley, of New Orleans, has been furnished the publisher by Lieutenant Franklin. The poem was sent to the lieutenant by its writer as a token of friendship for him, and is dedicated to

THE COLORED BOYS IN BLUE.

Brave men of color, rise! awake!
    And hasten to your country's call.
Your slothful bonds asunder break,
    Your latent spirit disenthrall,
And be the warriors you are;
Your sires of old were men of war.

An island lies across the main
    Whose sons have fought for many years
The sanguinary hosts of Spain,
    That drenched their soil with blood and tears.
Arise and help that patriot band
To drive the Spaniard from the land.

Your kinsmen there have shed their blood,
    And lost their lives in freedom's cause;
In tattered rags and meager form
    They fought, and won the world's applause.
Go! emulate their valor now,
And glory's wreath will crown your brow.

Go! seek the spot where Maceo fell,
    And strike his slayers; spare them not.
Your cheer shall be their funeral knell,
    Your vengeance shall be swift and hot.
From Spanish misrule purge and clear
The occidental hemisphere.

America demands your aid,
    Wards of the land of liberty!
Behold his grand, benignant shade
    Who strove to set your fathers free.
It beams upon you from above,
Shedding its blessings and its love.

Ye scions of a warlike race,
    Renew the prestige of your sires,
And by your valor win the place
    Where glory flames with radiant fires,
With those great heroes, brave and pure,
Men like Maceo, Toussaint L'Ouverture.

STERLING PRICE BROWN, First Lieutenant, commanding Co. D.

STERLING PRICE BROWN.

.. .. ..

HE subject of this sketch, Sterling Price Brown, was born in Atlanta, Ga., December 23, 1863. He attended the public schools of Atlanta until he reached the age of fourteen. He attended the Central Tennessee College, at Nashville, Tennessee, where he completed the academic course in four years. He entered the Meharry Medical College in 1881, and after three years of faithful study graduated with distinguished honors, and was unanimously selected by the faculty to be the valedictorian of his class. After receiving the degree of M.D. he went to New Orleans, La., and passed the examination that admitted him to the practice of his profession.

When the first call was made for volunteers to take up arms in defense of their country, Dr. Brown gave up his practice, and assisted in organizing the 9th U. S. V. Infantry. After the regiment was organized, its services were offered to the Governor of the state, as part of that state's quota called for by the Secretary of War. The Governor refused to accept the regiment, as the laws of Louisiana forbid a military organization of negroes. The regiment was then offered to the President of the United States, who had already appointed Col. Charles J. Crane to organize a regiment in the states of Louisiana and Texas. When Colonel Crane went to New Orleans to organize the 9th U. S. V. Infantry, Dr. Brown was among the first to be appointed a first lieutenant, and was assigned to duty with Company D.

During the labor strike in New Orleans in 1895, when the colored screwsmen and many longshoremen were driven from the wharf by a mob of white hoodlums, and their tools thrown into the Mississippi river, Dr. Brown was among the first of his race to offer his services to the laboring men of that city. He gave them the use of his office, which was near the Cotton Exchange, and acted as secretary of the joint conference committees that were selected by the colored and white organizations to settle the labor trouble. At that time fighting was going on continuously, and the cowards made it a point to shoot at every colored man that came in range of their guns. Carey, Allen & Co., two of the most prominent colored labor leaders in the city, organized a stevedore firm, and signed a contract with M. J. Saunders, agent of the West India Steamship Company, to load and unload all the ships of that line. When the first ship, the William Cliffe, came into port, and the men went to Southport to see to the unloading of their tools, which they had secured from Mobile, Ala., they were surrounded by over five hundred men in ambush, who began firing upon the men with Winchester rifles, killing and wounding a great many. Among the many wounded was H. H. Carey, the senior partner of the colored stevedore firm. Carey was deserted by most of his comrades, who were unarmed, and not prepared to meet such a body of armed foes. Carey, single-handed and alone, stood off the entire mob and sent many of the hoodlums to their last resting place. Dr. Brown took up the fight that had been started by Carey, and, with the colored screwsmen and longshoremen, loaded the first ship that was loaded during the entire labor troubles. It is needless to say that it required a man who had no fear of his personal safety to undertake so dangerous a task. But, loving his people, he was willing to sacrifice his life in their behalf. Today the laboring men of his race are enjoying the fruits of his daring.

Lieutenant Brown is among the most efficient lieutenants of the regiment. He

THOMAS C. BUTLER, Second Lieutenant, Co. D.

was peculiarly fortunate in being in temporary command of the second battalion at the time of the official inspection by Gen. C. J. Breckenbridge, U. S. A. That officer said that he had long desired to see a battalion or regiment officered by colored men. The battalion was drilled by the lieutenant in the school of the battalion with so great efficiency, and passed in review with so perfect cadence, that it won for its young officer and itself the respect and high laudation of this veteran of two wars.

THOMAS C. BUTLER.

THE subject of this sketch, Second Lieutenant Thomas C. Butler, was born in the city of Baltimore. He left his home when quite young, and attended school at the St. Mary College for priests, in Annapolis, Maryland, under the most austere and religious of teachers, Jesuit priests. At an early age he became a sailor, and followed the sea until 1887, when, after being shipwrecked on Cape Hatteras, N. C., he joined the now famous 9th U. S. Regular Cavalry, colored. The Lieutenant speaks with undisguised but pardonable pride of the part his regiment took during the Sioux campaign of 1890-91. He was then a non-commissioned officer of Troop D of that regiment, which company was "rear guard" during the night the regiment made the forced march from Harney Springs to Pine Ridge Agency, to be engaged next morning, December 30, 1890, and had not brought in their lost when, on the same day, in the evening, they were ordered to the rescue from probable annihilation of the gallant but unlucky 7th U. S. Regular Cavalry.

During the Spanish-American war he served his country as private in Company H, 25th U. S. Infantry, which made the famous charge against the stone fort at El Caney. The *Army and Navy Journal* of October 22, 1898, says : "He and another man, on their own responsibility, quietly worked their way in front of the general line, and captured the Spanish flag," for which brave act he was appointed a second lieutenant in the 9th U. S. V. Infantry.

Company A, 9th United States Volunteer Infantry.

1st BATTALION, LIEUT. COL. D. M. SELLS COMMANDING.

C. D. WOOD. *Captain.**

G. H. NELSON. *First Lieutenant.*   E. H. PHILLIPS, *Second Lieutenant.*

Name	Rank	Date of Enrollment	Place of Enrollment	Remarks	Date of first illness
FAIRLEY, SOLOMON, JR.	First Sergeant	July 8, '98	New Orleans, La.		July 5, '98
LE BLANC, ISIDORE	Q. M. Sergeant	June 10, '98	New Orleans, La.		July 14, '98
JONES, NICHOLAS, JR.	Sergeant	June 10, '98	New Orleans, La.		July 5, '98
PENDLETON, JOHN W.	Sergeant	June 14, '98	New Orleans, La.	Changed from Quartermaster Sergeant to Duty Sergeant.	Oct. 10, '98
MADISON, JAMES	Sergeant	June 14, '98	New Orleans, La.		Mar. 4, '99
DORSEY, JOHN	Sergeant			Appointed Corporal July 15, '98; appointed Sergeant Mar. 14, '99.	
TATE, EUGENE	Corporal	June 10, '98	New Orleans, La.	Died Sept. 24, '98, at San Juan Hill, Cuba.	July 8, '98
DERRIGAN, THOMAS	Corporal	June 15, '98	New Orleans, La.	Vice Eugene Tate	Aug. 13, '98
RICHARDSON, WILLIAM	Corporal	June 11, '98	New Orleans, La.		Sept. 8, '98
ANDERSON, JOHN	Corporal	June 10, '98	New Orleans, La.	Vice James Madison	July 17, '98
BARGAMER, JESSE	Corporal	June 14, '98	New Orleans, La.		Oct. 29, '98
McLAIN, JOHN	Corporal	June 10, '98	New Orleans, La.	Vice John W. Pendleton	Aug. 16, '98
BROUSSARD, JOSEPH	Corporal	June 13, '98	New Orleans, La.		July 20, '98
CARTER, MILTON	Corporal	June 14, '98	New Orleans, La.	Vice Wallace Mitchell	July 5, '98
WILSON, JAMES	Corporal	June 11, '98	New Orleans, La.		Sept. 8, '98
MAYFIELD, JOSEPH A.	Musician	June 11, '98	New Orleans, La.	Transferred to Band August 1	

*C. D. Wood, Captain, vice James C. Simpson (resigned).

Name	Rank	Date	Place	Remarks	Date
DOMINGO, ALFRED	Musician	June 13, '98	New Orleans, La.	Vice John G. Williams	July 24, '98
JONES, PETER	Wagoner	June 10, '98	New Orleans, La.		Mar. 31, '99
PASCAL, JOSEPH	Artificer	June 14, '98	New Orleans, La.	Vice Thomas Derrigan	Aug. 4, '98
Allen, William	Private	June 13, '98	New Orleans, La.		July 6, '98
Antoine, Manuel	Private	June 10, '98	New Orleans, La.		Sept. 8, '98
Baker, George	Private	June 10, '98	New Orleans, La.		Aug. 13, '98
Baker, Frank	Private	June 10, '98	New Orleans, La.		Sept. 17, '98
Benjamin, Frank	Private	June 10, '98	New Orleans, La.		July 27, '98
Bibbs, Chas.	Private	June 13, '98	New Orleans, La.		Sept. 7, '98
Bryant, Joseph A.	Private	June 11, '98	New Orleans, La.	Transferred to Band August, '98	Aug. 3, '98
Burthlong, Robert E.	Private	June 10, '98	New Orleans, La.		July 13, '98
Clark, B. F.	Private	July 8, '98	New Orleans, La.	Reduced from Sergeant	July 13, '98
Clements, Dennis	Private	June 15, '98	New Orleans, La.		Sept. 14, '98
Daspit, Albert	Private	June 10, '98	New Orleans, La.		July 7, '98
Davis, John	Private	June 10, '98	New Orleans, La.	Died Sept. 17, '98, at San Juan Hill	July 5, '98
Dixon, Joseph	Private	June 10, '98	New Orleans, La.		Aug. 29, '98
Dunn, John H.	Private	June 11, '98	New Orleans, La.	Appointed Company Tailor	Sept. 21, '98
Dupre, Geo.	Private	June 13, '98	New Orleans, La.		Aug. 13, '98
Dyer, Ellis	Private	June 10, '98	New Orleans, La.		Sept. 9, '98
Gaspard, Lafayette	Private	June 10, '98	New Orleans, La.		July 22, '98
Grant, Ferdinand	Private	June 11, '98	New Orleans, La.		July 13, '98
Greer, John	Private	June 10, '98	New Orleans, La.		July 22, '98
Hagan, John	Private	June 13, '98	New Orleans, La.		July 5, '98

(87)

Company A, 9th United States Volunteer Infantry—continued.

Name	Rank	Date of Enrollment	Place of Enrollment	Remarks	Date of first illness
Henderson, George	Private	June 10, '98	New Orleans, La.	Reduced from Sergeant	July 5, '98
Hodges, Will	Private	June 14, '98	New Orleans, La.		Aug. 29, '98
Irwin, Oscar	Private	June 10, '98	New Orleans, La.		Aug. 13, '98
Jackson, William	Private	June 10, '98	New Orleans, La.		Sept. 14, '98
Johnson, Samuel	Private	June 10, '98	New Orleans, La.		July 5, '98
Jackson, S.	Private	June 10, '98	New Orleans, La.	Reduced from Corporal	Sept. 9, '98
Jones, Henry	Private	June 11, '98	New Orleans, La.		July 12, '98
Jones, Joseph	Private	June 13, '98	New Orleans, La.		July 28, '98
Jones, John	Private	June 13, '98	New Orleans, La.		July 30, '98
L'Esperance, Paul	Private	June 14, '98	New Orleans, La.		July 22, '98
Logan, Henry P.	Private	June 14, '98	New Orleans, La.		July 6, '98
Macon, David	Private	June 14, '98	New Orleans, La.		Sept. 6, '98
Milanez, Marshall	Private	June 10, '98	New Orleans, La.		July 26, '98
Mitchell, Wallace	Private	June 14, '98	New Orleans, La.	Reduced from Corporal	Sept. 11, '98
Montana, Joseph	Private	June 10, '98	New Orleans, La.		Sept. 8, '98
Morales, Harry	Private	June 11, '98	New Orleans, La.		July 26, '98
Morris, Alphonse	Private	June 14, '98	New Orleans, La.		July 5, '98
Moody, Willis	Private	June 10, '98	New Orleans, La.		Nov. 7, '98
Murry, Adolph M.	Private	June 11, '98	New Orleans, La.		Sept. 12, '98
Manuel, Alfred	Private	June 13, '98	New Orleans, La.		Aug. 1, '98
Philips, Charles	Private	June 13, '98	New Orleans, La.	Appointed Company Musician	July 7, '98

Name	Rank	Enlisted	Place	Remarks	Mustered Out
Putney, Joseph	Private	June 13, '98	New Orleans, La.		July 26, '98
Raggas, Lucien	Private	June 13, '98	New Orleans, La.		July 22, '98
Richardson, Daniel	Private	June 20, '98	New Orleans, La.		Aug. 29, '98
Robertson, John F.	Private	June 15, '98	New Orleans, La.	Reduced from Wagoner	Aug. 29, '98
Schofield, Samuel	Private	June 10, '98	New Orleans, La.		July 5, '98
Soucy, Joseph	Private	June 13, '98	New Orleans, La.		Aug. 29, '98
Stephens, Joseph	Private	June 10, '98	New Orleans, La.		Sept. 26, '98
Telemaque, Joseph	Private	June 10, '98	New Orleans, La.	Appointed Company Cook	July 24, '98
Terrel, Robert	Private	June 13, '98	New Orleans, La.		July 5, '98
Vincent, Eugene	Private	June 13, '98	New Orleans, La.		Aug. 13, '98
Volsin, Joseph	Private	Aug. 9, '98	New Orleans, La.		Aug. 29, '98
Washington, Henry	Private	June 11, '98	New Orleans, La.		Aug. 13, '98
Watson, Samuel	Private	June 10, '98	New Orleans, La.		July 6, '98
White, Benjamin, Jr.	Private	June 14, '98	New Orleans, La.		Sept. 7, '98
White, Spencer	Private	June 10, '98	New Orleans, La.	Died Feb., '98, at El Cobre, Cuba	July 8, '98
Williams, Jesse	Private	June 14, '98	New Orleans, La.		July 31, '98
Williams, Louis F.	Private	June 10, '98	New Orleans, La.		July 27, '98
Williams, John G.	Private	June 13, '98	New Orleans, La.	Reduced from Musician	July 18, '98
Winbush, Daniel	Private	June 17, '98	New Orleans, La.		Sept. 8, '98
Young, Edward	Private	June 13, '98	New Orleans, La.		July 28, '98

Company B, 9th United States Volunteer Infantry.

1st BATTALION, LIEUT. COL. D. M. SELLS COMMANDING.

SIDNEY GOODE, *Captain.*

WILLIAM H. FRANKLIN, *First Lieutenant.*   J. W. BROWN, *Second Lieutenant.* *

Name	Rank	Date of Enrollment	Place of Enrollment	Remarks	Date of first illness
HARRIS, WM. J.	First Sergeant	June 14, '98	New Orleans, La.		Nov. 20, 98
LAWRENCE, ANDREW	Q.M. Sergeant	June 15, '98	New Orleans, La.		Sept. 29, 98
THOMAS, HENRY C.	Sergeant	June 13, '98	New Orleans, La.		Sept. 17, '98
HALL, WILLIS	Sergeant	June 10, '98	New Orleans, La.	Discharged Dec. 17, '98, by order of War Dept.	
MOORE, WILLIAM, JR.	Sergeant	June 15, '98	New Orleans, La.		Sept. 14, '98
PERKINS, MOSES	Sergeant	June 11, '98	New Orleans, La.		Sept. 17, '98
THOMPSON, GEORGE	Sergeant	June 15, '98	New Orleans, La.		
WARWICK, THOMAS	Corporal	June 15, '98	New Orleans, La.		Sept. 22, '98
EVANS, PETER	Corporal	June 15, '98	New Orleans, La.		Oct. 5, '98
CHURCHILL, OLIVER	Corporal	June 15, '98	New Orleans, La.		Sept. 17, '98
GRIFFIN, WASHINGTON	Corporal	June 13, '98	New Orleans, La.		Nov. 15, '98
THURSTON, A. L. J.	Corporal	June 11, '98	New Orleans, La.		Sept. 16, '98
SCOTT, GEORGE F.	Corporal	June 15, '98	New Orleans, La.		Sept. 8, '98
WESLEY, JOHN	Corporal	June 15, '98	New Orleans, La.		Oct. 10, 98
BOUDREAU, CLEMON	Musician	June 15, '98	New Orleans, La.		Oct. 22, '98
LEWIS, GEORGE	Musician	June 10, '98	New Orleans, La.		Sept. 4, '98

*J. W. Brown, Second Lieutenant, vice J. C. Allen (died in Officers' Hospital at Santiago).

Name	Rank	Enlisted	Place	Notes	Date
WISHAM, J. H.	Artificer	June 14, '98	New Orleans, La.		Oct. 10, '98
JACKSON, CHAS. H.	Wagoner	June 13, '98	New Orleans, La.	Died Nov. 12, '98, at Santiago	
ROBICHEAU, JOSEPH	Wagoner	Oct. 6, '98	San Luis, Cuba		
Alcorn, Philip	Private	Aug. 4, '98	New Orleans, La.		Sept. 10, '98
Ambras, Charles	Private	June 10, '98	New Orleans, La.		Nov. 9, '98
August, Joseph	Private	June 13, '98	New Orleans, La.		Dec. 31, '98
Baptiest, John	Private	June 13, '98	New Orleans, La.		Oct. 6, '98
Bashaw, Baptiste	Private	June 20, '98	New Orleans, La.		Sept. 28, '98
Bolden, Isaau	Private	June 11, '98	New Orleans, La.		
Bell, James	Private	June 13, '98	New Orleans, La.		Oct. 10, '98
Benjamin, Albert	Private	June 11, '98	New Orleans, La.		Sept. 7, '98
Bolvia, Gus	Private	June 14, '98	New Orleans, La.		July 26, '98
Buchanan, Joseph	Private	June 14, '98	New Orleans, La.	Died Sept. 16, '98, at Santiago, Cuba	Sept. 24, '98
Butler, Lewis	Private	June 11, '98	New Orleans, La.	Died Sept. 28, '98	Sept. 7, '98
Cole, Henry	Private	June 11, '98	New Orleans, La.		Oct. 10, '98
Carter, Samuel	Private	June 15, '98	New Orleans, La.	Died Oct. 28, '98, at Santiago	
Christian, Martin	Private	June 15, '98	New Orleans, La.		Sept. 20, '98
Crader, Joseph	Private	June 15, '98	New Orleans, La.		Sept. 11, '98
Davis, John H.	Private	June 10, '98	New Orleans, La.		July 20, '98
Decurie, George	Private	June 13, '98	New Orleans, La.		Sept. 10, '98
Dennis, Albert	Private	June 14, '98	New Orleans, La.		July 28, '98
Edwards, R. L.	Private	June 15, '98	New Orleans, La.		Oct. 10, '98
Evans, Walter	Private	June 15, '98	New Orleans, La.		

Company B, 9th United States Volunteer Infantry — continued.

Name	Rank	Date of Enrollment	Place of Enrollment	Remarks	Date of first illness
Gardener, James	Private	June 10, '98	New Orleans, La.	Died—date uncertain	Sept. 11, '98
Givhan, Thomas	Private	June 13, '98	New Orleans, La.	Died Feb. 7, '99	
Hacher, William	Private	June 20, '98	New Orleans, La.	Discharged April 4, '99, at Santiago	Sept. 6, '98
Hall, James	Private	June 13, '98	New Orleans, La.		Dec. 15, '98
Holmes, Frank A.	Private	June 20, '98	New Orleans, La.		Sept. 12, '98
Harris, Louis	Private	June 12, '98	New Orleans, La.		Sept. 22, '98
Jackson, William	Private	June 11, '98	New Orleans, La.		Sept. 8, '98
Johnson, Harvey	Private	June 11, '98	New Orleans, La.		July 26, '98
Johnson, George	Private	June 19, '98	New Orleans, La.	Died Sept. 19, '98, at Santiago, Cuba	
Jones, Eugene	Private	June 15, '98	New Orleans, La.		Sept. 12, '98
Joseph, John H.	Private	June 11, '98	New Orleans, La.		Sept. 14, '98
Joyce, Alfred H.	Private	June 13, '98	New Orleans, La.		Sept. 7, '98
Lewis, Levy	Private	June 14, '98	New Orleans, La.		
Lewis, William	Private	June 13, '98	New Orleans, La.	Died Oct. 12, '98, at San Luis, Cuba	
Long, Frederick	Private	June 20, '98	New Orleans, La.		Sept. 12, '98
McGraw, Isaac H.	Private	June 14, '98	New Orleans, La.		Sept. 10, '98
Martin, Edward	Private	June 14, '98	New Orleans, La.		
Maxwell, Charles	Private	June 13, '98	New Orleans, La.		Oct. 6, '98
Miles, James A.	Private	June 10, '98	New Orleans, La.		
Mitchell, William	Private	June 11, '98	New Orleans, La.		Feb. 12, '98
Nelson, Benjamin	Private	June 13, '98	New Orleans, La.		Sept. 17, '98

Name	Rank	Date	Place	Remarks	Date
Noyra, Eugene	Private	June 14, '98	New Orleans, La.		Sept. 17, '98
Papin, Willie	Private	June 17, '98	New Orleans, La.		Sept. 12, '98
Petaway, Willie B.	Private	June 10, '98	New Orleans, La.	Deserted July, '98	
Penn, James A.	Private	June 10, '98	New Orleans, La.	Discharged April 26, '99	Oct. 29, '98
Peterson, Edward	Private	June 15, '98	New Orleans, La.		Oct. 14, '98
Piper, Louis	Private	June 15, '98	New Orleans, La.		Sept. 7, '98
Richardson, Oliver	Private	June 15, '98	New Orleans, La.		Oct. 27, '98
Robertson, David	Private	June 13, '98	New Orleans, La.		
Scales, J. B.	Private	June 13, '98	New Orleans, La.		Oct. 21, '98
Spencer, George	Private	June 15, '98	New Orleans, La.		
Stovall, Louis	Private	June 13, '98	New Orleans, La.		July 25, '98
Sullivan, George	Private	June 15, '98	New Orleans, La.		Sept. 11, '98
Thompson, Charles I.	Private	June 15, '98	New Orleans, La.		Oct. 27, '98
Thompson, Matt	Private	June 15, '98	New Orleans, La.		Oct. 26, '98
Veazie, Arthur	Private	June 15, '98	New Orleans, La.	Died Sept. 16, '98, at Santiago, Cuba	
Vinet, Peter	Private	June 15, '98	New Orleans, La.		Sept. 11, '98
Wagner, Daniel	Private	June 15, '98	New Orleans, La.		Sept. 17, '98
Washington, George	Private	June 15, '98	New Orleans, La.		Oct. 25, '98
Washington, John	Private	June 15, '98	New Orleans, La.		Sept. 20, '98
Weeks, Reuben	Private	June 15, '98	New Orleans, La.		July 11, '98
White, Tom	Private	June 15, '98	New Orleans, La.		July 30, '98
Williams, John	Private	June 15, '98	New Orleans, La.		Sept. 5, '98
Williams, Robert	Private	June 15, '98	New Orleans, La.		Sept. 6, '98

Company C, 9th United States Volunteer Infantry.

1st BATTALION. LIEUT. COL. D. M. SELLS COMMANDING.

E. J. SHEARMAN, *Captain.**

J. T. BECKAM. *First Lieutenant.*   H. O. FRANKLIN, *Second Lieutenant.†*

Name	Rank	Date of Enrollment	Place of Enrollment	Remarks	Date of first Illness
Jackson, Adam	First Sergeant	June 16, '98	New Orleans, La.		July 25, '98
Brooks, Oscar	Q.M.Sergeant	June 16, '98	New Orleans, La.		Sept. 8, '98
Mora, Octave B	Sergeant	June 11, '98	New Orleans, La.		July 10, '98
Flowers, Mitchell	Sergeant	June 18, '98	New Orleans, La.	Died Sept. 29, at Santiago, Cuba	July 25, '98
Eugene, Charles H.	Sergeant	June 16, '98	New Orleans, La.		July 17, '98
Van Vactor, Arthur	Sergeant	June 15, '98	New Orleans, La.	Transferred to Band Sept. 3, '98	June 22, '98
Bruschamp, J.	Sergeant	June 16, '98	New Orleans, La.	Appointed Sergeant Sept. 1, '98, vice Flowers, reduced.	Sept. 4, '98
Buchanan, James	Corporal	June 17, '98	New Orleans, La.	Appointed Corporal Dec. 8, '98, vice Corporal Nelson, reduced.	July 6, '98
Robinson, Thomas	Corporal	June 16, '98	New Orleans, La.	Killed Jan. 26, '99, at El Cobre, Cuba	Sept. 5, '98
Grace, Manuel	Corporal	June 16, '98	New Orleans, La.		July 5, '98
Mayfield, James A.	Corporal	June 18, '98	New Orleans, La.		Sept. 4, '98
Newman, Joseph H.	Corporal	June 11, '98	New Orleans, La.		July 22, '98
Duvernay, Andrew B.	Corporal	June 17, '98	New Orleans, La.		July 20, '98
Dugay, Charles	Corporal	June 12, '98	New Orleans, La.		Sept. 6, '98
Hamilton, Louis	Corporal	June 17, '98	New Orleans, La.	Appointed Corporal March 9, '99, vice Robinson, discharged.	Nov. 10, '98
Ownes, Ernest	Corporal	June 17, '98	New Orleans, La.	Appointed Corporal Sept. 1, '98, vice Thompson, reduced.	Sept. 6, '98

*Date of first illness, Sept. 4, '98.   †Sept. 11, '98.

Name	Rank	Date	Place	Remarks	Date
GASPARD, ETIENNE	Musician	June 12, '98	New Orleans, La.	Transferred to Band Aug. 1, '98	July 5, '98
LEWIS, JOSEPH	Musician	June 16, '98	New Orleans, La.		
JACKSON, J. W.	Artificer	June 17, '98	New Orleans, La.		Aug. 1, '98
Armstead, Louis	Private	June 17, '98	New Orleans, La.		
Batou, Jacob	Private	June 16, '98	New Orleans, La.		July 14, '98
Boyd, William	Private	June 16, '98	New Orleans, La.	Died Sept. 29, '98, at Santiago, Cuba	Sept. 5, '98
Boyd, Joseph	Private	June 18, '98	New Orleans, La.	Appointed Company Cook	Sept. 4, '98
Bradford, Henry	Private	June 19, '98	New Orleans, La.		July 13, '98
Brodes, William M.	Private	June 11, '98	New Orleans, La.		July 23, '98
Chatard, Maximilian	Private	June 20, '98	New Orleans, La.		July 4, '98
Chatman, Willie	Private	June 18, '98	New Orleans, La.		July 20, '98
Clark, Charles	Private	June 17, '98	New Orleans, La.		July 14, '98
Clark, Matthew C.	Private	June 17, '98	New Orleans, La.		Aug. 28, '98
Clark, Willie	Private	June 16, '98	New Orleans, La.	Killed Nov. 14, '98, at San Luis, Cuba	July 9, '98
Clinch, Eddie	Private	June 17, '98	New Orleans, La.		July 8, '98
Color, Quazine	Private	June 17, '98	New Orleans, La.		July 25, '98
Davis, Bartholomew	Private	June 16, '98	New Orleans, La.	Died Oct. 30, '98, at San Luis, Cuba	Sept. 6, '98
Drake, Sanford	Private	June 16, '98	New Orleans, La.		Sept. 9, '98
Dunn, Aaron	Private	June 18, '98	New Orleans, La.		July 7, '98
Dupas, Peter H.	Private	June 13, '98	New Orleans, La.		Sept. '98
Edwards, Adam	Private	June 18, '98	New Orleans, La.		
Ellis, Arthur	Private	June 17, '98	New Orleans, La.	Transferred to Band Aug. 1, '98	July 12, '98
English, Frank	Private	June 16, '98	New Orleans, La.		Aug. 30, '98

Company C, 9th United States Volunteer Infantry—continued.

Name	Rank	Date of Enrollment	Place of Enrollment	Remarks	Date of first Illness
Ernest, Joseph	Private	June 16, '98	New Orleans, La.		June 18, '98
Eulen, Anathole	Private	June 18, '98	New Orleans, La.		July 28, '98
Falfair, Julius	Private	June 16, '98	New Orleans, La.		July 24, '98
Farron, Joseph	Private	June 19, '98	New Orleans, La.		Aug. 9, '98
Francis, Taylor	Private	June 11, '98	New Orleans, La.		June 18, '98
Gardner, Henry R.	Private	June 17, '98	New Orleans, La.	Pioneer	Sept. 7, '98
Gordon, Albert	Private	June 25, '98	New Orleans, La.		July 3, '98
Grant, Alexander	Private	June 18, '98	New Orleans, La.		July 12, '98
Hamilton, Sheridan	Private	June 17, '98	New Orleans, La.		Sept. 6, '98
Harris, John	Private	June 17, '98	New Orleans, La.		Sept. 6, '98
Harrison, Henry	Private	June 16, '98	New Orleans, La.		July 24, '98
Hills, Auguste	Private	June 17, '98	New Orleans, La.		July 30, '98
Huber, Gustave	Private	June 17, '98	New Orleans, La.		Sept. 6, '98
Jackson, Morrice	Private	June 16, '98	New Orleans, La.		Aug. 14, '98
Jessamine, Placide	Private	June 16, '98	New Orleans, La.	Died Sept. 13, '98, at Santiago, Cuba	July 14, '98
Jenkin, Joseph	Private	June 18, '98	New Orleans, La.		July 30, '98
Johnson, Thomas	Private	June 13, '98	New Orleans, La.		July 7, '98
Jones, August	Private	June 20, '98	New Orleans, La.	Appointed Company Musician Oct. 20, '98	July 5, '98
Kennedy, Charles	Private	June 17, '98	New Orleans, La.	Appointed Company Musician Oct. 20, '98	Sept. 6, '98
Love, Gilbert	Private	June 17, '98	New Orleans, La.		July 11, '98
Mabry, Harry	Private	June 17, '98	New Orleans, La.		Sept. 5, '98

(96)

Name	Rank	Date	Place	Notes	Date
Mack, Henry	Private	June 17, '98	New Orleans, La.		Sept. 6, '98
Martin, William	Private	June 17, '98	New Orleans, La.		July 25, '98
Minor, John R.	Private	June 10, '98	New Orleans, La.	Pioneer	July 6, '98
Monette, Albert	Private	June 18, '98	New Orleans, La.		Aug. 29, '98
Monie, Joseph	Private	June 18, '98	New Orleans, La.		July 3, '98
Moret, Alcide	Private	June 18, '98	New Orleans, La.		Sept. 5, '98
Morris, Joseph	Private	June 18, '98	New Orleans, La.	Died Oct. 16, '98, at San Luis, Cuba	Aug. 31, '98
Narcisse, Joseph	Private	June 18, '98	New Orleans, La.	Died Nov. 7, '98, at San Luis, Cuba	
Nelson, Louis	Private	June 17, '98	New Orleans, La.	Reduced from Corporal to ranks	Sept. 6, '98
Patterson, Noah	Private	June 18, '98	New Orleans, La.		Aug. 30, '98
Profeit, Eugene	Private	June 16, '98	New Orleans, La.		Sept. 5, '98
Roan, Alexander	Private	June 16, '98	New Orleans, La.		July 28, '98
Robinson, Daniel	Private	June 10, '98	New Orleans, La.		Aug. 5, '98
Ross, William	Private	June 17, '98	New Orleans, La.		Jan. 7, '99
Sanders, William	Private	June 17, '98	New Orleans, La.	Company Tailor	Aug. 14, '98
Sarofield, George	Private	June 18, '98	New Orleans, La.		Aug. 30, '98
Saulsbury, William J.	Private	June 15, '98	New Orleans, La.	Company Clerk	July 6, '98
Small, Villere	Private	June 17, '98	New Orleans, La.		July 7, '98
Smith, Henry	Private	June 16, '98	New Orleans, La.		July 15, '98
Thompson, Henry	Private	June 17, '98	New Orleans, La.	Reduced from Corporal to ranks	July 25, '98

Company D, 9th United States Volunteer Infantry.

1st BATTALION, LIEUT. COL. D. M. SELLS COMMANDING.

GEORGE LEA FEBIGER, *Captain.**

S. P. BROWN, *First Lieutenant.*†   T. C. BUTLER, *Second Lieutenant.*‡

Name	Rank	Date of Enrollment	Place of Enrollment	Remarks	Date of first Illness
JONES, ROBERT	First Sergeant	June 20, '98	New Orleans, La.	Excellent non-commissioned officer. Appointed July 10, '98. vice Thomas H. Jones, dishonorably discharged.	July 11, '98
LAWSON, H. P.	Q. M. Sergeant	June 18, '98	New Orleans, La.	Excellent non-commissioned officer	July 22, '98
DORSEY, FRANK	Sergeant	June 20, '98	New Orleans, La.	. . . .	Aug. 11, '98
LABROSSIERS, Wm.	Sergeant	June 20, '98	New Orleans, La.	Discharged from service Mar. 20, '99, from Josiah Simpson Hospital, Fortress Monroe, Va., per sur. cert. of disability.	July 14, '98
HENDERSON, JOHN W.	Sergeant	June 10, '98	New Orleans, La.	Appointed Jan. 1, '99	Sept. 7, '98
ALEXANDER, HENRY	Sergeant	June 20, '98	New Orleans, La.	Appointed Sergt Jan. 1, '99. Rec'd. special commendation at discharge for bravery in assisting in capture of Cuban bandits.	July 5, '98
ROBINSON, ADOLPH	Sergeant	June 21, '98	New Orleans, La.	Died Oct. 22, '98, at San Luis, Cuba	July 6, '98
DOUGLASS, JOHN	Sergeant	June 20, '98	New Orleans, La.	Appointed Sergeant April 20, '99	July 25, '98
BALLARD, WILLIAM	Corporal	June 13, '98	New Orleans, La.	. . . .	July 22, '98
JOHNSON, HENRY	Corporal	June 20, '98	New Orleans, La.	Appointed Corporal Jan. 1, '99. Regimental Mail Carrier, per orders regimental com'r.	July 5, '98
DOLPHUS, HARVEY	Corporal	June 20, '98	New Orleans, La.	. . . .	Sept. 9, '98
LAVMORE, ALFRED	Corporal	June 20, '98	New Orleans, La.	Appointed March 12, '99	Sept. 7, '98
FOX, EMILE	Corporal	June 21, '98	New Orleans, La.	Appointed March 23, '99	Aug. 1, '98
MASSON, EDWARD	Corporal	June 17, '98	New Orleans, La.	Appointed March 12, '99	. . . . . .
JOHNSON, REUBEN F.	Corporal	June 20, '98	New Orleans, La.	Appointed April 11, '99	Sept. 15, '98
GRAY, EDGAR	Corporal	June 20, '98	New Orleans, La.	Appointed April 20, '99	July 5, '98

*George Lea Febiger, Captain, vice W. A. Payton, resigned. †S. P. Brown, First Lieut., commanding company. ‡T. C. Butler, Second Lieut., vice Philip Phillipson, resigned.

Name	Rank			Remarks	
Downs, Robert H., Jr.	Corporal	June 21, '98	New Orleans, La.	Died Feb. 2, '99, at camp near San Luis, Cuba	July 5, '98
Pullam, Alexander	Corporal	June 17, '98	New Orleans, La.	Died Sept. 15, '98, at San Juan Hill	July 22, '98
Thomas, Peter	Musician	June 21, '98	New Orleans, La.	Appointed Nov. 1, '98	Sept. 6, '98
Bowden, Albert W.	Musician	June 20, '98	New Orleans, La.	Reduced to ranks Nov. 1, '98. Discharged from service March 12, '99, surgeon's certificate of disability.	Sept. 6, '98
Peters, Charles	Artificer	June 20, '98	New Orleans, La.	. . . . .	July 26, '98
Robinson, Edward	Wagoner	June 20, '98	New Orleans, La.	. . . . .	July 6, '98
Baker, Charles	Private	June 20, '98	New Orleans, La.	Detached service Santiago, Cuba, from Feb. 12 to April 26, '99.	Aug. 14, '98
Benjamin, Felix	Private	June 20, '98	New Orleans, La.	. . . . .	Sept. 10, '98
Benoit, Louis	Private	June 21, '98	New Orleans, La.	. . . . .	Sept. 10, '98
Black, Joseph	Private	June 20, '98	New Orleans, La.	. . . . .	July 5, '98
Boniswail, Philip	Private	June 20, '98	New Orleans, La.	Died Sept. 18, '98, at Santiago, Cuba	July 10, '98
Brown, Lewis	Private	June 20, '98	New Orleans, La.	. . . . .	July 10, '98
Buddymoore, William	Private	June 20, '98	New Orleans, La.	. . . . .	July 9, '98
Carter, John	Private	June 20, '98	New Orleans, La.	. . . . .	Oct. 27, '98
Carter, William C.	Private	June 20, '98	New Orleans, La.	. . . . .	July 10, '98
Coleman, Henry	Private	June 21, '98	New Orleans, La.	. . . . .	Aug. 3, '98
Collier, John	Private	June 20, '98	New Orleans, La.	Detached service Santiago, Cuba, from Feb. 12 to April 26, '99.	July 5, '98
Conway, Charles B.	Private	June 20, '98	New Orleans, La.	Transferred to Regimental Band, Aug. 1, '98 per order regimental commander.	
Crump, Amile	Private	June 20, '98	New Orleans, La.	. . . . .	July 9, '98
Davis, George E.	Private	June 21, '98	New Orleans, La.	Died Sept. 22, '98, San Luis, Cuba	Aug. 1, '98
Davis, James	Private	June 20, '98	New Orleans, La.	Died Sept. 24, '98, Santiago, Cuba	July 9, '98
De Lisle, Alphonse	Private	June 13, '98	New Orleans, La.	Appointed Sergeant June 22, '98; reduced to ranks Jan. 1, '99.	July 5, '98
Diggs, Anadie	Private	June 18, '98	New Orleans, La.	Nurse, Regimental Hospital	Sept. 14, '98

Company D, 9th United States Volunteer Infantry — continued.

Name	Rank	Date of Enrollment	Place of Enrollment	Remarks	Date of first Illness
Dormer, Emile	Private	June 21, '98	New Orleans, La.	Appointed Company Clerk April 20, '99	
Drayton, Lewis	Private	June 21, '98	New Orleans, La.	Transferred to Regimental Band, Aug. 1, '98 per order regimental commander.	
Fernandez, Julius	Private	June 20, '98	New Orleans, La.		Aug. 20, '98
Foster, Louis	Private	June 21, '98	New Orleans, La.		July 26, '98
Gaudines, Jules	Private	June 21, '98	New Orleans, La.		July 15, '98
Garrett, William	Private	June 21, '98	New Orleans, La.	Killed Aug. 21, '98, at New Orleans, La., while resisting arrest by civil authority.	Aug. 10, '98
Guichard, Peter	Private	June 18, '98	New Orleans, La.		July 5, '98
Hope, George	Private	June 20, '98	New Orleans, La.		July 6, '98
Hubert, Thomas	Private	June 21, '98	New Orleans, La.		July 5, '98
Hunter, Frank	Private	June 21, '98	New Orleans, La.		Sept. 9, '98
Jackson, Gus	Private	June 21, '98	New Orleans, La.		Sept. 8, '98
Jackson, Wright	Private	June 20, '98	New Orleans, La.		Oct. 1, '98
Johnson, Willie	Private	June 20, '98	New Orleans, La.		July 31, '98
Labarrosiers, Ernest	Private	June 21, '98	New Orleans, La.	Reduced from Corporal to ranks, Oct. 8, '98.	
Lavaux, Lucien	Private	June 21, '98	New Orleans, La.		July 15, '98
Lecouq, Octave	Private	June 20, '98	New Orleans, La.	Transferred to Band Aug. 1, '98	
Lewis, Robert	Private	June 21, '98	New Orleans, La.	Reduced from Corporal to ranks, Jan. 3, '99	
Martin, Richard	Private	June 21, '98	New Orleans, La.		July 15, '98
McKinney, Abson	Private	June 21, '98	New Orleans, La.	Detached service, Santiago de Cuba, from Feb. 12 to April 26, '99.	July 5, '98
McWay, Briscoe	Private	June 21, '98	New Orleans, La.		Aug. 14, '98
Moore, Willie	Private	June 21, '98	New Orleans, La.	Nurse in regimental hospital	

Name	Rank	Date	Place	Remarks	Date
Morse, Joseph D.	Private	June 21, '98	New Orleans, La.	. . .	July 24, '98
Mosoly, Joseph	Private	June 21, '98	New Orleans, La.	Died Oct. 3, '98, at San Luis, Cuba	July 30, '98
Neal, Elmore	Private	June 21, '98	New Orleans, La.	Third Company Cook	Aug. 31, '98
Patterson, George W.	Private	June 20, '98	New Orleans, La.	Appointed Hospital Steward April 20, '99	July 9, '98
Peterson, Van	Private	June 19, '98	New Orleans, La.	. . .	July 7, '98
Pierre, Edward	Private	June 20, '98	New Orleans, La.	Discharged at San Luis, Cuba, April 26, '99	July 5, '98
Posey, Eugene	Private	June 15, '98	New Orleans, La.	Reduced from Corporal April 20, '99	July 5, '98
Powell, William	Private	June 18, '98	New Orleans, La.	Died Oct. 9, '98, at San Luis, Cuba	July 6, '98
Ridgley, Emanuel	Private	June 21, '98	New Orleans, La.	Transferred to Band Aug. 1, '98, per orders regimental commander.	
Simpson, John	Private	June 20, '98	New Orleans, La.	. . .	Sept. 6, '98
Stamps, Willie	Private	June 21, '98	New Orleans, La.	Deserted Aug. 5, '98, at New Orleans, La. Died at Brookhaven, Miss.	
St. Smith, Webster	Private	June 20, '98	New Orleans, La.	Reduced to ranks July 10, '98. Promoted to musician Nov. 1, '98	
Thomas, Jackson	Private	June 21, '98	New Orleans, La.	. . .	July 5, '98
Thomas, Peter	Private	June 21, '98	New Orleans, La.	. . .	July 22, '98
Vincent, Paul	Private	June 20, '98	New Orleans, La.	Died Sept. 29, '98, San Luis, Cuba	Sept. 9, '98
Ward, John	Private	June 21, '98	New Orleans, La.	Second Company Cook	
Washington, Joseph	Private	June 20, '98	New Orleans, La.	. . .	July 26, '98
Williams, John	Private	June 16, '98	New Orleans, La.	. . .	July 7, '98
Williams, Arthur	Private	June 21, '98	New Orleans, La.	. . .	Sept. 9, '98
Williams, Jacob	Private	June 21, '98	New Orleans, La.	. . .	
Wilson, Robert	Private	June 21, '98	New Orleans, La.	. . .	July 6, '98
Willis, Landry	Private	June 20, '98	New Orleans, La.	Chief Company Cook	Sept. 7, '98

JOHN FARRELL, First Sergeant, Co. E.

A born soldier and an excellent non-commissioned officer. Upon the efficiency
of the first sergeant the strength of a company depends.

Second Battalion

MAJOR DUNCAN B. HARRISON COMMANDING.

EDWARD WILLIAMS.

•• •• ••

EDWARD WILLIAMS, First Lieutenant 9th United States Volunteer Infantry, was born in Centerville, Hickman county, Tenn. He enlisted for service in the 24th Infantry, U. S A., on January 19, 1876. He served continuously in that regiment as a private, corporal, sergeant and first sergeant until October 26, 1898, on which date he was appointed to a first lieutenancy in the 9th U. S. Volunteer Infantry, which commission he accepted. At the time of his appointment as first lieutenant he was first sergeant of Co. L, 24th Infantry. He was appointed to the first lieutenancy of Co. E, 9th United States Volunteer Infantry, and assumed the command of that company on December 6, 1898 (the captain being absent on sick leave), per Special Order No. 111, headquarters of the 9th United States Volunteer Infantry, at camp near San Luis, Cuba. He was in the engagements of the Fifth Army Corps, and served in Cuba from June 25 to July 15, 1898. His continuous service in the United States army has embraced twenty-three years, six months and twelve days.

★
★   ★
★

LAFAYETTE THARP.

•• •• ••

LAFAYETTE THARP was born in Lafayette county, Ark. At the time of the raising and mustering of the 9th Regiment United States Volunteer Infantry, he was president of the C. L. M.'s Alliance, an organization of 12,000 men, of New Orleans. By this position of influence he was able to and rendered to the organizing officer, Col. C. J. Crane, invaluable assistance, and was by him recommended for a second lieutenancy, to which he was appointed, and assigned to Company E. He acted as chaplain of the regiment until the Rev. T. Walker was appointed, and was then assigned to special duty.

W. H. Robinson, First Lieutenant, Co. F.

W. H. ROBINSON.

* * *

FIRST LIEUT. W. H. ROBINSON was born in the city of New Orleans on January 24, 1866, of a combination of Georgia and Mississippi ancestry, his grandmother, Lucy Gordon, at the time of her death (1880) being one of the oldest citizens of the city of Savannah, having spent a while under Governor Oglethorpe's administration as British Governor of the colonies. He received the greater portion of his education in the public schools of the city, and partially completed the same at the Straight University (an institution founded by the American Congregational Society for the education of the colored race in Louisiana.) He has held several positions of trust. Upon the organization of the 9th United States Volunteers, he joined as a second lieutenant, coming to Cuba and sharing the fate of the boys at San Juan hill, having had a spell of yellow fever for twenty-one days, and expected at one time to be left to sleep the sleep that knows no waking. Recovering, he rejoined his command, which had moved up to San Luis, a mountain town. On October 15, First Lieutenant Charles W. Fillmore resigned and left Second Lieutenant Robinson in command of the company, he being the only officer with the command, Captain Patrick having resigned at Camp Corbin, before leaving New Orleans. He served as commander of the company until the arrival of Capt. Edw. B. Markley, deceased, son of Major Markley, of San Juan hill fame, who commanded a battalion of the 24th Infantry. He served as assistant regimental quartermaster, and was appointed regimental treasurer by Col. Chas. J. Crane. He removed with a detachment to Songo, another town higher up in the mountains, and was appointed detachment quartermaster and acting commissary of subsistence. While thus serving, he was promoted to the position of first lieutenant, April 13, 1899, through the recommendation of Colonel Crane.

*
*   *
*

WILLIAM WILKES.

* * *

WILLIAM WILKES was born in Columbia, Maury county, Tenn., June 29, 1856. He enlisted January 10, 1876, at Nashville, Tenn., and from there was sent to Columbus Barracks, Ohio, and later to Fort Duncan, Texas, a small army post, where he was assigned to Company F, 24th Infantry, March 31, 1876. He was appointed corporal August 1, 1876, and sergeant January 1, 1877. The regiment changed stations from Texas to Indian Territory November, 1880. He was discharged January 9, 1881, at the cantonment at North Fork, Canadian River, Indian Territory. He reënlisted at St. Louis, Mo., February 4, 1881, was assigned to the 9th Cavalry, and joined Troop L, March 24, 1881, at Fort Bliss, Texas. From May 20 to November he was in the field in New Mexico, scouting for Indians. The regiment changed stations, December, 1881, to Fort Riley, Kansas, where he saw field service in Colorado in 1882. He was appointed corporal

WILLIAM WILKES, First Lieutenant, Co. G

August 7, 1883, and saw field service in the Indian Territory. The regiment left Fort Riley June 13, 1885, on an overland march through Kansas and Nebraska, arriving at Fort McKinney, Wyoming, August 19, 1885 Appointed sergeant December 2, 1885. Discharged February 3, 1886. Reënlisted at Fort Leavenworth, Kansas, February 26, 1886, for Company F, 24th Infantry. Appointed sergeant May 7, 1886. Changed stations from Fort Elliot, Texas, to Fort Bayard, New Mexico, June, 1888. Discharged at Fort Bayard February 25, 1891. Reënlisted at Fort Bayard February 26, 1891. Discharged at Fort Bayard February 25, 1896. Reënlisted at Fort Bayard February 26, 1896. Changed station to Fort Douglas, Utah, October, 1896. Left this post April 20, 1898, for Chickamauga Park, Georgia. Left there for Tampa, Fla., April 30. The regiment, receiving orders about June 7 to embark for Cuba, boarded the transport City of Washington at Tampa, and a few days later sailed for Cuba, arriving at Santiago about June 21, and debarking at Siboney, June 25. In the battles at San Juan, Cuba, from July 1 to July 14, the officers of Company F were both wounded in the early part of the first day's fight. William Rainey, first sergeant of the company, bravely conducted the company to the top of San Juan hill, aided by the other non-commissioned officers. July 14 the regiment was ordered back to Siboney, to act as nurses at the fever hospital. August 3, Lieutenant Wilkes took the fever, left the Island August 25 for the United States, debarked at Montauk Point, L. I., September 3, and from there went to Fort Douglas, Utah. He was appointed first lieutenant of the 9th United States Volunteer Infantry October 24, 1898, and joined the regiment December 7, 1898, in camp near San Luis, Cuba.

WALLACE D. SEALS.

•• •• ••

SECOND LIEUT. WALLACE D. SEALS was born in Cherokee, Cherokee county, Texas, December 5, 1862, and shortly after was conveyed to a little town called Cedar Bayou. After six years had passed his parents became convinced, from the flying bullets of the so-called Ku-Klux, that it was time to find a new hiding place, Galveston being their choice. Sacrifice sales were made of both land and stock. Then, in company with other families, they made their escape by night on board the schooner Hard Times. After a night and day's sail they reached Galveston, where they located. After the death of his father, he entered the employ of the G C. and S. F. R. R., where he served fifteen years in the freight department. During that time he joined a military company known as the "Lincoln Guards," of Galveston. Soon he became the best in the company in drill, a fact which was tested by a drill for a gold medal. Shortly after he was appointed first sergeant, in which capacity he served four years. He was then elected second lieutenant. After the expiration of his commission he was asked to accept the captaincy of the company, but his work would not allow it. Being a member of the Cotton Jammers' and Longshoremen's Association, he was forced to quit the G. C. and S. F. R. R. to jam cotton. Shortly afterward he was appointed cotton clerk. The next season the associa-

11 HERMAN BLUNT, First Lieutenant, Co. H

tion received a new line of ships, when he was elected cotton clerk and paymaster, with a pay-roll of thirty and forty dollars per week. He remained in this business until he joined the army for the Spanish-American war. In June his company, known as the "Hawley Rifles," left Galveston to join the regiment at New Orleans. On the 17th day of August the regiment boarded the steamship Berlin for Cuba. After a five days' voyage the Berlin anchored in the harbor of Santiago. On the evening of the 23d the troops disembarked and marched to San Juan hill, where they camped in the road that night and climbed the hill next morning. In about two weeks nearly the entire regiment was taken sick. This was a distressful time, men sickening and dying rapidly. The regiment put in eight hard months in Cuba and lost a large number of men, including two lieutenants and one captain.

Lieutenant Seals is of the opinion that Americans can endure the climate of Cuba, provided they are not overzealous in work and drill.

H. HERMAN BLUNT.

•• •• ••

PROMINENT among the brave soldier boys who have had the distinction of representing the African race in the late unpleasantness with Spain, few of those who have gone bravely to the front are so deserving of most respectful mention as the subject of this sketch. It argues little whether a man who has voluntarily enlisted in defense of his country sees active service or not. The fact that he offers himself a willing sacrifice should the necessity demand, fully entitles him to a share of whatever glory attaches to the arms of his country. But it is to be doubted whether active service in the field requires more heroism than garrison duty in such a plague-stricken country as Cuba, where Lieutenant Blunt's regiment was stationed.

Aside from any hero worship, it is a double pleasure to contemplate one who combines so many excellent qualities for a place of authority in the service as Lieut. H. Herman Blunt. Col. Charles J. Crane says of him that he was one of the best officers in his regiment. But those who know him best need no evidence to convince them that he does nothing without making it harder for somebody else to give satisfaction at the same job. Lieutenant Blunt can feel well and justly assured of the admiration of every loyal American by reason of the high post of honor which he occupied in the war with Spain, and the splendid manner in which he executed the trust.

Lieutenant Blunt enjoys the distinction of being the only colored officer assigned to command a military post, among the many assignments made by Col. Charles J. Crane; viz., Cristo, Cuba. On account of the efficiency developed he was placed in command of Company E, to straighten out its affairs, which was done very creditably. Later, the captain of Company H being absent, he was assigned to command the company, and prepared it for the muster-out, at Camp Meade, near Middletown, Penna. Cool, suave, courageous and discreet, he adroitly accom-

STEPHEN G. STARL, Second Lieutenant, Co. H.

plished that which many considered impracticable, and bridged over difficulties which seemed impossible to others, thus evincing administrative abilities of a high order. Lieutenant Blunt's record thus far gives promise of a career highly beneficial to his people and honorable to himself as well as the race he represents.

STEPHEN GALVESTON STARR.

STEPHEN G. STARR was born Feb. 5, 1845, in the Republic of Mexico, in the city of Buena Vista, of African and Mexican parentage. From the age of 10 to 16 years he served as a sheep herder and cowboy. He came to the United States in 1863, enlisted in the Federal army Dec. 9, 1864, and was assigned to the Sixty-fifth Volunteer Infantry Dec. 12, 1864. Went to the front with his regiment Dec. 20; was in action Dec. 27; wounded in the battle of Port Hudson, Dec. 29; discharged Sept. 14, 1865. Reënlisted in the 41st Regular Infantry Jan. 7, 1867; discharged Jan. 6, 1870. Reënlisted in the 24th Infantry July 16, 1870; discharged July 15, 1875. Reënlisted Sept. 20, 1877; discharged Sept. 19, 1882. Reënlisted Oct. 16, 1882; discharged Oct. 15, 1887. Reënlisted in the General Service, Detachment of Messengers, in 1887; discharged Oct. 15, 1892. Reënlisted in General Service, Detachment of Messengers, Oct. 16, 1892; discharged by an Act of Congress Aug. 6, 1894. Reënlisted in the 24th Infantry Nov. 5, 1894; discharged Nov. 4 1897. Reënlisted Nov. 5, 1897; went to the front with the 24th Infantry; was in action at San Juan hill July 1, 2 and 3; ordered to the United States Aug. 25, 1898. Received a commission as second lieutenant Nov. 28, 1898. He served in all the grades of a non-commissioned officer in the 64th, 41st and 24th Infantry, General Service, Detachment of Messengers, Tenth Cavalry, and 9th United States Volunteer Infantry.

He has seen service all over the south and northwest; he has taken part in all the Indian wars in the United States from 1868 to 1885. There is but one court-martial recorded against him in all his service. As for education, he has but little, his only opportunity having been a post school.

HOBSON TREE, AND GRAVES OF MEN OF 9TH U. S. V. I. AT SAN JUAN.

ARSENAL WHERE LIEUTENANT HOBSON WAS FIRST IMPRISONED. LATER
USED AS A GENERAL HOSPITAL FOR AMERICAN SOLDIERS.

Company E, 9th United States Volunteer Infantry.

2nd BATTALION, MAJOR DUNCAN B. HARRISON COMMANDING.

C. G. BECKHAM, *Captain.*

EDWARD WILLIAMS, *First Lieutenant.** LAFAYETTE THARP, *Second Lieutenant.*

Name	Rank	Date of Enrollment	Place of Enrollment	Remarks	Date of first Illness
FARRELL, JOHN	First Sergeant	June 25, '98	New Orleans, La.	Vice John V. Oliver, discharged	Sept. 8, '98
ROBINSON, NELSON B.	Q.M.Sergeant	June 21, '98	New Orleans, La.		Nov 26, '98
WHALEY, HORACE O.	Sergeant	June 23, '98	New Orleans, La.		Nov 4, '98
JONES, ACHILLES	Sergeant	June 23, '98	New Orleans, La.	Vice Victor Miller, died Oct. 7, '98, at Santiago, Cuba.	
JOHNSON, HENRY	Sergeant	June 23, '98	New Orleans, La.	Died Sept 18, '98, at Santiago, Cuba	
LEE, DAVID P.	Sergeant	June 23, '98	New Orleans, La.		
BONNEY, GRANT S.	Corporal	June 23, '98	New Orleans, La.		
CAMMACK, JOSEPH A.	Corporal	June 23, '98	New Orleans, La.	Vice James N. Benjamin, reduced	Oct. 20, '98
WILLIAMS, EDWARD	Corporal	June 23, '98	New Orleans, La.		Sept. 24, '98
ASHFORD, WILLIAM J.	Corporal	June 23, '98	New Orleans, La.		Nov 26, '98
BUTLER, WARREN E.	Corporal	June 23, '98	New Orleans, La.		Feb. 22, '98
ODS, FRANK	Corporal	June 20, '98	New Orleans, La.	Vice Robert Cooper, died Dec. 29, '98, at camp near San Luis, Cuba.	
GONZALEZ, ADOLPHE	Corporal	June 25, '98	New Orleans, La.	Vice William Smith, resigned	
LOVE, HENRY	Corporal	June 27, '98	New Orleans, La.		Dec. 2, '98
HILL, JOSEPH	Musician	June 23, '98	New Orleans, La.		

*Edward Williams, First Lieutenant, vice L. J. Barnett (died at Santiago Hospital Sept. 19, '98).

Names not on Roster at time of first publication: Victor Miller, died Oct. 7, '98, at Santiago; Robert Cooper, died Dec. 28, '98, at camp near San Luis, Cuba; Ferdinand Bermoly, died Dec. 20, '98, at camp near San Luis, Cuba.

Name	Rank	Date	Place	Remarks	Date
LEMOS, SOLOMON	Musician	June 25, '98	New Orleans, La.	Vice Ferdinand Bermudy, died Dec. 20,'98, at camp near San Luis, Cuba.	Nov. 6, '98
MOISE, FERDINAND	Artificer	June 24, '98	New Orleans, La.	Vice Jules Peters, relieved	
WILLIAMS, SANDY	Wagoner	June 24, '98	New Orleans, La.		Sept. 24, '98
Banks, James R.	Private	June 23, '98	New Orleans, La.	Died Sept. 17, '98, at San Juan, Cuba	
Benjamin, James N.	Private	June 22, '98	New Orleans, La.		Nov. 7, '98
Berry, Alfred	Private	June 23, '98	New Orleans, La.		
Celestan, Bremer	Private	June 23, '98	New Orleans, La.		Nov. 25, '98
Chatman, Thomas	Private	June 24, '98	New Orleans, La.		Nov. 18, '98
Dabuery, William	Private	June 24, '98	New Orleans, La.		Sept. 11, '98
Davis, Oliver	Private	June 17, '98	New Orleans, La.		Sept. 18, '98
Dawkins, Elihu S.	Private	June 23, '98	New Orleans, La.		Apr. 5, '99
Fargo, Emile	Private	June 24, '98	New Orleans, La.		Sept. 21, '98
Ferrand, Frederick	Private	June 27, '98	New Orleans, La.	Discharged	Oct. 10, '98
Flood, Horace R.	Private	June 24, '98	New Orleans, La.		Dec. 14, '98
Fortnonin, Edgar	Private	June 24, '98	New Orleans, La.		Dec. 14, '98
François, Victor	Private	June 24, '98	New Orleans, La.		Oct. 13, '98
Frivol, Arthur	Private	June 24, '98	New Orleans, La.		Oct. 24, '98
Gaines, Matthew	Private	June 24, '98	New Orleans, La.		
Gottschalk, Andrew	Private	June 22, '98	New Orleans, La.	Killed Mar. 22, '99, at San Luis, Cuba	
Green, Joseph	Private	June 24, '98	New Orleans, La.		Sept. 18, '98
Griffin, William	Private	June 24, '98	New Orleans, La.		Apr. 10, '98
Hall, George A.	Private	June 24, '98	New Orleans, La.		
Henderson, Alfred	Private	June 24, '98	New Orleans, La.		Oct. 10, '98

Company E, 9th United States Volunteer Infantry — continued.

Name	Rank	Date of Enrollment	Place of Enrollment	Remarks	Date of first Illness
Hill, Nathaniel P.	Private	June 24, '98	New Orleans, La.		Sept. 29, '98
Jackson, James	Private	June 23, '98	New Orleans, La.		Sept. 18, '98
James, Adolphe	Private	June 23, '98	New Orleans, La.		Sept. 18, '98
Johnson, Henry	Private	June 27, '98	New Orleans, La.		Sept. 18, '98
Johnson, John	Private	June 23, '98	New Orleans, La.		Sept. 2, '98
Johnson, Walter	Private	June 27, '98	New Orleans, La.		Oct. 6, '98
Jones, Emile	Private	June 25, '98	New Orleans, La.		Nov. 28, '98
Jones, Lewis	Private	June 23, '98	New Orleans, La.	Died Sept. 28, '98, at San Luis, Cuba	
Jones, Robert	Private	June 23, '98	New Orleans, La.		
Jones, Robert B.	Private	June 27, '98	New Orleans, La.		
Kennedy, John	Private	June 23, '98	New Orleans, La.		Jan. 6, '99
Lasbostrie, George	Private	June 22, '98	New Orleans, La.		Sept. 18, '98
Learson, Henry	Private	June 24, '98	New Orleans, La.		Sept. 20, '98
Leday, Foster	Private	June 25, '98	New Orleans, La.		Oct. 8, '98
Lee, Sedley E.	Private	June 22, '98	New Orleans, La.		Oct. 6, '98
Lewis, David	Private	June 22, '98	New Orleans, La.		
Long, William	Private	June 17, '98	New Orleans, La.	Discharged	
McAllister, Jack	Private	June 23, '98	New Orleans, La.		Sept. 3, '98
McCormick, Walter	Private	June 23, '98	New Orleans, La.		Sept. 21, '98
Marmillion, Joseph	Private	June 27, '98	New Orleans, La.		Sept. 25, '98
Marshall, John	Private	June 27, '98	New Orleans, La.		

Name	Rank	Enlisted	Place	Remarks	Mustered Out
Miller, James A.	Private	June 24, '98	New Orleans, La.		Sept. 27, '98
Mitchell, Henry	Private	June 24, '98	New Orleans, La.		Sept. 10, '98
Montrell, Charles	Private	June 27, '98	New Orleans, La.		Sept. 16, '98
Nelson, Alfred	Private	June 24, '98	New Orleans, La.		Sept. 18, '98
Newton, William	Private	June 23, '98	New Orleans, La.		Nov. 16, '98
Owens, Charles	Private	June 17, '98	New Orleans, La.		
Patrick, Austin	Private	June 25, '98	New Orleans, La.		Dec. 1, '98
Peters, Jules	Private	June 25, '98	New Orleans, La.		
Ridgley, Usan	Private	June 27, '98	New Orleans, La	Transferred to Band Oct 27, '98	Sept. 24, '98
Robinson, David F.	Private	June 16, '98	New Orleans, La.		Sept. 18, '98
Simms, Lee	Private	June 25, '98	New Orleans, La.		
Sparks, Robert	Private	June 27, '98	New Orleans, La.	Died Feb. 4, '99, camp near San Luis, Cuba	
Stevens, George	Private	June 24, '98	New Orleans, La.	Died Sept. 18, '98, San Luis, Cuba	
Taylor, James	Private	June 23, '98	New Orleans, La.		Nov. 21, '98
Terrell, Silas	Private	June 23, '98	New Orleans, La.		Sept. 10, '98
Vincent, Ferman	Private	June 27, '98	New Orleans, La.		
Waterman, Oliver	Private	June 25, '98	New Orleans, La.		Sept. 24, '98
Williams, Harry	Private	June 22, '98	New Orleans, La.		Dec. 19, '98

Company F, 9th United States Volunteer Infantry.

2nd BATTALION, MAJOR DUNCAN E. HARRISON COMMANDING.

CHARLES C. D. GAITHER, *Captain.**

W. H. ROBINSON, *First Lieutenant.*‡   — — , *Second Lieutenant.**

Name	Rank	Date of Enrollment	Place of Enrollment	Remarks	Date of first Illness
CORNISH, WILLIAM	First Sergeant	June 28, '98	New Orleans, La.	Vice Stephen Burrell	July 8, '98
HILL, CLARENCE H.	Q.M.Sergeant	June 28, '98	New Orleans, La.		Sept. 9, '98
BURRELL, STEPHEN	Sergeant	June 28, '98	New Orleans, La.	Relieved from duty as First Sergeant and re-appointed Sergeant May 1, '99.	Sept. 7, '98
MARIGNY, JOSEPH	Sergeant	June 28, '98	New Orleans, La.		Sept. 10, '98
DESSALLE, ALBERT	Sergeant	June 28, '98	New Orleans, La.		July 14, '98
ST. AVIDE, GEORGE	Sergeant	June 29, '98	New Orleans, La.		July 11, '98
LEE, WILLIAM	Corporal	June 28, '98	New Orleans, La.		July 8, '98
GOBRIDGE, JOSEPH	Corporal	June 28, '98	New Orleans, La.		July 9, '98
GROOMS, DANIEL	Corporal	June 28, '98	New Orleans, La.		July 14, '98
LAWSON, WILEY	Corporal	June 28, '98	New Orleans, La		July 5, '98
DAVIS, RICHARD	Corporal	June 28, '98	New Orleans, La		Aug. 15, '98
THOMAS, PAUL	Corporal	June 28, '98	New Orleans, La		July 7, '98
FOREST, HENRY	Corporal	June 28, '98	New Orleans, La		July 8, '98
HILDEBRAND, CHARLES	Corporal	June 28, '98	New Orleans, La		Sept. 10, '98
LINSDEY, NOBLE	Musician	June 28, '98	New Orleans, La		Sept. 7, '98
LAWSON, CHARLES	Musician	June 28, '98	New Orleans, La.		July 18, '98

*Charles D. Gaither, vice Edward B. Markley (died Jan. 6, '99, Officers' Hospital, Santiago, Cuba, of typhoid malaria).

‡W. H. Robinson, First Lieutenant, vice Charles W. Fillmore (resigned Oct. 2, '98), who was appointed to take the place of Lieut. Frank Patrick, who resigned at New Orleans.

Name	Rank	Date	Place	Notes
ZAPHER, EDWARD	Musician	June 28, '98	New Orleans, La.	
ANTONIE, PETER	Artificer	June 28, '98	New Orleans, La.	
THOMPSON, STEPHEN	Wagoner	June 28, '98	New Orleans, La.	
Alexander, Dennis	Private	June 28, '98	New Orleans, La.	Died Nov. 7, '98, at Post Hosp., San Luis, Cuba
Aston, Henry	Private	June 28, '98	New Orleans, La.	
Bell, Albert	Private	June 28, '98	New Orleans, La.	
Blanchard, Charles	Private	June 28, '98	New Orleans, La.	
Bonaparte, Napoleon	Private	June 28, '98	New Orleans, La.	
Bridges, Jackson	Private	June 28, '98	New Orleans, La.	
Brooks, George	Private	June 28, '98	New Orleans, La.	
Brown, Paul	Private	June 28, '98	New Orleans, La.	
Brown, Peter	Private	June 28, '98	New Orleans, La.	
Butler, Aaron	Private	June 28, '98	New Orleans, La.	
Campbell, John	Private	June 28, '98	New Orleans, La.	
Cook, Charles	Private	June 28, '98	New Orleans, La.	
Craig, Isaac	Private	June 28, '98	New Orleans, La.	
Davis, Robert	Private	June 28, '98	New Orleans, La.	
Fascio, John	Private	June 28, '98	New Orleans, La	
Ferrand, Arthur	Private	June 28, '98	New Orleans, La.	
Forest, Eugene	Private	June 28, '98	New Orleans, La.	
Gaines, Manuel	Private	June 28, '98	New Orleans, La.	
Gipson, Charles	Private	June 28, '98	New Orleans, La.	
Gray, Thomas	Private	June 28, '98	New Orleans, La.	

Company F, 9th United States Volunteer Infantry — continued.

Name	Rank	Date of Enrollment	Place of Enrollment	Remarks
Hamilton, Richard	Private	June 28, '98	New Orleans, La.	
Henry, George	Private	June 28, '98	New Orleans, La.	
Hill, Henry	Private	June 28, '98	New Orleans, La.	
Holmes, Joseph	Private	June 28, '98	New Orleans, La.	Died Sept. 27, '98, at Santiago
Johnson, Washington	Private	June 28, '98	New Orleans, La.	
Johnson, Andrew	Private	June 28, '98	New Orleans, La.	
Jones, William	Private	June 28, '98	New Orleans, La.	
Lacy, William	Private	June 28, '98	New Orleans, La.	
Louis, John H.	Private	June 28, '98	New Orleans, La.	
Louis, Victor	Private	June 28, '98	New Orleans, La.	
Louis, Paul	Private	June 28, '98	New Orleans, La	
Massay, James	Private	June 28, '98	New Orleans, La.	
Mason, Joseph	Private	June 28, '98	New Orleans, La.	
McHamilton, Patrick	Private	June 28, '98	New Orleans, La.	
McKensie, Samuel	Private	June 28, '98	New Orleans, La.	
McCoy, William	Private	June 28, '98	New Orleans, La.	
Miles, Charles	Private	June 28, '98	New Orleans, La.	
Philips, Alfred	Private	June 28, '98	New Orleans, La.	
Raymond, George	Private	June 28, '98	New Orleans, La.	
Rheinhardt, Charles	Private	June 28, '98	New Orleans, La.	
Richardson, Benjamin	Private	June 28, '98	New Orleans, La.	

Name	Rank	Date	Place	
Robinson, Frank	Private	June 28, '98	New Orleans, La.	July 12, '98
Ross, William	Private	June 28, '98	New Orleans, La.	July 18, '98
Scannell, Isaac	Private	June 28, '98	New Orleans, La.	July 21, '98
Scott, Joseph C.	Private	June 28, '98	New Orleans, La.	July 12, '98
Simmons, Charles	Private	June 28, '98	New Orleans, La.	July 10, '98
Simms, Abraham	Private	June 28, '98	New Orleans, La.	Sept. 7, '98
Simms, James	Private	June 28, '98	New Orleans, La.	July 11, '98
Smith, Charles A.	Private	June 28, '98	New Orleans, La	July 12, '98
Smith, Robert	Private	June 28, '98	New Orleans, La.	Died Oct. 11, '98, at San Luis, Cuba
Thomas, Charles	Private	June 28, '98	New Orleans, La.	Sept. 10, '98
Washington, George	Private	June 28, '98	New Orleans, La.	Aug. 31, '98
Washington, Henry	Private	June 28, '98	New Orleans, La.	July 11, '98
Watts, James	Private	June 28, '98	New Orleans, La.	Sept. 14, '98
Webb, Calvin	Private	June 28, '98	New Orleans, La.	July 25, '98
Wells, Jacob	Private	June 28, '98	New Orleans, La.	Mar. 10, '99

Company G, 9th United States Volunteer Infantry.

2nd BATTALION, MAJOR DUNCAN B. HARRISON COMMANDING.

WILLIAM M. BROWN, *Captain.**

WILLIAM WILKES, *First Lieutenant.*   WALLACE D. SEALS, *Second Lieutenant.†*

Name	Rank	Date of Enrollment	Place of Enrollment	Remarks	Date of first illness
BREED, GEORGE W.	First Sergeant	June 30, '98	Galveston, Texas	Vice Mapson Burnett	July 18, '98
BRANTLEY, DENNIS	Q.M. Sergeant	June 29, '98	Galveston, Texas		Sept. 9, '98
BURNETT, MAPSON	Sergeant	June 28, '98	Galveston, Texas	Vice Batise Jice, discharged	July 18, '98
SMITH, TONEY A.	Sergeant	June 30, '98	Galveston, Texas		July 28, '98
KENNEDY, WALTER	Sergeant	June 30, '98	Galveston, Texas	Vice William Holman	July 13, '98
HELMS, GEORGE	Sergeant	June 29, '98	Galveston, Texas	Vice George W. Breed	July 11, '98
JOHNSON, HUMPHREY	Corporal	June 29, '98	Galveston, Texas	Vice William Robinson	July 23, '98
CALDWELL, WALTER	Corporal	June 29, '98	Galveston, Texas	Vice Beverly Chaney	Aug. 12, '98
CUMMINGS, ISAII	Corporal	June 30, '98	Galveston, Texas	Vice Clarence Burke, discharged	July 18, '98
GILES, WILLIAM	Corporal	June , '98	Galveston, Texas	Vice Walter Kennedy	Sept. 6, '98
SHIELDS, WILLIAM	Corporal	June , '98	Galveston, Texas	Vice Charles Lemons	July 12, '98
LYONS, EDWARD	Corporal	June 29, '98	Galveston, Texas	Vice George Helms	July 12, '98
McCASTLE, HENRY	Corporal	June 28, '98	Galveston, Texas	Vice Edward Seymour	July 24, '98
JACKSON, RICHARD	Corporal	June 30, '98	Galveston, Texas	Vice Jesse Anderson, discharged	July 12, '98
RICHARDSON, SAMUEL	Musician	June 28, '98	Galveston, Texas	Transferred to Band	

*William M. Brown, Captain (first illness Nov. 28, '98), vice H. A. Chanler (first illness July 27, '98).

†Wallace D. Seals, Second Lieutenant (first illness Sept. 9, '98), resigned April 7, '99, vice Nelson Smiley (first illness July 7, '99), resigned.

Name	Rank	Date	Place	Remarks	Discharge
Irving, Daniel	Musician	June 28, '98	Galveston, Texas	Transferred to Band	July 22, '98
Holman, Wilson	Artificer	June 28, '98	Galveston, Texas	Vice Humphrey Johnson	July 5, '98
Nash, William	Wagoner	June 30, '98	Galveston, Texas		July 21, '98
Adams, Joseph	Private	June 29, '98	Galveston, Texas		Sept. 9, '98
Akels, Albert	Private	June 29, '98	Galveston, Texas		July 25, '98
Alberts, Isaac	Private		Galveston, Texas		
Allen, John	Private	June 29, '98	Galveston, Texas		July 27, '98
Augustan, Charles W.	Private	June 30, '98	Galveston, Texas	Died at Santiago	July 12, '98
Bailey, George	Private	June 29, '93	Galveston, Texas	Permission to enlist	Oct. 9, '98
Chaney, Beverly	Private	June 28, '98	Galveston, Texas	Reduced from Corporal	Aug. 30, '98
Chase, Charles	Private	June 29, '98	Galveston, Texas		July 5, '98
Coleman, Henry	Private	June 29, '98	Galveston, Texas	Permission to enlist	July 18, '98
Dorsey, George	Private	June 29, '98	Galveston, Texas		Aug. 5, '98
Duke, Samuel	Private	June 30, '98	Galveston, Texas	Died at San Luis	July 11, '98
Eddore, John	Private	June 29, '98	Galveston, Texas		July 8, '98
Ford, James A.	Private	June 28, '98	Galveston, Texas		July 18, '98
Gamble, Arthur	Private	June 29, '98	Galveston, Texas	Permission to enlist	July 6, '98
Grasty, Robert J.	Private	June 28, '98	Galveston, Texas	Deserted camp near San Luis, Cuba	Oct. 8, '98
Grays, Adam	Private	June 30, '98	Galveston, Texas		July 9, '98
Green, George	Private	June 29, '98	Galveston, Texas		
Hardin, Sandy	Private	June 30, '98	Galveston, Texas		July 5, '98
Hayes, Richard	Private	June 30, '98	New Orleans, La.		July 11, '98
Henry, William	Private	June 29, '98	Galveston, Texas		Sept. 6, '98

Company G, 9th United States Volunteer Infantry continued.

Name	Rank	Date of Enrollment	Place of Enrollment	Remarks	Date of first illness
Hudson, Toney	Private	June 28, '98	Galveston, Texas		Aug 3, '98
Isaac, Albert	Private	June 29, '98	Galveston, Texas		July 6, '98
Jackson, Stonewall	Private	June 30, '98	Galveston, Texas		July 26, '98
Johnson, Thomas T.	Private	June 29, '98	Galveston, Texas	Discharged	July 26, '98
Jones, Ned	Private	June 28, '98	Galveston, Texas		
Jones, Samuel	Private	June 29, '98	Galveston, Texas	Discharged per Order	July 9, '98
Jones, Zack	Private	June 29, '98	Galveston, Texas		Aug 15, '98
Letons, Charles	Private	June 29, '98	Galveston, Texas	Reduced from Corporal	July 11, '98
Lewis, Sol	Private	June 30, '98	Galveston, Texas		Aug 10, '98
Lucas, William	Private	June 30, '98	Galveston, Texas		July 5, '98
McIntyre, John	Private	June 29, '98	Galveston, Texas		July 16, '98
Madison, Henry	Private	June 30, '98	Galveston, Texas		June 14, '98
Manning, Jesse	Private	June 30, '98	Galveston, Texas		July 16, '98
Manning, Fred	Private	June 29, '98	Galveston, Texas		July 16, '98
Moxie, William	Private	June 29, '98	Galveston, Texas	Died at San Luis	July 11, '98
Neal, James	Private	June 29, '98	Galveston, Texas		July 5, '98
Ovide, Charles	Private	June 28, '98	New Orleans, La		Sept 8, '98
Robinson, William	Private	June 29, '98	Galveston, Texas	Reduced from Corporal	Aug 13, '98
Rodville, Thomas	Private	June 29, '98	Galveston, Texas		Sept. 7, '98
Rogers, William	Private	June 29, '98	Galveston, Texas		July 6, '98
Roundtree, Robert	Private	June 29, '98	Galveston, Texas		July 5, '98

Name	Rank	Date	Year	Place	Remarks	Date
Sears, John	Private	June	'98	Galveston, Texas		July 11, '98
Seymour, Edward	Private	June 29, '98		Galveston, Texas	Reduced from Corporal	July 5, '98
Simms, Alfred	Private	June	'98	New Orleans, La.		July 19, '98
Smith, Brisco	Private	June 28, '98		Galveston, Texas		Aug. 9, '98
Smith, Jesse	Private	June 29, '98		Galveston, Texas		July 15, '98
Smith, William	Private	June	'98	Galveston, Texas		July 5, '98
Smithers, Alexander	Private	June 29, '98		Galveston, Texas		Aug. 28, '98
Solomon, Lewis	Private	June	'98	Galveston, Texas		July 13, '98
Stewart, Robert	Private	June	'98	Galveston, Texas		July 6, '98
Stores, Frank	Private	June	'98	Galveston, Texas		July 6, '98
Taylor, Grant	Private	June	'98	Galveston, Texas		Oct. 9, '98
Thomas, William	Private	June	'98	Galveston, Texas		July 5, '98
Thomas, Edward	Private	June	'98	Galveston, Texas	Permission to enlist	July 12, '98
Todmann, Alphonse	Private	June	'98	Galveston, Texas	Discharged, disability	Sept 27, '98
Tolley, J. C.	Private	June 30, '98		New Orleans, La	Discharged by Order	Aug. 30, '98
Trevason, Gaston	Private	June	'98	New Orleans, La		July 11, '98
Walker, Thomas	Private	June	'98	Galveston, Texas		July 21, '98
Weston, Frederick	Private	June	'98	Galveston, Texas	Deserted	July 6, '98
Williams, William	Private	June	'98	Galveston, Texas		July 6, '98
Williams, Charles	Private	June	'98	Galveston, Texas		July 22, '98
Williams, Joseph	Private	June	'98	Galveston, Texas		July 22, '98
Williams, Hiram A.	Private	June	'98	Galveston, Texas		July 11, '98
Wilson, Alonzo	Private	June	'98	Galveston, Texas		Sept 1, '98

Company H, 9th United States Volunteer Infantry.

2nd BATTALION, MAJOR DUNCAN B. HARRISON COMMANDING.

R. M. NOLAN, *Captain.*
H. HERMAN BLUNT, *First Lieutenant.*   S. G. STARR, *Second Lieutenant.*

Name	Rank	Date of Enrollment	Place of Enrollment	Remarks	Date of first illness
HALL, GEORGE W.	First Sergeant	June 29, '98	New Orleans, La.		July 20, '98
SMITH, ROBERT	Q.M. Sergeant	June 29, '98	New Orleans, La.		July 10, '98
BAPTISTE, ANTONIE L.	Sergeant	June 30, '98	New Orleans, La.		July 30, '98
BRUCE, NAPOLEON D.	Sergeant	July 2, '98	New Orleans, La.		July 28, '98
VAUGHN, DANIEL	Sergeant	June 29, '98	New Orleans, La.		July 28, '98
HARRIS, PHILIP	Sergeant	July 2, '98	New Orleans, La.		July 6, '98
WILLIAMS, HENRY H.	Corporal	July 1, '98	New Orleans, La.		July 9, '98
LEWIS, STEPHEN	Corporal	June 29, '98	New Orleans, La.		July 16, '98
SHERFIE, HENRY	Corporal				
NASH, ROBERT	Corporal	June 30, '98	New Orleans, La.		July 30, '98
BLANCHARD, BENJAMIN F.	Corporal	June 29, '98	New Orleans, La.		Sept. 9, '98
JACOE, WILLIAM	Corporal				
THOMAS, WILLIAM	Corporal		New Orleans, La.		
DANIELS, LEONCE	Corporal	June 27, '98	New Orleans, La		July 14, '98
MATHEWS, SAMUEL	Musician	June 29, '98	New Orleans, La.		July 7, '98
HENDERSON, STERLING	Musician	June 3, '98	New Orleans, La.	Died Nov. 26, '98, camp near San Luis, Cuba	July 8, '98
HILLARD, WILLIAM	Artificer	July 1, '98	New Orleans, La.		July 30, '98

Name	Rank	Date	Place	Remarks	Date
Alford, Henry	Wagoner	July 1, '98	New Orleans, La.		Aug 4, '98
Baptiste, Joseph	Private	June 30, '98	New Orleans, La		Sept 9, '98
Baptiste, George	Private	July 1, '98	New Orleans, La.		July 30, '98
Baptiste, James	Private	July 1, '98	New Orleans, La.		July 13, '98
Bazile, Thomas	Private	June 30, '98	New Orleans, La.	Permission to enlist	July 30, '98
Bernard, Murray	Private	June 29, '98	New Orleans, La.		Aug. 31, '98
Blanchard, Louis P.	Private	June 30, '98	New Orleans, La.		July 30, '98
Breashear, Joseph	Private	June 29, '98	New Orleans, La.		Sept. 8, '98
Breshear, Allen	Private	July 1, '98	New Orleans, La.		July 7, '98
Brent, Robert	Private	June 29, '98	New Orleans, La.		July 20, '98
Briggs, Robert	Private	June 29, '98	New Orleans, La.		July 28, '98
Brown, James H.	Private	June 30, '98	New Orleans, La.	Permission to enlist. Died Dec 1, '98	July 26, '98
Brown, Fletcher	Private	July 2, '98	New Orleans, La.		July 16, '98
Butcher, James	Private	July 1, '98	New Orleans, La.		Aug. 4, '98
Carter, William	Private	July 30, '98	New Orleans, La.		July 8, '98
Chase, Frederick	Private	July 2, '98	New Orleans, La.		July 8, '98
Curry, Oscar	Private	June 28, '98	New Orleans, La.	Permission to enlist	July 26, '98
Curtis, John B.	Private	July 1, '98	New Orleans, La.		July 30, '98
Davis, Richard	Private	June 29, '98	New Orleans, La.		July 14, '98
Douglass, John	Private	July 1, '98	Baton Rouge, La.		July 2, '98
Dula, John S.	Private	June 29, '98	New Orleans, La.	Discharged order War Dep't	July 30, '98
Foster, George	Private	June 30, '98	New Orleans, La.		July 29, '98
Gaiton, Louis	Private	July 1, '98	New Orleans, La.		July 30, '98

Company H, 9th United States Infantry   continued.

Name	Rank	Date of Enrollment	Place of Enrollment	Remarks	Date of first Illness
Garret, Lee	Private	July 1, '98	New Orleans, La		July 7, '98
Goodrich, Albert	Private	June 30, '98	New Orleans, La.	Died Nov. 26, '98, at San Juan, Cuba	Sept. 8, '98
Griffin, Arthur	Private	June 31, '98	New Orleans, La.	Permission to enlist. Died (?)	Sept. 7, '98
Hall, Joseph	Private	July 1, '98	New Orleans, La.		July 30, '98
Hatch, Edgar	Private	June 29, '98	New Orleans, La.		July 10, '98
Jacobs, Louis	Private				July 30, '98
Jenkins, William	Private	July 29, '98	New Orleans, La.		July 26, '98
Jessie, Willie	Private	June 30, '98	New Orleans, La.		July 13, '98
Johnson, Moses	Private	July 1, '98	New Orleans, La.		July 19, '98
Johnson, Robert	Private	June 29, '98	New Orleans, La.		July 19, '98
Johnson, William	Private	July 1, '98	New Orleans, La.		July 7, '98
Kane, William	Private	July 1, '98	New Orleans, La.		July 30, '98
Kerner, Moses	Private	July 1, '98	New Orleans, La.		July 9, '98
King, William	Private	July 1, '98	New Orleans, La.		July 30, '98
Le Day, Ernest	Private	June 28, '98	New Orleans, La.		July 29, '98
McCann, Isadore	Private	July 1, '98	New Orleans, La.		Sept. 8, '98
McGee, Edgar	Private	June 29, '98	New Orleans, La.		July 14, '98
Mason, Nathan	Private	June 29, '98	New Orleans, La.		July 13, '98
Miles, Wilson	Private	June 27, '98	New Orleans, La.		July 8, '98
Mitchell, Henry	Private	June 29, '98	New Orleans, La.		July 16, '98
Parker, Noel	Private	June 29, '98	New Orleans, La.		July 28, '98

Name	Rank	Date	Place	Notes	Date
Rene, Alcie R.	Private	July 2, '98	New Orleans, La.		July 20, '98
Robinson, Joseph	Private	June 29, '98	New Orleans, La.		July 30, '98
Rock, Frank	Private	July 1, '98	New Orleans, La.	Discharged	July 6, '98
Ross, Ananias	Private	June 30, '98	New Orleans, La.		July 30, '98
Rouchon, Baptiste	Private	July 2, '98	New Orleans, La.		July 30, '98
Russell, William	Private	June 30, '98	New Orleans, La.		July 6, '98
Shearfie, Henry	Private	June 30, '98	New Orleans, La.		July 7, '98
Smith, Robert	Private	June 29, '98	New Orleans, La.		July 28, '98
Spillers, Noah	Private	June 30, '98	New Orleans, La.	Discharged	Aug. 3, '98
Taylor, Joseph	Private	June 30, '98	New Orleans, La.	Died Dec. 11, '98, near San Luis, Cuba	July 29, '98
Thomas, Edward	Private	July 1, '98	New Orleans, La.		July 21, '98
Thomas, Wallace	Private	July 1, '98	New Orleans, La.	Permission to enlist	July 10, '99
Thomas, William	Private	June 30, '98	New Orleans, La.		July 30, '98
Luciana, Toney	Private	June 29, '98	New Orleans, La.		July 6, '98
Train, Raners	Private	June 29, '98	New Orleans, La.	Permission to enlist	July 22, '98
Trevalon, William	Private	June 29, '98	New Orleans, La.		July 20, '98
Tripagnier, Peter	Private	June 28, '98	New Orleans, La.		Aug. 13, '98
Ubern, Joseph	Private	June 30, '98	New Orleans, La.		July 30, '98
Walker, James	Private	July 1, '98	New Orleans, La.		July 9, '98
Washington, Henry	Private	July 1, '98	New Orleans, La.		Aug. 4, '98
Waterman, Paul	Private	June 29, '98	New Orleans, La.		July 16, '98
Weaver, Charles	Private	June 29, '98	New Orleans, La.		July 30, '98
Williams, William	Private	July 2, '98	New Orleans, La.		Aug. 28, '98
Wilson, Elijah	Private	June 29, '98	New Orleans, La.		July 13, '98
Winn, Andrew	Private	July 1, '98	New Orleans, La.		July 6, '98

PIERRE L. CARMOUCHE, First Lieutenant, Co. I.

Third Battalion

CLARON A. WINDUS.

. . .. ..

CAPTAIN WINDUS was born January 10, 1850, at Janesville, Wisconsin, enlisted as drummer in the 5th Wisconsin Infantry in July, 1862, and was sent to the rear in August, 1862, because of being too small and young. He afterward served five years in the 6th U. S. Cavalry, and was honorably discharged October 12, 1871, with a medal of honor for meritorious conduct in fighting the Indians. He has lived in Texas since that time—twenty-five years at Fort Clark, and still resides there. He was assigned to command of the Ferguson Rifles, of Houston, Texas, on June 25, 1898, joined the 9th regiment at New Orleans, and was mustered into the U. S. volunteer service July 1, 1898. The regiment left New Orleans for Santiago de Cuba August 17, and landed on the 23d of August, 1898. Captain Windus was taken ill September 6 with yellow fever, and returned to duty September 20, 1898, having fully recovered from the fever, and has since been in the enjoyment of excellent health.

★
★ ★
★

ADOLPHE J. WAKEFIELD.

. . .. ..

ADOLPHE J. WAKEFIELD was born in New Iberia, La., the son of Hon. Samuel Wakefield and Mrs. Amelia Wakefield. He was educated at Straight University, New Orleans, La. His father was one of the famous "Old Guard" 306, who went down at Chicago with ex-President Grant, in the Republican National Convention of 1880.

Lieutenant Wakefield was elected clerk of the District Court in and for the Twenty-first Judicial District of Louisiana, and held a number of positions in the New Orleans Custom House, and has been in business, off and on, the better part of his life. He was appointed second lieutenant by President McKinley, June 29, 1898, and joined the 9th United States Volunteer Infantry at New Orleans, July 3, 1898. His regiment was ordered to Santiago, Cuba, on the 17th of August, and arrived at that point on the 22d of that month.

In February, 1899, at Santiago, his company was mounted, and was ordered to suppress the bandits around San Ana and Mayari, Cuba. It was he who found Private Goodchaux two miles from San Ana, murdered by bandits, after which he

R. G. Woods, Second Lieutenant, Co. L

had two or three sharp fights in the mountains of San Ana, the home of the bandits, in which he displayed a cool courage which won him the esteem of rank and file alike, and showed him to be of heroic mould. He was appointed first lieutenant May 22, 1899.

JACOB CLAY SMITH.

JACOB CLAY SMITH was born June 25, 1857, at Taylorsville, Kentucky. He enlisted January 20, 1880; assigned to and joined Co. I, 24th U. S. Infantry, at Ringgold Barracks, March 16, same year; transferred to Co. F, same regiment, March 31, 1881; appointed corporal August 4, 1882; promoted sergeant February 23, 1883; served continuously in this grade until October, 1887, when he was transferred to the 10th U. S. Cavalry, serving in said regiment as private, sergeant and regimental saddler-sergeant until commissioned a second lieutenant of the 9th United States Volunteer Infantry, October 27, 1898; was assigned to Co. K January 1, 1899; reported for duty with said company at Cristo, Cuba, January 2, 1899; appointed quartermaster and commissary of post same day.

PIERRE L. CARMOUCHÉ.

PIERRE L. CARMOUCHÉ was born in the town of Donaldsonville, La., parish of Ascension, on November 20, 1862. He obtained a common school education. At the age of 14 he was a fine barber; later on he acquired much of the dental profession. Becoming dissatisfied with this profession, he learned the blacksmithing and farrier's trades. Young as he was, he became a skillful workman, and in course of time was the owner of the establishment where he learned his trade. He has been successful in his business. He is one of the most particular in matters pertaining to the race, is very patriotic; believes in perfection first, and elevation next.

His war or army record is quite limited, being simply that of the volunteer army. Cuba libre and the success of Maceo, in Cuba, was the height of his ambition. On February 25, 1898, he tendered to Secretary Alger his services and that of 250 colored Americans from his section of the country for the defence of his country at home or abroad. In the meantime, he neglected his business in order to enthuse his people and to instruct them as to their duties as defenders of the country. In that he succeeded, for on July 8, 1898, he furnished a company from his section, Ascension parish, for the 9th U. S. V. I. On the 13th of the same month his Company, L, was mustered into service. He was appointed one of the first lieutenants of the 9th, stood by the men on San Juan hill all through

Alexander V. Richardson, First Lieutenant, Co. M.

the afflictions which befell them, an ordeal long to be remembered, and one which makes the 9th U. S. V. I. famous.

Lieutenant Carmouché is known in his regiment to be a strict disciplinarian, and much credit is due him for the condition and discipline in the 9th U. S. V. I. He is much liked by his regiment. He holds two commissions from Ex-Governor Sam'l D. McHenry, of Louisiana, one dated May 1, 1886, as assessor of the town of Donaldsonville, and the other as an evidence of his reëlection to the same position May 7, 1887.

Lieutenant Carmouché claims to be the first colored man to offer his services to his country in the war with Spain, and has documentary evidence to substantiate the claim. On page 218 we print a number of communications to and from the lieutenant, which indicate very clearly that the colored men of Louisiana were just as patriotic as those in other parts of the country, and at the first call for help were willing, ready and anxious to respond.

★
★ ★
★

R. G. WOODS.

• • • • •

THE subject of this sketch was born in Starkville, Miss., March 31, 1870, and was educated at the University of Holly Springs, Miss. He enlisted at Memphis, Tenn., July 6, 1889, joined the 24th United States Infantry, and was assigned to Company G January 10, 1890, at San Carlos, A. T., or Indian Reservation. He was discharged at Fort Bayard, N. M., July 5, 1894, with character "excellent." He reënlisted July 23, 1894, at St. Louis, Missouri, rejoined his regiment September 17, 1894, was assigned to Company G, 24th Infantry, September 18, 1894, was appointed corporal September 26, 1894, and company clerk September 27, 1894. He was detailed as clerk in the Quartermaster's Department July 25, 1895. Relieved from this duty, he was detailed as company clerk March 1, 1896. Appointed sergeant and first sergeant August 27, 1896. The regiment moved to Salt Lake City, Utah, October 19, 1896; remained there until ordered to Chickamauga Park, Ga., April 20, 1898, where it remained from April 25 to 29, 1898, when ordered to Tampa, Fla., and later to Cuba. Arrived in front of Santiago June 20. Disembarked at Siboney, Cuba, June 25, remained in camp till June 27, when the regiment was ordered to Las Guasismas, to join the 3d Brigade, with the 9th, 13th, and 24th Regular Infantry,—the brigade that charged San Juan hill, July 1, 1898. By virtue of rank, Lieutenant Woods' company was on the right of the regiment, and, as first sergeant thereof, he was the first man on the firing line. After crossing the point in the river where so many men of his brigade fell (now called Bloody Ford), he was ordered by his captain (Brereton) to establish the firing line, which was promptly done. The concensus of opinion is that the advanced position taken by his company caused the charge up San Juan hill to be forced. Two men killed and twelve wounded, were the number lost in his company in this terrible combat. Lieutenant Woods, then first sergeant, was in the trenches in front of Santiago from July 1 to 15, inclusive, and in the fierce combats of July 1, 2, 3, 10, and 11, 1898. On July 15, 1898, his regiment volunteered to go to

W. A. PINCHBACK, Second Lieutenant, Co. M.

Siboney, Cuba, as attendants in the yellow fever hospital. At this place the whole company, with the exception of Sergeants J. T. Williams, W. H. Carroll, Private Samuel Bradshaw, and himself, were stricken down with this plague. At this place the regiment remained for forty days, laboring under adverse circumstances and seemingly forgotten, toiling with the sick and wounded, losing about one-fifth of the regiment. Finally relief came. The 3d Immunes and the 24th Infantry were ordered to proceed to Montauk Point, L. I., at which place they remained until September 23, 1898, when they were ordered back to their old station, Fort Douglas, Utah. During this campaign Lieutenant Woods, then first sergeant, conducted himself so as to win the respect of his superior officers, and in three weeks after arriving at Fort Douglas he was rewarded for his faithful services by an appointment as second lieutenant in the 9th United States Volunteer Infantry (Immunes). On November 5, 1898, he proceeded to Santiago to join his regiment, which was at San Luis, Cuba. On December 28 he was ordered to Songo, Cuba, at which place he was appointed adjutant of the 3d battalion, which position he held with satisfaction and credit.

Lieutenant Woods was the youngest first sergeant in the 24th Infantry. In his capacity as battalion adjutant, the office and its vexatious work were so well conducted that the commanding officer of his battalion, and other officers, complimented him for his thorough knowledge of the regulations and the forms governing army matters.

ALEXANDER VICTORIA RICHARDSON.

A LEXANDER VICTORIA RICHARDSON, First Lieutenant, Co. M, 9th United States Volunteer Infantry, was born in or near Gallatin, Tenn., December 13, 1858, received in all about six months' schooling, left home at the age of 16 years, enlisted in the regular army March 10, 1876, was appointed corporal May 1, 1877, sergeant July 28, 1880, first sergeant May 31, 1889. This position he held until his appointment as first lieutenant 9th United States Volunteer Infantry, October 26, 1898. He was 21 years and 10 months a non-commissioned officer in Co. B, 24th U. S. Infantry.

WALTER A. PINCHBACK.

W ALTER A. PINCHBACK, the youngest son of ex-Gov. P. B. S. Pinchback, was born in New Orleans, La., October 21, 1871. He attended "Southern" and "Columbia" Universities, in New Orleans. In 1889 he went to Andover, Mass., where he finished his education in 1891, and went to Washington, D. C., where he was appointed to a clerkship in the recorder's office, which position he resigned in July, 1898, to accept an appointment as a lieutenant

NOAH H. JOHNSON, First Sergeant, Co. M.

in the 9th United States Volunteer Infantry. In July, 1898, he joined his regiment at New Orleans, and was assigned to Co. M. During his stay in Cuba he suffered much from illness, and after being confined in the general military hospital at Santiago, where he was placed in what was known as the "dangerous ward," obtained a sick leave and returned to the United States, where he remained two months. Upon the recovery of his health, he returned to Songo, Cuba, where upon arrival he was made post adjutant, and remained such until his regiment left for home. He was an honest and faithful officer.

NOAH H. JOHNSON.

• • •• ••

NOAH H. JOHNSON, First Sergeant of Co. M, is an efficient non-commissioned officer. He was most useful in recruiting the regiment, having recruited Co. M, and has been faithful in the discharge of the exacting duties of his important position. He apparently comes from a patriotic family, two of his brothers having served during the war of the rebellion.

ARTHUR V. HARANG.

• • •• ••

ARTHUR V. HARANG, First Lieutenant of Co. K, was born at New Orleans November 19, 1869. He attended Straight University, after which he entered the government employ, and later that of a prominent commercial house He was assigned to Co. K, and has been faithful in the discharge of the duties of his office. He takes particular pleasure in the fact that he has been faithful to his government and yet has retained the confidence and love of the men of his company.

Company I, 9th United States Volunteer Infantry.

3rd BATTALION, MAJOR ARMAND G. ROMAIN COMMANDING.

CLARON A. WINDUS, *Captain.*

ADOLPHE J. WAKEFIELD, *First Lieutenant.** POOLE S. HALL, *Second Lieutenant.*†

Name	Rank	Date of Enrollment	Place of Enrollment	Remarks	Date of first illness
PERFAULT, AUGUST	First Sergeant	July 1, '98	Houston, Texas		Sept. 13, '98
POE, WILLIAM J.	Q.M. Sergeant	July 1, '98	Houston, Texas		July 7, '98
WESTON, SAXON A.	Sergeant	July 2, '98	Houston, Texas		Aug. 3, '98
COHEN, THOMAS	Sergeant	July 1, '98	Houston, Texas		
DAVIS, ALONZO	Sergeant	July 2, '98	Houston, Texas		July 20, '98
MURRY, DANIEL	Sergeant	July 1, '98	Houston, Texas		Aug. 1, '98
JEFFERSON, SETH	Corporal	July 2, '98	Houston, Texas		July 8, '98
WASHINGTON, OWEN	Corporal	July 1, '98	Houston, Texas		
WILLIAMS, JAMES	Corporal	July 1, '98	Houston, Texas		
COLEMAN, FRANK	Corporal	July 2, '98	Houston, Texas		July 6, '98
JENKISS, HENRY	Corporal	July 2, '98	Houston, Texas		July 5, '98
COLEMAN, CHARLES	Corporal	July 2, '98	Houston, Texas		
JACKSON, ALEXANDER	Corporal	July 2, '98	Houston, Texas		July 8, '98
WINFREE, AUSTIN	Corporal	July 2, '98	Houston, Texas		July 12, '98
MERMILLION, CORNELIUS	Musician	July 2, '98	New Orleans, La.		July 5, '98

* By A. G. O. May 22, '99, vice Louis E. Brown, dismissed from service Feb. 17, '99. First illness Aug. 29, '98.

† Poole S. Hall was promoted from private to Corporal July 1, '98; to Sergeant Sept. 15, '98. Later, promoted to Sergeant-Major, and, on May 22, '98, appointed, by A. G. O., Second Lieutenant.

Name	Rank	Date	Place	Notes	Discharged
BEUCHLEY, WALTER J.	Artificer	July 1, '98	Houston, Texas		July 5, '98
MILES, BERDIE	Wagoner	July 1, '98	Houston, Texas		July 8, '98
Alexander, Frank	Private	July 1, '98	Houston, Texas		July 6, '98
Alexander, Cornelius	Private	July 1, '98	New Orleans, La.	Died Oct. 23, '98, at San Luis, Cuba	
Anderson, Joseph	Private	June 2, '98	New Orleans, La.		July 12, '98
Barnett, William	Private	July 2, '98	Houston, Texas		
Birden, Alexander	Private	July 1, '98	Houston, Texas		July 8, '98
Booker, Richard	Private	July 1, '98	Houston, Texas		July 8, '98
Carpenter, John H.	Private	July 2, '98	New Orleans, La.		
Ceaser, John	Private	July 2, '98	Houston, Texas		
Clark, William	Private	July 1, '98	Houston, Texas	Died Jan. 4, '99, at Songo, Cuba	
Collins, Walter	Private	July 1, '98	Houston, Texas		
Dunbar, Austin	Private	July 1, '98	New Orleans, La.	Died Oct. 1, '98, Yellow Fever Hospital, Santiago.	
Dougherty, Henderson	Private	July 2, '98	New Orleans, La.		
Easter, Henry	Private	July 2, '98	Houston, Texas		July 25, '98
Franklin, Charles L.	Private	Aug. 4, '98	New Orleans, La.		
Gladden, Nuric	Private	July 2, '98	Houston, Texas		
Gordon, Solomon	Private	July 1, '98	Houston, Texas		
Gray, James	Private	July 1, '98	Houston, Texas		
Hall, Poole S.	Private	July 1, '98	Houston, Texas	See note at foot of page 140	
Harris, Edward	Private	July 1, '98	Houston, Texas	Died Sept. 15, '98, Yellow Fever Hospital, Santiago.	
Herne, Joseph H.	Private	July 1, '98	Houston, Texas		
Hurd, Louis	Private	July 1, '98	Houston, Texas		Jan. 6, '99

Company I, 9th United States Volunteer Infantry—continued.

Name	Rank	Date of Enrollment	Place of Enrollment	Remarks	Date of first illness
Jackson, Henry T.	Private	July 1, '98	Houston, Texas		
Johnson, Joseph H.	Private	July 1, '98	Houston, Texas		
Kertwood, Bernard	Private	July 2, '98	Houston, Texas		July 5, '98
Kittrell, Robert S.	Private	July 1, '98	Houston, Texas		
Lee, Wallace	Private	July 1, '98	Houston, Texas		
Lewis, Charles	Private	July 1, '98	Houston, Texas		July 8, '98
McCabe, James	Private	July 1, '98	New Orleans, La.		
Miles, Henry	Private	July 1, '98	Houston, Texas		
Minor, John S.	Private	June 10, '98	New Orleans, La.	Appointed Q. M. Sergt. same date; see p 62 .	
McCarthy, John S.	Private	July 18, '98	New Orleans, La.	Transferred to Co. L	Oct. 22, '98
Mason, George	Private	July 2, '98	Houston, Texas		July 12, '98
Massie, Adam	Private	July 1, '98	Houston, Texas		
Mathews, John	Private	July 2, '98	Houston, Texas		July 7, '98
Mathews, Jack	Private	July 1, '98	Houston, Texas		July 12, '98
Montgomery, Nelson L.	Private	July 1, '98	Houston, Texas	Regimental Q. M. Sergeant	July 8, '98
Moseley, Daniel	Private	June 30, '98	New Orleans, La.		July 26, '98
President, Harry	Private	July 1, '98	Houston, Texas		July 8, '98
Procter, Frank E.	Private	July 2, '98	Houston, Texas		July 12, '98
Pyatt, John M.	Private	July 1, '98	Houston, Texas		July 12, '98
Reed, Forest	Private	July 3, '98	Houston, Texas		July 26, '98
Richmond, Gabriel	Private	July 1, '98	Houston, Texas		July 24, '98

Name	Rank	Date	Place	Notes	Mustered out
Roscoe, Edward L.	Private	July 1, '98	Houston, Texas		July 6, '98
Ross, Josiah	Private	Sept. 1, '98	New Orleans, La.		
Smith, David	Private	July 1, '98	Houston, Texas		July 14, '98
Stanley, Jesse L.	Private	July 1, '98	Houston, Texas		July 5, '98
Sparks, Adam	Private	July 1, '98	Houston, Texas		
Thomas, Edward	Private	July 1, '98	Houston, Texas		July 19, '98
Thompson, William	Private	July 2, '98	Houston, Texas		July 8, '98
Walton, William	Private	July 1, '98	Houston, Texas		
Washington, George	Private	July 2, '98	Houston, Texas	Appointed Sergeant; died Oct. 1, '98, at Yellow Fever Hospital, Santiago.	
Washington, A. Philip	Private	July 1, '98	Houston, Texas		
Wiggins, Gus	Private	July 1, '98	Houston, Texas		July 6, '98
Williams, Edward	Private	July 1, '98	Houston, Texas		July 5, '98
Williams, Henry	Private	July 2, '98	Houston, Texas		July 6, '98
Williams, Joe	Private	July 1, '98	New Orleans, La.	Died Oct 13, '98, at San Luis	
Wilson, John	Private	July 1, '98	Houston, Texas	Died Sept. 22, '98, at San Juan Hill	
Wilson, Charles B.	Private	July 2, '98	Houston, Texas		July 25, '98
Woods, Louis	Private	June 28, '98	Houston, Texas		
Young, Thomas	Private	July 1, '98	Houston, Texas		July 26, '98

Company K, 9th United States Volunteer Infantry.

3rd BATTALION, MAJOR ARMAND G. ROMAIN COMMANDING.

WILLIAM LOWERY, *Captain.*

ARTHUR V. HARANG, *First Lieutenant.*   JACOB C. SMITH, *Second Lieutenant.**

Name	Rank	Date of Enrolment	Place of Enrollment	Remarks	Date of first Illness
ROSS, JAMES	First Sergeant	July 8, '98	New Orleans, La.		
JOHNSON, SPENCER	Q. M. Sergeant	July 2, '98	New Orleans, La.		
NEWMAN, ALBERT	Sergeant	July 4, '98	New Orleans, La.		
WOODSON, JOSHUA	Sergeant	July 4, '98	New Orleans, La.	Vice Lemuel Jones	Mar. 28, '99
BURTON, JOHN	Sergeant	July 8, '98	New Orleans, La.		
CHILDRES, DENNIS	Corporal	July 6, '98	New Orleans, La.	Vice George Smith	
COTTON, HENRY	Corporal	July 4, '98	New Orleans, La.	Vice William T. Tate	
BLACKBURN, HORACE	Corporal	July 8, '98	New Orleans, La.		Oct. 18, '98
BROWN, JOHN	Corporal	July 8, '98	New Orleans, La.	Vice Leonard Rainey	Sept. 10, '98
WHITE, ROBERT	Corporal	July 6, '98	New Orleans, La.		
BANKS, JOHN	Corporal	July 6, '98	New Orleans, La.	Vice Jonas Wiggins	
MAYSE, RICHARD	Corporal	July 4, '98	New Orleans, La.	Vice Jefferson Green	
REAMS, SANDY	Corporal	July 8, '98	New Orleans, La.	Vice John Smith	
JACKSON, JAMES	Musician	July 6, '98	New Orleans, La.		
PALAO, EDGAR J.	Musician	July 6, '98	New Orleans, La.		
CAPENY, MONROE	Artificer	July 8, '98	New Orleans, La.		Sept. 19, '98

* Appointed Jan. 2, '99, from First Sergeant 10th U. S. Cavalry.

Name	Rank	Date	Place	Remarks
SMITH, JOHN	Company Clerk	July 4, '98	New Orleans, La.	Dec. 17, '98
WIGGINS, C.	Wagoner	July 4, '98	New Orleans, La.	Sept. 10, '98
Abadie, Walter	Private	July 4, '98	New Orleans, La.	Jan. 1, '99
Allen, Moses	Private	July 6, '98	New Orleans, La.	
Anderson, William	Private	July 6, '98	New Orleans, La.	Oct. 1, '98
Bailey, Thomas	Private	July 6, '98	New Orleans, La.	Sept. 7, '98
Barnes, George	Private	July 8, '98	New Orleans, La.	
Benoid, Benjamin	Private	July 8, '98	New Orleans, La.	Sept. 11, '98
Berthelemy, Lucian	Private	July 8, '98	New Orleans, La.	Apr. 7, '99
Boyd, Edward	Private	July 4, '98	New Orleans, La.	Aug. 14, '98
Bradley, Noel	Private	July 8, '98	New Orleans, La.	Sept. 10, '98
Brown, Henry	Private	July 4, '98	New Orleans, La.	
Brown, William	Private	July 8, '98	New Orleans, La	
Campbell, James	Private	July 4, '98	New Orleans, La.	
Chatman, Richard	Private	July 6, '98	New Orleans, La	
Clark, Louis	Private	July 4, '98	New Orleans, La.	Died April 13, '99, at San Luis, Cuba
Duggan, Joseph	Private	July 4, '98	New Orleans, La.	
Dupas, Gustave	Private	July 4, '98	New Orleans, La.	
Edmonds, August	Private	July 8, '98	New Orleans, La.	
Edwards, Frank	Private	July 6, '98	New Orleans, La.	
Fields, Norman	Private	July 4, '98	New Orleans, La	
Frederick, William	Private	July 4, '98	New Orleans, La.	Died at Santiago, Cuba
Gamble, William	Private	July 4, '98	New Orleans, La.	Nov. 20, '98

Company K, 9th United States Volunteer Infantry—continued.

Name	Rank	Date of Enrollment	Place of Enrollment	Remarks	Date of first illness
Gaspard, Robert	Private	July 8, '98	New Orleans, La.		
Green, Jefferson	Private	July 8, '98	New Orleans, La.	Reduced from Corporal	Jan. 6, '99
Harrand, William	Private	July 6, '98	New Orleans, La.		
Harris, Michel	Private	July 8, '98	New Orleans, La.		Sept. 10, '98
Harris, Samuel	Private	July 8, '98	New Orleans, La.		Sept. 24, '98
Honor, Nelus	Private	July 8, '98	New Orleans, La.		Sept. 19, '98
Jackson, Emile	Private	July 6, '98	New Orleans, La.		
James, Thomas	Private	July 8, '98	New Orleans, La.		Nov. 12, '98
Jones, Lemuel	Private	July 8, '98	New Orleans, La.	Reduced from Sergeant	Sept. 10, '98
Landry, Felix	Private	July 4, '98	New Orleans, La.		Sept. 10, '98
Lawson, John	Private	July 6, '98	New Orleans, La.	Died at Santiago Hospital	Sept. 19, '98
Lee, Henry	Private	July 8, '98	New Orleans, La.		Sept. 16, '98
Lee, William	Private	July 6, '98	New Orleans, La.		Sept. 10, '98
Long, Robert	Private	July 6, '98	New Orleans, La.		Sept. 19, '98
Marshall, Alphonse	Private	July 4, '98	New Orleans, La.		Sept. 24, '98
Miller, Henry	Private	July 8, '98	New Orleans, La.		Apr. 9, '99
Miller, Timothy	Private	July 6, '98	New Orleans, La.		
Morgan, James	Private	July 4, '98	New Orleans, La.		Oct. 18, '98
Moseley, Barney	Private	July 6, '98	New Orleans, La.		
Pernell, Louis	Private	July 8, '98	New Orleans, La.		
Preston, Peter	Private	July 4, '98	New Orleans, La.		Sept. 19, '98

Name	Rank	Date	Place	Note	Date
Powell, Mack	Private	July 6, '98	New Orleans, La.		Nov. 30, '98
Primrose, Albert	Private	July 6, '98	New Orleans, La.		
Racque, Paul	Private	July 8, '98	New Orleans, La.		Sept. 17, '98
Rainey, Leonard	Private	July 6, '98	New Orleans, La.	Reduced from Corporal	
Randolph, George	Private	July 8, '98	New Orleans, La.		
Shelly, Marion	Private	July 6, '98	New Orleans, La.		
Smith, George	Private	July 2, '98	New Orleans, La.	Reduced from Corporal	
Smith, Beverley	Private	July 5, '98	New Orleans, La.		Sept. 10, '98
Tate, William T.	Private	July 6, '98	New Orleans, La.	Reduced from Corporal	Sept. 19, '98
Thomas, John R.	Private	July 21, '98	Chicago, Ill.	Transferred from 8th Illinois Vols.	
Thomas, Simon	Private	July 6, '98	New Orleans, La.		Sept. 10, '98
Thompson, Henry	Private	July 6, '98	New Orleans, La.		Sept. 10, '98
Thompson, Louis	Private	July 5, '98	New Orleans, La.		Sept. 19, '98
Turner, Alphonse	Private	July 5, '98	New Orleans, La.		Aug. 4, '98
Vance, James M.	Private	July 6, '98	New Orleans, La.	Reduced to ranks	
West, William	Private	July 8, '98	New Orleans, La.		Nov. 13, '98
White, William	Private	July 8, '98	New Orleans, La.		Sept. 10, '98
Wiggins, Jonas	Private	July 4, '98	New Orleans, La.	Reduced from Corporal	
Williams, Cyrus	Private	June 27, '98	New Orleans, La.		
Willis, Walter	Private	July 4, '98	New Orleans, La.		Oct. 1, '98
Wilson, Louis	Private	July 6, '98	New Orleans, La.		
Wilson, Willis	Private	July 4, '98	New Orleans, La.		
Wood, Joseph	Private	July 2, '98	New Orleans, La.		Sept. 10, '98

Company L, 9th United States Volunteer Infantry.

3rd BATTALION, MAJOR ARMAND G. ROMAIN COMMANDING.

W. PRAGUE COLEMAN. *Captain.*

P. L. CARMOUCHE. *First Lieutenant.**   ROBERT G. WOODS, *Second Lieutenant*

Name	Rank	Place of Enrollment	Date of Enrollment	Remarks	Date of first Illness
LONGS, JAMES R.	First Sergeant	Donaldsonville, La.	July 6, '98	Appointed 2d Lieut. by A. G. O., May 23, '99	July 20, '98
WALKINS, EUGENE C.	Q.M. Sergeant	Donaldsonville, La.	July 5, '98		Aug. 12, '98
GRIGSBY, ELIE A.	Sergeant	Donaldsonville, La.	July 5, '98		July 27, '98
RANDOLPH, C. LEWIS	Sergeant	Donaldsonville, La.	July 6, '98	Vice Joseph Ayo, died at San Luis, Cuba	Sept. 6, '98
CLANTON, T. WALKER	Sergeant	New Orleans, La.	July 11, '95	Vice Philip J. Brown	Aug. 12, '98
BROMAN, JOHN W.	Sergeant	Donaldsonville, La.	July 6, '98	Appointed Corporal Oct 3. '98; appointed Sergeant Dec. 14, '98	July 13, '98
ROBERSON, CHARLES	Corporal	Donaldsonville, La.	July 5, '98		July 24, '98
CAMILLE, FRANK C.	Corporal	New Orleans, La.	July 12, '98		July 25, '98
PERRIN, PLACIO	Corporal	New Orleans, La.	June 30, '98		July 26, '98
BROWN, PHILIP J.	Corporal	Donaldsonville, La.	July 5, '98	Reduced from Sergeant to ranks Sept. 6, '98; subsequently appointed Corporal.	July 20, '98
GRADY, NACE	Corporal	Donaldsonville, La.	July 5, '98		July 29, '98
INMAN, AMOS	Corporal	Donaldsonville, La.	July 13, '98	Appointed Corporal Feb. 23, '99, vice Scott Simmonds.	July 29, '98
WHITE, DANIEL	Corporal		July 11, '98	Appointed Corporal Feb. 23, '99, vice Sonny H. Granville.	Aug. 13, '98
LAWSON, WILLIAM	Corporal	Donaldsonville, La.	July 5, '98	Died Jan. 17, '99, at Songo, Cuba.	Sept. 8, '98
PERRY, CHARLES G.	Musician	Donaldsonville, La.	July 6, '98		July 11, '98
SENEGAL, A. J.	Musician	Donaldsonville, La.	July 13, '98	Transferred to Band July 31, '98.	

* P. L. Carmouche, First Lieutenant, commissioned July 21, '98.   † Robert G. Woods, Second Lieutenant, vice O. S. Duncan (resigned Oct. 15, '98).

Name	Rank	Date Enlisted	Place	Remarks	Date Discharged
BROWN, ARTHUR	Artificer	July 13, '98	Donaldsonville, La.		Sept. 5, '98
LA COSTA, ROBERT	Wagoner	July 6, '98	New Orleans, La.		Aug. 1, '98
Alger, Silvon	Private	July 13, '98	New Orleans, La.		Sept. 5, '98
Arcidore, Alphonse	Private	July 8, '98	New Orleans, La.	Died Feb. 9, '99, Santiago, Cuba	July 14, '98
Augustine, David	Private	July 11, '98	Donaldsonville, La.	Died Sept. 20, '98, San Luis, Cuba	Aug 19, '98
Ayo, Joseph	Private	July 6, '98	Donaldsonville, La.	Died Oct. 9, '98, San Luis, Cuba. Had been appointed Sergeant prior to his death.	July 30, '98
Baker, Joseph	Private	July 28, '98	New Orleans, La		Aug. 21, '98
Bernard, H.	Private	July 11, '98	New Orleans, La.		Sept. 1, '98
Bishop, Edward	Private	July 7, '93	Donaldsonville, La.		July 19, '98
Boone, Fedia	Private	July 8, '98	New Orleans, La.		Sept. 11, '98
Brooks, George	Private	July 11, '98	New Orleans, La.		Aug. 29, '98
Bush, Nelson	Private	July 11, '98	New Orleans, La		Aug. 21, '98
Carter, Wilson	Private	July 6, '93	Donaldsonville, La.		Aug. '98
Davis, Abe	Private	July 6, '98	Donaldsonville, La.		July 23, '98
Davis, Henry	Private	July 6, '98	Donaldsonville, La.		Aug. 27, '98
Dean, John P.	Private	July 12, '98	New Orleans, La		Sept. 2, '98
Delane, Albert	Private		New Orleans, La.	Died Oct 7, '98, San Luis, Cuba	Sept 6, '98
Dozier, Silas	Private	July 11, '98	New Orleans, La.		Aug 21, '98
Ford, Basil	Private	July 11, '98	New Orleans, La		Sept. 10, '98
Frances, Mack	Private	July 6, '98	Donaldsonville, La.		July 23, '98
Frerette, Joseph	Private	July 8, '98	New Orleans, La.		Aug. 13, '98
Granville, Sonny H.	Private	July 2, '98	Donaldsonville, La.	Reduced from Corporal to ranks Aug. 8, '98.	Aug. 27, '98
Gregour, Leonce	Private	July 23, '98	New Orleans, La.		July 30, '98

Company L, 9th United States Volunteer Infantry—continued.

Name	Rank	Date of Enrollment	Place of Enrollment	Remarks	Date of first Illness
Haines, Joseph	Private	July 13, '98	New Orleans, La.		July 19, '98
Harris, James	Private	July 7, '98	Donaldsonville, La.		July 28, '98
Harrison, Frank	Private	July 11, '98	New Orleans, La.	Appointed Corporal Aug. 8, '98; reduced to ranks Jan. 14, '99.	
Jackson, Daniel	Private	July 6, '98	Donaldsonville, La.		Sept. 4, '98
Jackson, Felix	Private	June 13, '98	New Orleans, La.		Aug. 13, '98
Johnson, Alfred	Private	July 11, '98	New Orleans, La.		July 19, '98
Jones, Sandy	Private	July 24, '98	New Orleans, La.		July 23, '98
Jones, Edward	Private		New Orleans, La.		Aug. 14, '98
Joseph, Armeda	Private	July 12, '98	New Orleans, La.	Transferred to Band July 21, '98	
Julian. Silas	Private	July 6, '98	New Orleans, La.		Sept. 14, '98
Longs. Dennis	Private	July 13, '98	New Orleans, La.		Sept. 10, '98
Marvel, William	Private	July 24, '98	New Orleans, La.		Aug. 12, '98
McCane, Isadore	Private	June 29, '98	New Orleans, La.		Aug. 26, '98
McCarty, J. D.	Private	July 18, '98	New Orleans, La.	Transferred from Co. I.	Aug. '98
Mosely, William	Private	July 3, '98	New Orleans, La.		Oct. 22, '98
Neams, W. J.	Private	July 13, '98	Donaldsonville, La.		Aug. '98
Nore. Amile	Private	July 6, '98	New Orleans, La.		July 28, '98
Patterson, Joseph	Private	July 11, '98	New Orleans, La.		Aug. 4, '98
Pierce, William	Private	July 13, '98	New Orleans, La.		July 29, '98
Porter, Nick.	Private	July 11, '98	New Orleans, La.		Aug. 8, '98
Powell, John	Private	July 11, '98	New Orleans, La.		Aug. 12, '98
					July 11, '98

Name	Rank	Enlisted	Place	Remarks	Date
Primons, Wille	Private	July 11, '98	New Orleans, La	Died Sept. 10, '98	Sept. 10,'98
Rencher, Thomas	Private	July 1, '98	New Orleans, La		July 13, '98
Richardson, Albert	Private	July 6, '98	New Orleans, La	Died Sept. 17, '98, San Juan Alta	July 8, '98
Roberson, Peter	Private	July 11, '98	New Orleans, La		July 25, '98
Sanders, Edward	Private	July 11, '98	New Orleans, La		Aug. 5, '98
Sanders, John	Private	July 11, '98	New Orleans, La		Aug. 27, '98
Simmons, Scott	Private	July 27, '98	New Orleans, La	Reduced from Corporal Aug. 10, '98. Reappointed Corporal May 3, '99.	Sept. 8, '98
Silvan, Victor	Private	July 11, '98	New Orleans, La		July 26, '98
Smith, George	Private	July 1, '98	New Orleans, La		July 28, '98
Solomon, Rufe	Private	July 13, '98	New Orleans, La	Dishonorably discharged	July 15, '98
Tillis, Jefferson	Private	July 1, '98	New Orleans, La		July 20, '98
Turner, James	Private	July 7, '98	New Orleans, La		Aug. 27, '98
Victor, Charles	Private	July 4, '98	New Orleans, La		July 27, '98
Villevasso, Jerome	Private	July 6, '98	New Orleans, La	Died Sept. 15, '98, San Juan Alta	July 29, '98
Waren, Joseph	Private	July 11, '98	New Orleans, La		July 16, '98
Washington, Henry	Private	July 11, '98	New Orleans, La		Sept. 7, '98
Washington, John	Private	July 21, '98	New Orleans, La		Sept. 10, '98
Washington, Robert	Private	July 11, '98	New Orleans, La		July 27, '98
Williams, Andrew	Private	July 12, '98	New Orleans, La		Sept. 1, '98
Williams, Curtis	Private	July 7, '98	New Orleans, La		Sept. 12, '98
Williams, George	Private	July 11, '98	New Orleans, La	Died Sept. 25, '98, Santiago	Sept. 3, '98
Williams, Charles	Private		New Orleans, La		Sept. 4, '98
Williams, Willie	Private	July 2, '98	New Orleans, La		Aug. '98
Wilson, Alexander	Private	July 5, '98	New Orleans, La	Died Sept. 17, '98, San Juan Alta	Sept. 5, '98
Winn, Alfred	Private	July 8, '98	New Orleans, La	Died Oct. 8, '98, San Luis	Sept. 6, '98
Zedore, Elex	Private	July 11, '98	New Orleans, La		Aug. 10, '98

Company M, 9th United States Volunteer Infantry.

3rd BATTALION, MAJOR ARMAND G. ROMAIN COMMANDING.

JAMES H. ALDRICH. *Captain.*

ALEXANDER RICHARDSON. *First Lieutenant.*   W. A. PINCHBACK. *Second Lieutenant.*

Name	Rank	Date of Enrollment	Place of Enrollment	Remarks	Date of first Illness
JOHNSON, NOAH H.	First Sergeant	July 16, '98	New Orleans, La.		No date
BOUTTE, JOHN A.	Q.M.Sergeant	July 13, '98	New Orleans, La.		July 22, '98
HINKSON, AMOS	Sergeant	July 16, '98	New Orleans, La.		July 22, '98
JOHNSON, GILES	Sergeant	July 13, '98	New Orleans, La	Accidentally killed May 25, '99, at the Penn. R. R. Station in Harrisburg, Pa. See account elsewhere.	July 27, '98
FOREMAN, EDMOND B.	Sergeant	July 13, '98	New Orleans, La.		July 28, '98
JAMES, EDWARD R.	Sergeant	July 13, '98	New Orleans, La.		July 16, '98
HARVEY, RICHARD H.	Corporal	July 13, '98	New Orleans, La.		
BOUTTE, CHARLES S.	Corporal	July 13, '98	New Orleans, La.		
ROMAN, A. GUSTAVE	Corporal	July 11, '98	New Orleans, La.		July 27, '98
TILLMAN, ALEXANDER F.	Corporal	July 13, '98	New Orleans, La.		July 17, '98
OWENS, MACK	Corporal	July 13, '98	New Orleans, La.		
OBEE, SCOTT	Corporal	July 13, '98	New Orleans, La.		Aug. 2, '98
LEDO, ALEXIS	Corporal	July 15, '98	New Orleans, La.		No date
BATES, ALEXANDER	Corporal	July 13, '98	New Orleans, La.		July 26, '98
KINGSTON, CHARLES W.	Corporal	July 16, '98	New Orleans, La.	Died Sept. 16, '98 in Hospital at San Juan Hill, Cuba.	
DANIELS, FLOYD	Musician	July 13, '98	New Orleans, La.		July 15, '98
DANIELS, JOHN	Musician	July 13, '98	New Orleans, La.		No date

Name	Rank	Enlisted	Place	Remarks
HOLT, GEORGE W	Artificer	July 16, '98	New Orleans, La	
STELLAR, GUSTAVE	Wagoner	July 15, '98	New Orleans, La	Aug. 26, '98
Alexander, John	Private	July 15, '98	New Orleans, La	No date
Arnold, Edward	Private	July 13, '98	New Orleans, La	July 22, '98
Ashford, Beverly	Private	July 15, '98	New Orleans, La	July 22, '98
Belony, John	Private	July 13, '98	New Orleans, La	July 29, '98
Boswell, Walter	Private	July 15, '98	New Orleans, La	Died Nov. 19, '98, in hospital at San Luis, Cuba
Coleman, Israel	Private	July 15, '98	New Orleans, La	No date
Christmas, Brinkley	Private	July 27, '98	New Orleans, La	No date
Darbon, Amos	Private	July 13, '98	New Orleans, La	
Davis, John	Private	July 15, '98	New Orleans, La	July 18, '98
Decuir, Joseph	Private	July 13, '98	New Orleans, La	July 27, '98
Delahaunt, William	Private	July 11, '98	New Orleans, La	Died Sept. 16, '98, in detention hospital at Santiago, Cuba
Donot, Narcisse	Private	July 13, '98	New Orleans, La	
Dyer, Joseph	Private	July 14, '98	New Orleans, La	July 18, '98
Ewing, Henry	Private	July 13, '98	New Orleans, La	
Fieze, Frank	Private	July 14, '98	New Orleans, La	No date
Florron, Edward	Private	July 13, '98	New Orleans, La	
Flood, Eras	Private	July 14, '98	New Orleans, La	No date
Ford, George	Private	July 15, '98	New Orleans, La	July 28, '98
Ford, Julian M	Private	July 13, '98	New Orleans, La	July 17, '98
Francis, Baptiste	Private	July 13, '98	New Orleans, La	July 18, '98
Grant, William	Private	July 13, '98	New Orleans, La	July 22, '98

Company M, 9th United States Volunteer Infantry — continued.

Name	Rank	Date of Enrollment	Place of Enrollment	Remarks	Date of first Illness
Gibson, George	Private	July 16, '98	New Orleans, La.		July 27, '98
Gilmore, Aquila	Private	July 13, '98	New Orleans, La.		No date
Gilyard, Abram	Private	July 13, '98	New Orleans, La.		No date
Gregorie, Leonce	Private	July 16, '98	New Orleans, La.		
Harriss, James	Private	July 15, '98	New Orleans, La.		July 28, '98
Hill, Charles	Private	July 16, '98	New Orleans, La.		
Hills, Anthony	Private	July 16, '98	New Orleans, La.		Aug. 28, '98
Hilton, Thomas	Private	July 13, '98	New Orleans, La.		No date
Howard, Thomas	Private	July 14, '98	New Orleans, La.		No date
Hurst, Charles	Private	July 13, '98	New Orleans, La.		July 27, '98
Jeffrian, George	Private	July 12, '98	New Orleans, La.		No date
Johnson, Charles	Private	July 13, '98	New Orleans, La.		
Johnson, Menney	Private	July 16, '98	New Orleans, La.		July 20, '98
Johnson, William H.	Private	July 13, '98	New Orleans, La.		No date
Lepage, Joseph	Private	July 16, '98	New Orleans, La.		No date
Lawson, Edward	Private	July 13, '98	New Orleans, La.		July 22, '98
Lede, Charles	Private	July 13, '98	New Orleans, La.		No date
Louis, James	Private	July 11, '98	New Orleans, La.		July 17, '98
McGray, Joseph	Private	July 15, '98	New Orleans, La.		Aug. 28, '98
Marcou, Samuel	Private	July 15, '98	New Orleans, La.		Aug. 25, '98
Martin, Porter	Private	July 15, '98	New Orleans, La.		

Name	Rank	Date enlisted	Place	Remarks
Marvell, William	Private	July 11, '98	New Orleans, La.	No date
Murray, Alexander	Private	July 13, '98	New Orleans, La.	No date
Narcise, Thomas	Private	July 16, '98	New Orleans, La.	No date
Nethers, James	Private	July 13, '98	New Orleans, La.	No date
Nit, Antonie	Private	July 13, '98	New Orleans, La.	July 19, '98
Nit, Louis	Private	July 13, '98	New Orleans, La.	
Nolden, Edward	Private	July 13, '98	New Orleans, La.	Aug. 3, '98
Ollford, Peter	Private	July 15, '98	New Orleans, La.	
Perret, John	Private	July 16, '98	New Orleans, La.	July 25, '98
Reed, Louis	Private	July 16, '98	New Orleans, La.	July 22, '98
Rim, Henry	Private	July 14, '98	New Orleans, La.	Aug. 6, '98
Ross, Rudolph P.	Private	July 16, '98	New Orleans, La.	July 31, '98
Smith, Arthur	Private	July 14, 98	New Orleans, La.	Died Nov. 27, '98, in regimental hospital at Santiago, Cuba. Aug. 27, '98
Smith, Jessic	Private	July 14, '98	New Orleans, La.	July 14, '98
Smith, Cyrus	Private	July 16, '98	New Orleans, La.	July 27, '98
Smith, Milton	Private	July 16, '98	New Orleans, La.	Aug. 25, '98
Thomas, Henry	Private	July 15, '98	New Orleans, La.	Aug. 29, '98
Thomas, John	Private	July 16, '98	New Orleans, La.	Died Sept. 22, '98, in general hospital at Santiago.
Thomas, Luke	Private	July 15, '98	New Orleans, La.	
Venable, Charles	Private	July 13, '98	New Orleans, La.	
Verrett, Walter	Private	July 16, '98	New Orleans, La.	Reduced to ranks. Died March 22, '99, in general hospital, Santiago. July 28, '98
Watkins, Philip	Private	July 15, '98	New Orleans, La	

L. J. Barnett, First Lieutenant, Co E.
Died at Santiago.

Necrology

Band

DANIEL IRVIN

Company A

JOHN DAVIS
SPENCER WHITE
EUGENE TATE

Company B

MARTIN CHRISTIAN
CHARLES H. JACKSON
LEWIS BUTLER
JAMES GARDENER
GEORGE JOHNSON
WILLIAM LEWIS
ARTHUR VEAZIE
JOSEPH BUCHANAN
THOMAS GIVHAM

Company C

JOSEPH NARCISSE
WILLIAM BOYD
JOSEPH MORRIS
PLACIDE JESSAMINE
THOMAS ROBINSON
MITCHELL FLOWERS
BARTHOLOMEW DAVIS
WILLIE CLARK

Company D

ADOLPH J. ROBINSON
JAMES DAVIS
GEORGE E. DAVIS
WILLIAM GARRETT
JOSEPH MOSELY

WILLIAM POWELL
PHILIP BOUISWAIL
PAUL VINCENT
ROBERT H. DOWNS Jr.
ALEXANDER PULLAM

Company E

ANDREW GOTTSCHALK
LEWIS JONES
HENRY JOHNSON
ROBERT SPARKS
GEORGE STEVENS

VICTOR MILLER
ROBERT COOPER
JAMES R. BANKS
LIEUT. L. J. BARNETT
FERDINAND BERMUDY

Necrology

Company F

JOSEPH HOLMES
CHARLES SIMMONS
DENNIS ALEXANDER

Company G

CHARLES W. AUGUSTAN
SAMUEL DUKE
WILLIAM MOXIE

Company H

JAMES H. BROWN
ARTHUR GRIFFIN
STERLING HENDERSON
JOSEPH TAYLOR
ALBERT GOODRICH

Company I

JOHN WILSON
P. A. WASHINGTON
EDWARD HARRISON
JOE WILLIAMS
WILLIAM CLARK
CORNELIUS ALEXANDER
AUSTIN DUNBAR

Company K

WILLIAM FREDERICK
JOHN LAWSON
LOUIS CLARK

Company L

JOSEPH AYO
ALPHONSE ARCIDORE
DAVID AUGUSTINE
ALBERT RICHARDSON
JEROME VILLEVASSO
ALEXANDER WILSON
WILLIAM LAWSON
ALBERT DELANE
WILLIE PRIMONS
ALFRED WINN
GEORGE WILLIAMS

Company M

WALTER BOSWELL
ARTHUR SMITH
WILLIAM DELAHAUNT
JOHN THOMAS
CHARLES W. KINGSTON
WALTER VERRETT

GROUP OF SPANISH ARMY OFFICERS, SANTIAGO

SPANISH BULL FIGHT, SANTIAGO.

GENERAL ANTONIO MACEO, THE CUBAN LEADER
Surprised and killed by Spaniards in 1898.

General Antonio Maceo.

THE GREATEST SOLDIER OF HIS RACE.

F ALL the interesting information gleaned by the Congressional delegation that visited Cuba some time ago, none is more interesting and romantic than that illustrative of the character and life of General Antonio Maceo.

It was gratifying to know that he was not killed by the treachery of the Spaniards, although they made several efforts to poison him, but the emissary who had been engaged to administer it reached Maceo's camp and disclosed the plot to him, begging him to be on his guard.

Maceo passed from the province of Pinar del Rio, by boat, into that of Havana, and was endeavoring to reach the headquarters of the insurgents in that province, when he unexpectedly met a Spanish force and was killed. The story that he was led into an ambuscade by Dr. Zertuccha evidently is without foundation. The Spaniards liberated the physician, who was Maceo's surgeon, because he took advantage of Weyler's proclamation, pardoning insurgents who should voluntarily surrender.

Maceo was undoubtedly the greatest general that the revolution produced. He was as swift on the march as Sheridan or Stonewall Jackson, and equally as prudent and wary. He had flashes of military genius whenever a crisis arose. It was to his sudden inspiration that Martinez Campos owed his final defeat at Colisco, giving the patriots the opportunity to overrun the richest of the western provinces and to carry the war to the very gates of Havana.

Maceo developed rapidly in the ten years' war, which closed twenty years ago. As a boy, his brightness and probity attracted the attention of General Gomez, who made him his protege. In him Gomez had the utmost confidence, and he loved him as he loved his son or brother. Maceo entered the patriot army as a lieutenant. His promotion was rapid, and he rose to the rank of major-general. In that war he developed the ability shown in the late war. He died a lieutenant-general. No one has ever questioned his patriotism. Money could not buy him; promises could not deceive him. His devotion to Cuban freedom was like the devotion of a father to his family. All his energies, physical and intellectual, were given freely to his country. He won the rank of colonel at Sacra, between Guimara and Puerto Principe.

This was the first and the only time that Maceo was ever driven back, but the odds against him were fearful.   Gomez was engaged in battle with General Valmesada, under whom Weyler learned cruelty and brutality.   Gomez at this time had 800 men, and Valmesada 1,500. Only 300 of the patriots were armed with rifles.   The others carried the machete, and used it with deadly effect.   Two hundred men were put under Maceo's command.   He was placed in an important position, and told to hold it as long as possible.   Meantime Gomez prepared an ambuscade for the Spaniards.   Maceo held the position for hours, and brought back 80 of his 200 men, 52 of the 80 being wounded.   The Spanish forces were caught in a ravine, and lost 600 men.   It was the most momentous battle of the ten years' war.   Maceo was then a captain, and Gomez commander-in-chief.

Maceo, though a mulatto, was a second cousin of Martinez Campos. His mother came from the town of Mayari, on the north coast of eastern Cuba.   Indian blood courses in the veins of its inhabitants — the Indians of whom Jesus Rabi, a prominent Cuban general, is so striking a representative.   Maceo's mother was half Indian and half negro.   Her family name was Grinan.   Col. Martinez del Campo, the father of Martinez Campos, was the military governor of Mayari. While in this station he had relations with a woman of Indian and negro blood, who was a first cousin of Maceo's mother.   It was in Mayari that Martinez Campos was born.   The father returned to Spain, taking his boy with him.   Campos was baptized and legitimatized in Spain, and, under Spanish law, the town in which one is baptized is recognized as his legal birthplace.

When Campos returned to Cuba as captain-general he made inquiries for his mother.   On discovering her residence, he established her at Campo Florida, near Havana, where she was tenderly cared for until her death.   The second cousins were on opposite sides in the fight at Sacra, in which Valmesada was defeated.   While the governments were conducting negotiations at Zanjon, under the promise of autonomy made by Campos, Maceo remained in the mountain district of eastern Cuba.   For a long time he refused to enter into any negotiations whatever with the Spanish authorities.

After Maceo became a major-general and Campos became captain-general, and while preliminaries were being discussed at Zanjon, a meeting between them was arranged.   Campos was very desirous of a conference with Maceo.   He sent word that he was coming, and they met on the plain of Barrajua.   There were two royal palms of extraordinary size on this plain, landmarks throughout the country, well known to everybody.   It was agreed that the two generals should meet in the shade of these palms at noon, accompanied by their staffs. The place of meeting was selected by Maceo, at the request of the Captain-General. Maceo's army was only a few miles away. The mulatto General arrived beneath the palm trees at noon, with an escort of thirty men. Raising his field-glass, he scanned the horizon, but could see nobody. Surprised that Campos did not keep his word, he dismounted, and found the Captain-General seated and propped against one of the palms, fast asleep. Before this discovery Maceo had seen a horse tethered in a clump of bushes 200 yards away. It had borne Campos to the rendezvous. When the Spanish General opened his eyes, Maceo said: "Why, General, where is your staff?"

"Between gentlemen, on occasions like this," Campos gravely replied, "there is no need of witnesses."

It is possible that the Captain-General did not desire the presence of his staff, preferring that the conversation should be strictly confidential. Strangers are not the only ones dogged by Spanish spies. The government itself maintains an espionage on all of its officers.

Describing the interview afterwards, Maceo said that never in his life did he feel more ashamed than when Campos remarked that gentlemen, on occasions like this, needed no witnesses. In reply, the patriot said: "General, pardon me;" and, turning to his staff, ordered them back several hundred yards. Among them was the noted negro commander, Flor Crombet, whose inflexible patriotism was sometimes sullied by atrocious acts. Maceo might justly be termed the Toussaint l'Ouverture of the insurrection and Crombet its Dessalines. Saluting Maceo, previous to retiring, Crombet said, "General, I hope you know your duty."

To this remark Maceo responded: "Retire, and return at 3 o'clock."

Crombet referred to a law enacted by the Cuban government providing for the shooting of any Spanish officer who approached a patriot general to treat for a surrender. In telling the story afterwards, Maceo said that he saw the devil in Crombet's eyes, and feared trouble.

At 3 o'clock the escort returned, but without Crombet. Quintin Bandera, the well-known negro general of the late war, came back with the escort, and reported that on reaching the camp Flor Crombet had mustered his forces and departed. This reduced Maceo's army at least one-third. Fearful that Crombet meant mischief, and knowing his savage disposition, Maceo was afraid that Campos might be attacked on his return to his headquarters. He offered to escort him back to his staff, and the offer was accepted. Crombet had really gone to ambuscade Campos and his escort. He planted the ambuscade at a point called Los Infiernos (Hell's Steps). When Campos reached his escort, Maceo shook hands with him and departed. He warily followed the Captain-General, however, until long after sunset. About 8 o'clock at night Campos was fiercely attacked by Crombet. The attack was stoutly resisted. Maceo closed up, on hearing the first shot, and vigorously defended Campos, much to the astonishment of the latter. The assault was repelled, and the Captain-General returned to Alto Songo, Maceo accompanying him as far as Jarajuica.

Flor Crombet never rejoined Maceo. He afterwards disbanded his forces, reached the southern coast and escaped to Jamaica. This story was told by Maceo to a friend while seated on a log on the plain of Barrajua, near the two royal palms where Martinez Campos took his nap.

Maceo had a second interview with Campos not long afterward. It was upon the estate of an English planter. Campos urged him to follow the example of others, and surrender on the promise of autonomy. Maceo stoutly refused to accept such terms. He proposed that he be allowed to secrete his arms and leave Cuba, feeling perfectly free to return to the island whenever he pleased. This proposal was finally accepted. Campos further guaranteed the freedom of the slaves in Maceo's army, promising that they should have the same rights in Cuba thereafter as Spanish citizens. He also solemnly promised that Maceo and his staff should be sent to Jamaica on a steamship furnished by Campos, and there released. These promises were made in the presence of the British Consul, who came to Songo with Maceo in a buggy. On his arrival at Songo, the patriot General was sent in a special train with the British Consul to Santiago de Cuba. From the train he went directly aboard the ship Thomas Brooks, chartered to take him to Jamaica. Somewhat to his surprise, his staff was placed aboard another steamer, called Los Angelos. In violation of the promise of Martinez Campos, the staff were taken, not to Jamaica, but to Porto Rico. There they were transferred to Spanish warships and taken to Ceuta. It is probable that Maceo would also have been sent there, despite the agreement of Campos, were it not for the friendship shown him by the British Consul, Mr. Ramsden, who was the owner of the Thomas Brooks. Some months later Campos became Prime Minister in Spain. He had guaranteed home rule to Cuba, but the Spanish Cortes refused to sanction the agreement. They were not, however, utterly lost to shame, for they did pass Moret's bill, freeing the negroes. This, however, looked like a stroke of policy. It was evidently done to curry favor with the negroes, whose bravery, devotion, and discipline were unquestioned.

Antonio Maceo neither smoked tobacco nor drank spirituous liquor. When he felt unwell, he took copious drafts of orange-leaf tea. It is said that he was also in the habit of taking arsenic in solution. He forbade all smoking in camp at nights, and no one had the hardihood to smoke in his presence, as he had a natural antipathy to the fumes of tobacco.

After the close of the ten years' war he became a civil engineer, and spent some years in Central America. He was in communication with Marti and Gomez, and received information of the late insurrection at Port Limon. From there he went to Venezuela, and from Venezuela to Cuba. In concert with Marti, Gomez, Flor Crombet, Rabi, Bandera, and others, he assisted in organizing the army and in developing a plan for operations. The final meeting was held upon a plantation owned by a relative of the Pope. It was Maceo who planned the attack upon Martinez Campos on the way from Manzanillo to Bayamo. It was in this attack that Gen. Santocildes was killed. Campos instinctively took an unused road, and escaped to Bayamo. He had previously escaped death by strategy. He was carried in a litter from the rear to the vanguard of his army. The Cubans, taking him for a wounded soldier, allowed him to pass without firing at him.

DEPARTURE OF SPANISH TROOPS FROM SANTIAGO.

The People of Cuba.

❧

HE CUBAN PEOPLE have been variously described
by different writers. each of whom, it is to be presumed. has written of them as observed and met.
They have. with hardly an exception. described
them as ingrates. dishonest. dissolute of character,
and altogether a reprobate and degenerate people.
After months of familiar, if not intimate. association
with the people of Cuba, I cannot subscribe to the
above, to me, wanton and groundless sentiment. I have found them.
fortunately with hardly an exception. honorable, grateful. though in
the most abjectly impoverished condition. True. I have found no
one who has intimated a desire to prostrate himself before an American. nor any who has offered to kiss his hand. They recognize their
poverty, and when this condition is referred to, simply say it is not
a dishonor. Their shacks. or houses. a picture of which is given, will
illustrate their de-
plorable condition.
No monument of
stone or of gold can
display the quality
of their courage or
the virtue of their
females. These may
be robbed of their
chastity, but the
pain of hunger, the
shame of nudity.
and the want of
shelter, have failed
to cause them to
prostitute them-
selves, as have the
seductive present-

A TYPICAL CUBAN DWELLING.

ments of the hitherto all-purchasing American gold. To rob these
virgin sisters of Eve, there must be brought into action the most
beastial power of the profligate. There are no "tenderloin" districts

in San Juan, Ponce, Porto Rico, San Luis, Havana, Santiago, or the other cities of Cuba, where will be found the daughters of Cuba. To what is this most remarkable distinguishing feature to be traced? Surely not to the civil policy of Spain, in its wanton treatment of its colonies. Is it due to the polity of the Roman Church? If so, it is an honor which must secure to it the lasting admiration of the moral and religious world.

In large, if not predominating numbers, the Cubans are Afro-Spanish. They differ from the Afro-American only in the quality of their courage. They would never submit to the abuses with which the Afro-American is so familiar. Recognizing their common mongrel origin and their common destiny, they neither encourage nor will they tolerate invidious distinctions among themselves, as we have them in our country. They are being transplanted, and, as a seed, they are seeking a place of growth. But the soil is American, and the new growth is repugnant to the rich and poor, and is being choked out by the wholesome and just sentiment of this people, who have lived centuries together, have enjoyed all civil privileges in common, have suffered together the onerous exactions of their parent country, and have alike fought for Cuba libre. It remains to simply express the wish that they may find peace, security and helpful consideration in and by our government, which has come to them as the highest and best expression of the love of Him who shapes the destiny of a nation not less than He does that of an individual.

The Cuban climate is not malignant. Nor is it unhealthy to those who have studied and adapted themselves to it. I remember of having read somewhere of the malignity of the climatic conditions which existed in this country, where now the most healthy people dwell. They have studied the climate, and instituted such sanitary improvements as to secure life in the enjoyment of the most complete health and longevity.

The soil of Cuba is rich, and produces fruits of various kinds. The rivers are numerous, and the water clear as crystal. Indeed, the country has such a wealth of natural resources as require only the touch of modern life, energy, genius and methods to have it to assume at once an increasingly growing prominence among the nations, and to prove to the world the wonderful riches which an All-provident Father has reserved for His children of all races in the clime where, in His providence, He has permitted them to settle.

The relatively small population of Cuba affords an opportunity to Afro-Americans for emigration which will assist materially in solving the American race question. The island's vast uncultivated fields :

its unimproved waterways; its unbuilt railroads; indeed, its needs of labor of all kinds, skilled and unskilled, which are almost incalculable, afford an opportunity for service that will not again present itself to the same generation. It needs all of our institutions for the making of a higher civilization—churches, schools, asylums, and penal institutions. It needs, therefore, persons of all professions and trades. It is thought that the Afro-American can in a large degree supply these demands—supply them by honest labor upon the farm and in the mine; in the church and in the school; in the construction of waterways, and the building of railroads. He would

A CUBAN FAMILY.

find happiness in his labor, and protection in an ever-increasing demand assured by the never-ceasing progression of advancing civilization.

The Cuban family is usually large. It is not difficult to find families of from eight to twenty members. A family of less than eight is considered exceptional. They are bound one to the other by the most primitive love. Poverty does not seem to deter them from marriage. Style has not stunted the maternal aptitude. Unlike the women of the more advanced countries, the desire for woman's rights—a right to become a monstrosity—has not possessed them.

The advanced (?) countries, such as France and the United

States, have questions of maternity which are demanding and not receiving the attention which the perversion upon which they rest warrants. The women of Cuba and Porto Rico are obedient; they are fruitful and multiply; they replenish the earth. The civilization of Cuba and Porto Rico has been friendly to the biblical injunction. Their domestic customs are, of course, an index of the civilization: indeed, it is of them.

The style of dress is nearly Adamic. This is especially true as regards the clothing of their children. Among the poorer class (and this is not confined to the colored, but includes alike the white,

STREET VIEW IN PALMA.

Cubans as well as Spaniards), they are allowed to grow for about 10 years, and I believe that I saw some a few years older, with but nature's clothing. Indeed, it was a strange sight to see these little ones clothed in nudity, running, as they do, and often with pigs and chickens, happy and apparently healthy.

One noticeable abnormality as to their anatomy is plainly evident. The abdomen of a large number of children is unnaturally extended. In quite a number of instances, the navel is of so unnatural shape and size as to suggest the sad need of physicians, as well as the ignorance of the Spanish doctors, by whom they have been too long afflicted. The shack, or house, is of the manor born. It is native, if not unique. It is made of the barks of trees and the grass of the fields. The floor is also primitive, being nothing but the bare ground. Of course, the domiciles of the better-to-do classes are of boards, and their houses may be of boards or brick. Though their homes are of so primitive material and construction, they are invariably neat in arrangement and scrupulously clean. In many cases the better-to-do classes have their houses built as in Spain and the United States. But those of the greater number are mostly one story, with window-openings, without glass. Glass, indeed, would be an obstacle, preventing the free ventilation which they mostly need and by which house building is regulated.

CUBAN SHACK AND COCOANUT TREES.

The houses are built from one to two feet from the ground, mostly upon posts, and in some cases upon stone pillars. Carpets are seldom used. They are considered a nuisance, if not a breeder of disease. Druggets are more common. The rule is to have everything movable; this is necessary, as small insects are a permanent pest, while reptiles are not a scarcity.

The villages and cities have been built without any plan, and in places where no possible reason for their location is apparent. They, indeed, suggest the wanton colonial policy of Spain. They have no sanitary arrangement whatever, no general water supply, no gas, nor other method for lighting of streets. Indeed, no attention to these matters, with a view to better the health conditions of the people, has been given in the slightest degree.

The absence of these and many other of the essentials which are considered absolutely needed in Spain, for the health and well-being of its people, force upon the visitor a consciousness of the awful wrongs that have been done this people. They have been taxed without representation, and they have paid the tax for centuries, receiving no other benefit than the privilege of paying it more frequently. They have covered every conceivable thing and every conceivable privilege; and hence they have been taxed for conceptions not yet materialized, but which have been considered possible. The taxation of thought is inconceivable, but here it has been fully exemplified.

It is not an easy duty that devolves upon our civilization. It will measure its asserted capacity; but the Father of nations, the portrait of whose son is photographed on our national purpose, will not withhold from it the required strength.

A Distressing Incident of the Mustering-Out.

PROBABLY the saddest event in the history of the regiment was the death of Sergeant Giles Johnson, who was accidentally shot and killed in the Pennsylvania railroad station at Harrisburg, Pennsylvania.

It was peculiarly sad in that he had gone through the ten months' service without serious illness, and had been mustered out. He was to have left Harrisburg for his home in less than three minutes after the time he was shot.

While his taking away was purely accidental, it was none the less criminal. Quite a number of the recently mustered-out men had congregated at the station, among whom was Sergeant Johnson, and in one corner of the waiting-room he and several others formed a group who were examining a revolver one of them had bought. The chaplain, not half a minute before the accident, had admonished the men for carrying their revolvers so carelessly, and had advised them of their power to make enemies for themselves by so doing, and to put them into their trunks. One of them replied that they were thankful for his advice, but they were now free and could take care of themselves. They persisted in "caring" for themselves, with the result that the sergeant was accidentally killed.

Sergeant Johnson was a good soldier, a competent officer, and, I believe, a gentleman.

The Cuban "Soldiers."

A CORRESPONDENT, describing his experiences while following the army in Cuba, gives the following description of the so-called Cuban soldier, which, to say the least, is not very flattering:

"On the way we met several groups of Cubans. I don't know what they are called—'insurgents,' 'patriots,' 'soldiers,' or what. All names are alike to me. Several correspondents, who are friendly to Cubans, have accentuated the fact that the men we saw there were not the real soldiers, but a sort of cave-dwellers, or something quite forsaken. It seems strange that not one was ever seen to be guilty

TYPICAL CUBAN SOLDIER.

of an act which was not selfish—and often criminal. However, they made a terrible bluff. Every day, during the week preceding the battle of July 1st, the main thoroughfare was the scene of many brave Cubans going to the front. After much hullabaloo they would march up and down, and then vanish from one end of the village or the other—on their way to battle. What they battled for was with each other—for food. They invariably went a short distance out of town, then turned 'into camp' behind a heavy hedge by the roadside. The greatest of these was Bigaro Chavaville, who commanded 200 men. He was a worker. At various times during the day he would go dashing through the crowds at Siboney, up to the 'Cuban head-

(174)

quarters.' Here he would obtain grave information, and then dash off into the mountains. But he would only dash a few hundred yards, when he would go into camp and await the time for a reappearance. If he ever received any information other than the fact that General Castillo and his brother, Doctor Castillo —who seemed to be running things to suit themselves—were eating and drinking, I've never heard what it was. Judging from the little I saw of Cuban officers, I would like to know the address of a single one who would bind himself not to accept a political office for a term of five years. From the highest officer to the lowliest 'soldier,' they were there for personal gain. On the way to the front that morning I met several Cuban groups. The first encountered had been nowhere near the battlefield. They had been 'in camp.' After a good mile's tramp, I met the first of several bands of thieves. Possibly thirty were in this party. Every single one of them had from one to three or four pieces of clothing, blankets, or tents which they had picked up on the roadside, where they had been thrown by the men of the '1st' and '10th' while on their forced march. They were all chattering and grinning."

I regret to be unable to defend the Cuban soldier. The above quotation is the general expression of newspaper correspondents who were there. What they considered cowardly may be owing to the different methods of fighting employed by the two armies. One fact is most prominent: They had practically won their own freedom when our rescuing army invaded the then territory of Spain, to secure to the Cubans liberty and the right to pursue happiness. If they are the cowards that our newspaper men represent them, their accomplishments, while at war with their enemies, prove an unsolvable mystery. It is fair to say that no other nation of "cowards," with larger resources and greater aid from sympathizing nations, have ever accomplished what they did.

— — —

The Market at San Luis.
❧ ❧

THE market at San Luis presents many of the features of those of which we read in oriental literature. The scene is not only chaotic, but it is also archaic. Apparently the confusion alike among people and animals is unregulated. But a study of the situation will discover a certain unison of action as well as uniformity in the prices, which are far beyond being exorbitant for the things upon which they are placed. Indeed, uniformity is apparent in the

cackling hen, tied to a stick or stone at your feet, and in the grunt-
ing pig tugging at your trousers leg.

It is a medley of sounds, of action or inaction, of colors or no
colors, of things to sell or things to be sold when they have come.

MARKET-PLACE, SAN LUIS, CUBA.

But the things absent have, in this confusion of confusions, equal opportunity with those present to be cried out at the Americans.

The ground is paved with unshapely stones, upon which the
sellers either sit or stand and torment the passer-by. The donkey
stands dozing, and occasionally keeps unison with the little pickaninnies
hanging from their mothers' back in the unique hammock arrangement which they have passing over their necks. Near by, and with
far more composure and independence, is the kneeling goat, rough
and gray, with long, shaggy tufts of his own peculiar growth of hair
under the elevated chin. His master, near by, solicits patronage in
a voice which only those acquainted with the Cuban dialect understand. His costume is most simple. His feet are bare and apparently unacquainted with water. He is a Cuban, small of stature,
lithe, and of a complexion of mixed dust and perspiration. He beg-
gars description with his coat of many colors, sleeveless and belted,
dropping loosely from his waist over his knees. The goat and donkey,
restless under their merciless loads, groan and occasionally neigh and
bleat, adding volume to the noise of master, hens, ducks, sheep and
birds of many kinds, while the master paces indifferently to and fro,
holding the driving straps as he advertises what no American would
buy, if it were not that he knew that he must do so or starve.

The only things that appeal to the American appetite are the

beautiful looking fruit,—grapes, dates, figs, mangoes and pome-
granates.

The picture shows some women sitting with their backs against
the pillars of the market building.   Their dress is most common, a
linen frock, extending the full length of the person, loosely gathered
at the waist and a veil of cloth for covering the head.   Their mer-
chandise consists of eggs, rice, herbs—the latter in stone jars such as
may have been used by Magdalene at the well.   Among the jars,
bottles and eggs, regardless of the crowd, a dozen or a hundred half-
naked children play and fight.   Their bodies are black, brown, light or
white, suggesting that amalgamation is going quietly on.   Scarcely less
blatant are the dealers in the other necessities of life.   In addition
to these, there are the Italian and Arabian peddlers of jewelry and
other odds and ends.   These are almost impossible of description.
They are ever present, and will be, until American capital shall have
introduced the modern department store of which this scene may have
been the developing idea.

REGIMENTAL CHURCH SHED, NEAR CAMP CHEEVER.

Church Shack, Camp Cheever.

❦ ❦

OUR church shed at Camp Cheever was unique but most satis-
factory.   The men came to regard it with a devotion that is
often prominent by its absence in some of our large cities.
It was made of bamboo sticks, palm leaves and grass.   The cut
shows the chaplain and a number of the men, with Lieut. E.
Williams, just after the close of a service.

A Cuban Funeral.

❦ ❦

A FUNERAL is an extremely sad affair in either Cuba or Porto Rico, as the custom is the same. The same coffin may have been used many times, as it is only rented for the occasion. The body of the deceased is rested in it only from the time of death until its arrival at the place of burial. It is then taken out and laid away in the spotless white linen in which it has been clothed. Hearses are not used, the body being borne upon the shoulders of the pall-bearers.

The religious sacredness of the dead is shown by the universal respect paid to dead as it passes slowly along, with the mourners

ENTRANCE TO CEMETERY, SANTIAGO,
Where many American soldiers were buried.

tearfully following with bowed heads and measured step. Graves or plots in the cemeteries are not sold, but leased; this explains the need and use of the "bone-house," shown at the right of the entrance to the cemetery in the accompanying cut. In it, if the relatives or those interested in the deceased fail to pay the perennial burial fee, the bones of the dead are placed. At the time the writer was there, it was more than half full of human bones. It is plain that, by this process of taking up the bones of the dead, their dust becomes a part of the soil, and one walks upon the actual dust of those who were once his friends.

BIRDS-EYE VIEW OF SANTIAGO DE CUBA.

MORRO CASTLE—Entrance to Bay of Santiago.

Santiago and Morro Castle.

✦ ✦

HAVING failed to satisfy myself with what I had written of the most beautiful of scenes. I destroyed it and take the words of another, who, also, I believe, fails to portray in any adequate measure the beautiful entrance to the harbor of this old and famous city. He says:

"Passing Morro Castle on the right, one will enter the harbor of Santiago, the entrance to which is only 600 feet wide. As the vessel passes up the harbor, the wreck of the Reina Mercedes and the masts and funnels of the 'cork in the bottle,' the collier Merrimac, sunk by Lieutenant Hobson and his men, will be seen.

"Before you looms up the entrance to the port of Santiago, an entrance so beautiful as to defy description.

"Suddenly you come upon an old yellow castle that almost makes you rub your eyes and doubt what they show you. The high green bank has broken off almost precipitously, and at the fractured edge is this ancient Moorish stronghold, with extensions like roots of masonry reaching down the steep incline to the very surface of the water. Morro Castle, at Havana, is modern beside it. It has little belfry arches every here and there, and singular towers and barred windows sifting light into cavernous dungeons, and stairs hollowed by the feet of half a score of generations or more. You see soldiers here and there, and learn that it is used as a political prison, prin-

MORRO CASTLE, FROM THE OCEAN.
The picture shows the effects of bombardment by Schley.

cipally. On the ocean side, under the fort, the sea has cut deeply into the rock, how far it is not known, though it is said by the natives that boatmen who ventured into the cave never returned.

"Now Santiago lies before you, a spreading mass of low houses on a mountain slope, presenting more than the colors of the rainbow, for the citizens have utilized nearly every shade and tint in decorating the plaster walls of their homes. It looks for all the world as if it might be in Algiers, Morocco, or Tripoli.

"You are in a city founded by Velasquez in 1514, the oldest in the West Indies, if not in America; certainly the oldest of any size on the continent. So old is it that in its broad details (its streets, houses and general external appearance), it would not astonish Columbus could he see it today. Where else could he go and not be astonished? Cortez started from it to make the conquest of Mexico, and in many places it is just as he left it."

INTERIOR OF MORRO CASTLE.

Cienfuegos.

❦ ❦

THE entrance to this port is also exceedingly pretty. though the
course is not so serpentine nor the view so grandly beautiful
as at Santiago. There are lovely little country houses, quaint
fishers' cottages, and gay-hued bathing-boxes in the rich setting of
abundant verdure; and a menacing fort, more modern than at Santiago, guards the channel. In the city are several two-story houses.
and scores of residences as modern and almost as fine as some of

MARKET SCENE, SANTIAGO, CUBA.

the nice homes in Havana. Of course, they are nothing like American houses. They are fronted with plaster, decked with monstrous
barred windows and solid wooden doors, and passers-by see, with a
side glance, the tesselated, stone-floored parlor, with its family portraits, piano, rows of rockers, broad-tiled window-seat and scant,
cool furniture, and beyond that the lace curtains of a bedroom or
two, and the brilliant foliage of an open court, which separates the
hot and odorous kitchen from the dwelling-rooms.

Cienfuegos has its promenades, where, in the cool of the evening, when the day's toil is ended, young and old take recreation.
The plaza is just as inevitable to one of those Spanish towns as the
blue sea and the bluer sky. The cathedral is a fine building, and

HARBOR OF SANTIAGO.

NAUTICAL CLUB HOUSE, SANTIAGO Used as an Emergency Hospital

ROMAN CATHOLIC CATHEDRAL, SANTIAGO.

RAILROAD STATION, SANTIAGO, CUBA.

the inhabitants flock to it on Sabbath morning.   It is by no means gorgeous or gaudy outside, but inside you are confronted with color and ornamentation strangely out of keeping with our northern ideas of dignified simplicity.   The bells in this Cienfuegos cathedral are not the deep-toned, solemn chimes that had just a sufficient number of silver coins thrown in at their casting to give a sweetness to their cadence, but they are jangling, strident and discordant.   Here, too, as elsewhere in the island, the volante, a large, curious-looking, two-wheel buggy, drawn by a pair of horses or mules, is the ordinary conveyance.

SAN PEDRO STREET, SANTIAGO, CUBA.

During the war a spirited engagement took place at Cienfuegos between the shore batteries and the Marblehead and the Nashville, while several boat crews were engaged in cutting cables.

Daiquiri and Siboney.

A T Daiquiri, June 22, the first of General Shafter's army landed, after the surrounding hills had been shelled by the New Orleans, Detroit, Castine, Wasp and Suwanee.   After the Spaniards had retreated toward Santiago, Siboney, about six miles west of Daiquiri, was occupied by our troops.   It was at La Guasima, a short distance from Siboney, that the first battle, between the Rough Riders and the enemy, took place.

The distance overland from Daiquiri to Santiago by way of the battlefields is about fourteen miles, and from Siboney, about ten miles.

PALACE AND CENTRAL PARK, SANTIAGO, CUBA.

STREET SCENE IN SANTIAGO, CUBA.

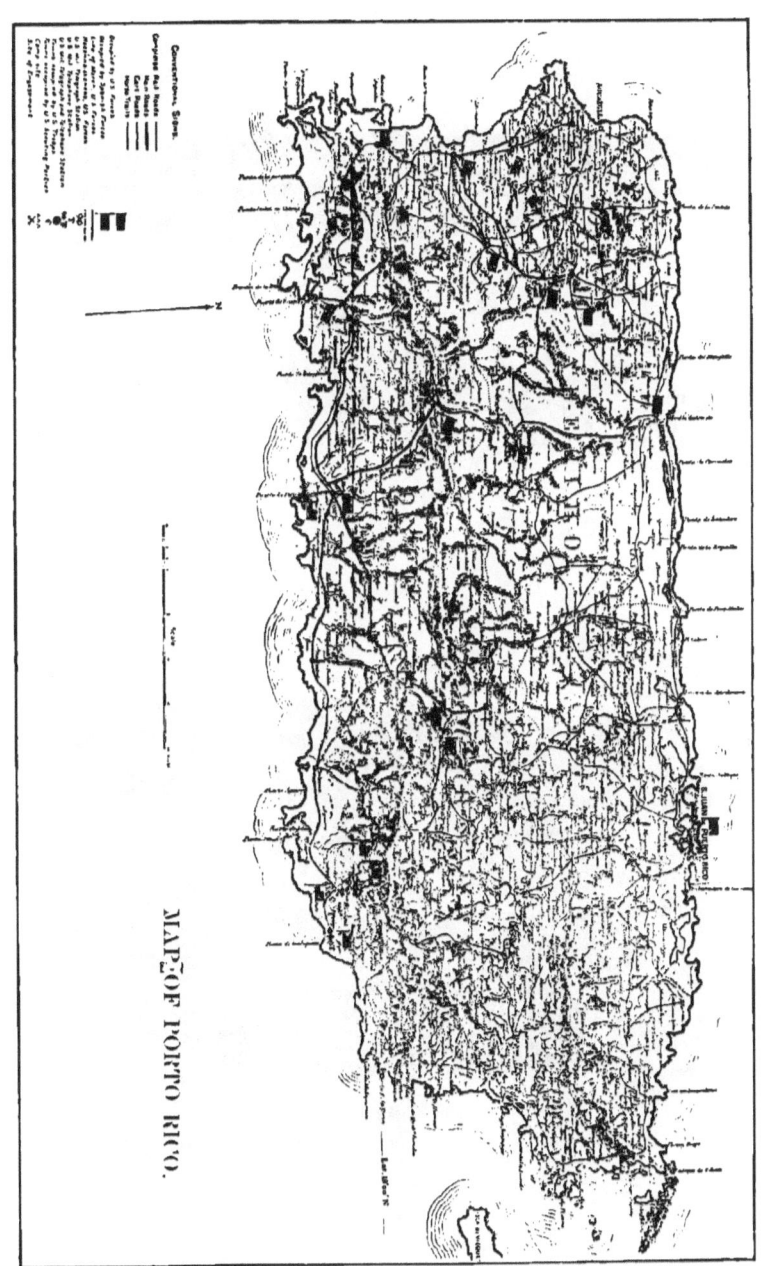

MAP OF PORTO RICO.

SAN JUAN HILL.—Santiago in distance

SAN JUAN HILL.

Spanish trenches, and graves of American soldiers: 9th and 10th Cavalry, 24th and
25th Infantry (the last two white), 2d Mass., Rough Riders, and 71st N. Y.

My Visit to San Juan, Porto Rico.

♥ ♥

PORTO RICO is the fourth island in point of size in the West Indies. and was. supposedly, at the time of its concession and annexation. the richest. It was discovered by Columbus in 1493. It is about 92 miles long from its eastern to its western extremity. and about 32 miles wide. comprising an area of 3,500 square miles. A magnificent mountain range extends through the island from east to west. its highest altitude being 4,000 feet above the sea. The climate is delightful, being more equable than

OLD GATE SAN JUAN.

that of the other islands. The entire island is under cultivation, the forests being mostly confined to the mountain regions. Its trade is mostly of tobacco. coffee and sugar. The population is largely mixed, and is estimated at 800,000.

San Juan. the capital, on the north side of the island. is a beautiful city. and has a population of 25,000. Morro Castle guards the entrance to the harbor. but is now shorn of its perennial authority. and has no terror for the foreigner. as it had during the reign of the Castilian monarchy.

ROAD TO SAN JUAN HILL.

On October 15, 1898, "the flag of Aragon and Castile" was low-ered for the last time, and the Stars and Stripes announced that it had become a part of the territory of the U. S. government.

It was the pleasure of the writer to preach at one service and to assist at another on Sunday, February 10, in San Juan. He assisted at a service held by a Baptist clergyman in the theater building on the plaza, and preached at a service held in a hall in one of the municipal buildings the same evening. He was told that he was the first colored clergyman or chaplain to preach upon the island.

GARCIA'S MEN ESCORTING AMERICAN OFFICERS,
NEAR EL COBRE, CUBA.

Port Au Ponce, Porto Rico.

THIS is a small town, two miles from the main city, and is called Playa, having a population of 3,000. The custom house, the office of the captain of the port, warehouses, cable offices and other official buildings are located here. The wharves are of stone, with plank covering. Here the ammunition of our troops and general supplies were landed, and then transferred to huge wagons of the quarter-master department of our army, or to native carts, which beggar description.

Here I witnessed for the first time some few of the necessities of war. There were soldiers everywhere, officers coming and going, and an absolute blockade of wagons, horses and mules, all the indescribable rush of war busy in the completion of arrangements for the taking of life.

To and from this beautiful little village, it was my pleasure to ride a bicycle upon the splendid road joining it and the camp. It was indescribably pleasant. The road is all that could be desired, being of a cement made of pounded stone, rounding from the center. On either side are cane fields, banana plantations, tropical fruits and flowers, houses, and the most hospitable people.

City of Songo.- Garrisoned by Cos. F, H, L and M, 9th U. S. V. I.

Songo.
❦ ❦

THE city of Songo is located upon Altar Songo, the highest hill in the province of Santiago. It is considered healthy, and the people are hospitable and industrious. They are mostly tobacco raisers. Here are found the most beautiful woods. They are being felled, dressed and exported to the United States, one American company having purchased thousands of acres of woodlands. Cocoanuts and bananas are raised in great quantities and find a ready market in Santiago, which is only twenty miles east. The people are quaint in their features, customs, and conduct. There is a nicety of behavior among them, the origin of which has been sought for and not found.

They have had no church and no school to refine them. And yet there is a comity existing among these people, a gentleness and felicity that have not always been found among a people of more favored surroundings.

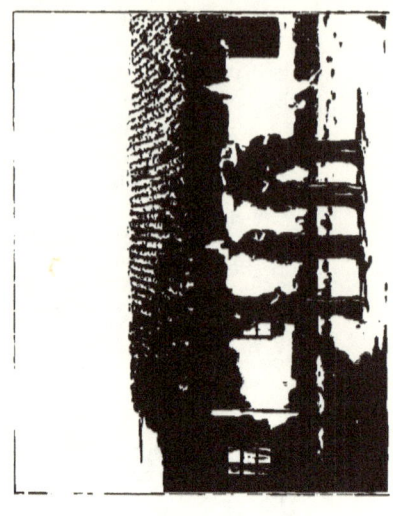

OFFICERS' QUARTERS, 9TH U. S. V. I., SAN LUIS, CUBA.

REGIMENTAL HOSPITAL, SAN LUIS, CUBA.

San Luis.

♥ ♥

SAN LUIS is a town of 4,000 inhabitants. It is the largest town in the province of Santiago. During the late insurrection it was the rendezvous of numerous bands of banditti. Though it is probably a hundred years old, it has no paved streets, none but the most recently established schools, and no church or religious societies of any kind. It is the habit of all the well-to-do people to send their children to school at Santiago, Madrid, or Paris. The very excellent relatives,—sisters, nephews, and nieces of General A. Maceo live here. They enjoy the respect and love of the entire community.

BARRACKS OF COS. A AND C AT EL COBRE.

and, while there may be many better situated families than this, there are none there or elsewhere, in which more refinement is manifested and truer devotion shown for Cuba libre. But it has cost them much, real estate and personal property as well as municipal and government bonds; to them the cost of patriotism has been great; and, most of all, these three sisters are widowed. Their husbands and several sons and other relatives, now dead, testify as to the quality of the Cuban people, and especially of this family. They were ever mindful of the fact that we were strangers, and their deeds of a kindly spirit were many.

Cristo.

♦ ♦

THE city of Cristo is located in a valley or what may have been a depression caused by volcanic action. This opinion is based upon the general character of its topography and upon the very fine specimens of quartz that are found there—jasper, amethyst, and agate. The people of this town resemble the others in most respects, but are apparently less ambitious and more contented. Their customs and habits are similar to those of the neighboring villages.

THOMAS GRAY, A PRIVATE OF CO. F, WHICH GARRISONED CRISTO.

El Cobre.

♦ ♦

THIS little town is noted for its mines, of both gold and iron and possibly of copper. It was burned by the Cubans during their insurrection against the Spanish government. It is especially noteworthy at this time on account of the altar in the church. It is of solid gold, having all of its appendages either of the same metal or of silver. It shows the deep religious sentiment of both Spaniards and Cubans. The former ransacked the city and the latter burned it; and yet this church, with its invaluable fixtures, escaped the ravages alike of the most destructive element and the rapacity of a rapacious people.

TOWN OF EL COBRE, CUBA,
Garrisoned by Cos. A and C, 9th U. S. V. I.

Havana.

❦ ❦

HAVANA has a fine harbor, separated from the sea by only a slender point of land. On the one hand is the low, many-colored city, and on the other, perched on a bluff, is the Morro Castle and the Cabanas. No one needs to be reminded that Morro is simply a reference to the style or manner in which the once-formidable fort was built. The Cabanas, stretching its grim walls behind the castle, was built after the English had captured Morro Castle in the eighteenth century. A yet more modern fortress is opposite, on the city side.

Wherever the eye rests, the scene is wholly unfamiliar to northern eyes. On the green hills, the graceful, umbrella-like palms and cocoanuts and huge-leaved bananas fling their branches to the breeze. The houses that are separated from the city and scattered about the surrounding shores are low and rambling, and are either white, or, more odd still, are blue, or pink, or green. Perhaps you do not notice it

at once, but you are able to see farther and better than at home, for
the air is usually as clear as crystal. You will notice, later on, that
the sky is similarly clear, and as for the nights, they are beautiful
beyond description.

The streets are very narrow: the sidewalks are seldom more than
two feet wide in the older parts of the city: the houses are mainly

MULE CART — HAVANA.

broad and low, three-story buildings being rare, and one-story struc-
tures quite common. You notice that everything is made to serve
comfort and coolness. Instead of having panes of glass, the windows
are open and guarded by light iron railings, and the heavy wooden
doors are left ajar. You see into many houses as you pass along,
and very cool and clean they look. There are marble floors, cane-
seated chairs and lounges, thin lace curtains, and glimpses of courts
in the center of each building, often with green plants or gaudy

flowers growing in them, between the parlor and the kitchen. You may walk in at the doors or the dining-room windows, just as you please, for the sides of the house seem capable of being all thrown open, while in the center of the building you see the blue sky overhead.

Havana is the metropolis of the West Indies. It has more life and bustle than all the rest of the Archipelago put together. The theaters astonish you by their size and elegance. They are the Tacon, Payret, Nuevo, Liceo, Verano, Cervantes, and the circus, called Circo de Jané. Some of these have five galleries, and one, the Tacon, can accommodate six thousand persons at a ball, or three thousand in the seats. It ranks fourth in size in the world. The Verano is a tropical establishment all open at the sides, and the circus can be thrown open to the sky. The aristocratic club is the Union, but the popular one is the Casino Espanol, whose club-house is a marvel of tropical elegance and beauty. Nearly all these attractions are on or near that broad, shady and imposing thoroughfare, the Prado—a succession of parks leading from the water opposite the Morro Castle almost across the city.

BLOODY BEND, NEAR EL CANEY.

TOWN OF EL CANEY

VIEW AT REAR OF EL CANEY.

Showing stream forded, with barbed wire fence, cut by Rough Riders and Tenth Cavalry (colored),
under fire, while singing "There'll be a hot time in the old town (Santiago) to-night."

The Nation's Tribute

TO ITS VALOROUS DEAD WHO DIED UPON SPANISH TERRITORY DEFENDING ITS FLAG.

GENERAL ORDERS
No. 60

HEADQUARTERS OF THE ARMY,
ADJUTANT GENERAL'S OFFICE,
WASHINGTON, April 3, 1899.

I. The following order of the President is published for the information of all concerned:

EXECUTIVE MANSION, April 3, 1899.

It is fitting that, in behalf of the Nation, tributes of honor be paid to the memories of the noble men who lost their lives in their country's service during the late war with Spain. It is the more fitting inasmuch as, in consonance with the spirit of our free institutions and in obedience to the most exalted promptings of patriotism, those who were sent to other shores to do battle for their country's honor, under their country's flag, went freely from every quarter of our beloved land. Each soldier, each sailor, parting from home ties and putting behind him private interests in the presence of the stern emergency of unsought war with an alien foe, was an individual type of that devotion of the citizen to the State which makes our Nation strong in unity and in action.

Those who died in another land left in many homes the undying memories that attend the heroic dead of all ages. It was fitting that with the advent of peace, won by their sacrifice, their bodies should be gathered with tender care and restored to home and kindred. This has been done with the dead of Cuba and Porto Rico. Those of the Philippines still rest where they fell, watched over by their surviving comrades, and crowned with the love of a grateful Nation.

The remains of many brought to our shores have been delivered to their families for private burial. But for others of the brave officers and men who perished, there has been reserved interment in ground sacred to the soldiers and sailors, amid the tributes of military honor and national mourning they have so well deserved.

Blockhouse at El Caney.

Inside Blockhouse at El Caney.

I therefore order that, upon the arrival of the cortege at the National Cemetery at Arlington, all proper military and naval honors be paid to the dead heroes; that suitable ceremonies shall attend their interment; that the customary salute of mourning be fired at the cemetery; and that on the same day, at 2 o'clock P. M., Thursday, the 6th day of April, the National Ensign be displayed at half staff on all public buildings, forts, camps, and public vessels of the United States; and that at 12 o'clock noon of said day all the departments of the Government at Washington shall be closed.

WILLIAM McKINLEY.

II. The following order from the War Department is published for the information and guidance of all concerned:

WAR DEPARTMENT, WASHINGTON, April 3, 1899.

The remains of officers and soldiers who lost their lives in the war with Spain during the operations in Cuba and Porto Rico will be interred, with due and fitting ceremonies, in the National Cemetery at Arlington, Va., on Thursday, April 6, at 2 P. M. By direction of the President, all of the United States troops serving in the vicinity of Washington, together with the National Guard of the District of Columbia, will be assembled at Arlington on the date in question, to participate in the funeral ceremonies.

G. D. MEIKLEJOHN,
Acting Secretary of War.

BY COMMAND OF MAJOR-GENERAL MILES:

H. C. CORBIN,
Adjutant-General.

CHURCH AT EL CANEY.

ROYAL PALM TREES.

SUGAR REFINERY OF COLONEL ROSSEAU, SPANISH ARMY.

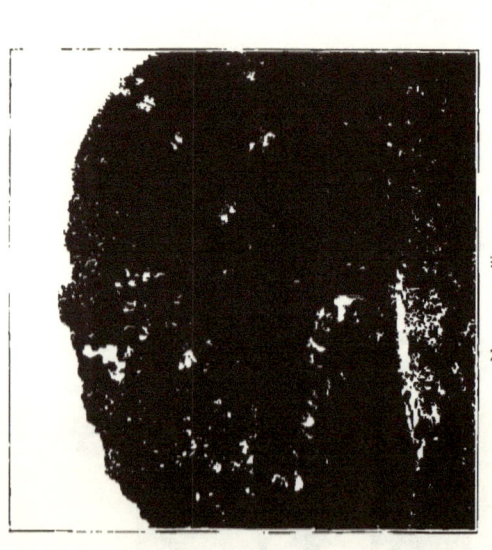

MANGROVE TREE.

Chronological History.

HAPPENINGS OF IMPORTANCE IN THE WAR
BETWEEN THE UNITED STATES AND SPAIN.

FEBRUARY 15 — Battleship Maine, U. S. Navy, destroyed in the harbor of Havana, with 248 of her officers and crew.

FEBRUARY 21 — Naval Court of Inquiry opened in harbor of Havana.

MARCH 5 — Both branches of the military being prepared for service.

MARCH 7 — The Montgomery ordered to Havana.

MARCH 27 — Board of Inquiry declares that the Maine was destroyed by external agencies.

APRIL 11 — President McKinley sends his message to Congress, advising armed intervention in Cuba.

APRIL 13 — House adopts Cuban resolution, directing the President to intervene.

APRIL 14 — Troops ordered to southern ports.

APRIL 20 — President's ultimatum sent to Spain. Spain expected to refuse. Spanish minister given his passports.

APRIL 21 — Minister Woodford given his passports by Spain.

APRIL 22 — North American squadron begins blockade of Cuba. United States gunboat Nashville captures freighter Buena Ventura, the first prize of the war.

APRIL 23 — Blockade of Havana begun. The President makes first call for 125,000 troops.

APRIL 25 — War formally declared by Congress. Asiatic squadron leaves Hong Kong to attack Manila.

APRIL 27 — First fight of the war. Bombardment of the Matanzas forts.

MAY 1 — Dewey's victory. Destroys Admiral Montijo's fleet at Manila. Sinks 11 Spanish ships.

MAY 5 — Sampson leaves for Porto Rico.

MAY 11 — Crusier Wilmington and torpedo-boat Winslow, in an attempt to silence the batteries at Cardenas, are repulsed. Ensign Worth Bagley, of North Carolina, and four seamen, attached to the Winslow, were killed by the bursting of a shell. Senate confirms nomination of Dewey to be a rear-admiral.

MAY 12 — Americans fail to land troops at Cienfuegos.

MAY 13 — North Atlantic squadron bombards San Juan. American troops land near Cabanas, Cuba. Commodore Schley, with flying squadron, sails from Old Point.

MAY 14—Steamer Gussie fails in an attempt to land troops and supplies in Cuba. First land fight.

MAY 17—Cervera's fleet reported off Venezuela.

MAY 19—Cervera's fleet enters harbor of Santiago.

MAY 25—The President calls for 75,000 additional volunteers.

MAY 31—Commodore Schley bombards the forts at the entrance of Santiago harbor.

17TH AND 25TH INFANTRY (COLORED) STORMING BLOCKHOUSE
AT EL CANEY, JULY 1, 1898.

JUNE 3 — Lieutenant Hobson and crew of seven heroes sink collier Merrimac in channel of Santiago harbor to prevent possible escape of Cervera's fleet.

JUNE 4—Cervera sends flag of truce to Admiral Sampson, announcing the safety of Lieutenant Hobson and crew, and complimenting them on their heroism.

JUNE 5—Americans land near Santiago.

JUNE 6—Santiago forts bombarded and Reina Mercedes sunk.

JUNE 7—Haitian cable cut by expedition from Marblehead, Yankee and St. Louis. Cuba now completely isolated.

JUNE 10 — Sampson's squadron bombards Baiquiri, near Santiago.

JUNE 12 — Spanish assault American marines encamped at Guantanamo, but are repulsed. Four men killed. General Shafter's expedition leaves Key West for Santiago.

JUNE 15 — Fight at Guantanamo Bay. 100 Spaniards killed.

JUNE 16 — Santiago bombarded.

JUNE 17 — Second Spanish squadron sails from Cadiz. Supposed destination, the Philippines.

JUNE 20 — Shafter's army appears before Santiago. Spanish troops forced to retire into fortified part of Manila.

JUNE 22 — Shafter's army lands at Baiquiri.

SPANISH TRENCH IN FRONT OF BLOCKHOUSE, EL CANEY.

JUNE 24 — Roosevelt's Rough Riders and First and Tenth United States Cavalry (less than 1,000 all told), after desperate battle with 2,000 Spanish troops, gained position within five miles of Santiago. "La Guasismas."

JUNE 27 — Orders issued for formation of eastern squadron, under command of Commodore Watson, to operate against Spanish coast. Admiral Camara's fleet in Suez Canal.

JULY 1 — United States troops, after an all-day engagement, occupy the outer works at Santiago.

JULY 2 — El Caney and San Juan captured, and 2,000 Spanish prisoners taken.

JULY 3 — Admiral Cervera's fleet destroyed by Schley. Spanish loss, about 300 killed, 1,300 prisoners.

JULY 4—The Ladrone Islands taken. First relief expedition reaches Manila.

JULY 6—Hobson and crew exchanged. German interference in the Philippines prevented by Admiral Dewey. Resolutions annexing Hawaii pass the Senate.

JULY 9—Major-General Miles leaves with reinforcements for Santiago.

JULY 10—Warships begin the bombardment of Santiago.

JULY 11—Armistice agreed on for twenty-four hours at Santiago.

JULY 14—General Toral formally surrenders Santiago.

JULY 17—Santiago occupied by Americans.

JULY 21—General Miles sails for Porto Rico.

JULY 23—Porto Rican expedition to reinforce General Miles leaves Tampa, Florida.

JULY 25—General Merritt arrives at Manila. General Miles' expedition lands on the southern coast of Porto Rico. Guantanamo surrenders to General Shafter.

JULY 26—French Ambassador, on behalf of Spain, asks the United States to name terms of peace.

JULY 30—United States Government's reply to Spanish peace proposals handed to French Ambassador.

AUGUST 3—Spanish troops in Manila attempt a sortie, but are driven back with heavy loss.

AUGUST 5—Secretary Alger orders the immediate return of General Shafter's army to the United States. Troops under General Brooke enter Guayamo. General Miles meets with little or no resistance in Porto Rico.

AUGUST 7—Spanish Cabinet accepts American peace proposals.

AUGUST 8—Spanish prisoners leave Santiago for Spain.

AUGUST 10—President submits a protocol to Spain on which peace can be arranged.

AUGUST 11—Spanish Cabinet accepts the peace protocol, practically ending the war.

AUGUST 12—The peace protocol signed, and President orders a cessation of hostilities, which had then lasted 110 days.

AUGUST 15—Manila surrenders unconditionally to Admiral Dewey, after a bombardment of two hours and a gallant assault by the American troops. News of the peace protocol had not reached Dewey.

AUGUST 17—The President appoints the Military Commissioners for Cuba and Porto Rico, as follows: For Cuba—Maj.-Gen. James F. Wade, Rear-Admiral William T. Sampson, and Maj.-Gen. Matthew C. Butler, U. S. Vols. For Porto Rico—Maj.-Gen. John R. Brooke, Rear-Admiral Winfield S. Schley, and Brig.-Gen. William W. Gordon, U. S. Vols.

AUGUST 30—United States representatives on Peace Commission appointed by the President, as follows: Wm. R. Day, of Ohio, late Secretary of State:

Senator C. K. Davis (Rep.), of Minn.; Senator Wm. P. Frye (Rep.), of Maine; Senator George Gray (Dem.), of Delaware; Hon. Whitelaw Reid, of New York.

OCTOBER 1 — Peace Commissioners meet with five commissioners on behalf of Spain, in Paris.

OCTOBER 18 — American flag raised permanently over Porto Rico.

DECEMBER 10 — Treaty of peace signed by Peace Commissioners of United States and Spain, at Paris.

DISEMBARKING AT JERSEY CITY.

The cost of the war to the United States up to the signing of the peace protocol was $150,000,000.

Casualties in killed and wounded during the war: Army — officers killed, 23; enlisted men killed, 257; total, 280; officers wounded, 113; enlisted men wounded, 1,464; total, 1,577. Navy — 1 officer and 18 enlisted men killed; 67 enlisted men wounded.

No officers or men of the army or navy captured, except the crew of the Merrimac, — 1 officer and 7 enlisted men.

MONUMENT TO JOHN FREDERIC HARTRANFT, Brevet Major-General,

Commander 3d Division 9th Corps, Army of Potomac, at the ceremony of the
unveiling of which, May 12, 1899, the 9th Regt. U. S. V. I.
was accorded the position of honor.

[Erected in Capitol Park, Harrisburg, Pa.]

Points of Information.

Our Pension System.

HE pension system of the United States dates from August 26, 1776, when the Continental Congress, by resolution, " recommended to the several assemblies or legislative bodies" of the states that provision be made for putting on "half pay," or less, those persons of the military or naval forces who lost limbs or became otherwise disabled in service; the amounts so paid to be charged to the United States. We hear nothing now-a days of pensions in connection with the Revolutionary war, and many have gained the impression that the patriots of those days were a supernatural order of men, having no thought or care for pensions. But, as shown above, in less than two months after the Declaration of Independence, the first pension provision was enacted, followed by a long series of subsequent laws relative to the soldiers and sailors, not only of the Revolution, but of the 1812 war, the various Indian wars, the Mexican war, the war of the rebellion, the Spanish war, and of the Regular Army and Navy in time of peace.

Many of our most prominent citizens, as well as many of our bravest leaders of the wars, such as Generals Scott, Grant, Sherman, Sheridan, Admirals Farragut and Porter, etc., are or have been the recipients of pensions, either in the form of pay on the retired list or in the ordinary form. So it is no detraction from one's patriotism to claim and receive what is provided by a grateful country for its defenders. The pension roll is indeed truly termed a roll of honor.

Pension is not a matter of favor or charity; it is a question of *title under the law*, and when title is shown, the pension is due, as a *matter of law*. Congress, acting for the whole people, has made the laws, and the essentials of pension title therein defined are all that need be considered in seeking the benefits of the law.

War of the Rebellion.—Union soldiers and sailors of the war of the rebellion, and their heirs, come under the general law, as hereinafter shown, and also under the *Act of June 27, 1890*, which does not apply to any Spanish war soldier or sailor, his widow or children.

Regular Army and Navy.—Officers and men of the Regular Army and Navy in time of peace, and in the various Indian wars and disturbances, etc., and the heirs of such, come under the general pension law, as hereinafter shown.

Spanish War.—The Act of April 22, 1898, provides : "Section 12. That all officers and enlisted men of the Volunteer Army, and of the Militia of the states when in the service of the United States, shall be in all respects on the same footing as to pay, allowances and *pensions* as that of officers and enlisted men of corresponding grades in the Regular Army." But wholly irrespective of the above provision, the soldiers and sailors of the Spanish war and their heirs come under the general law, which covers all claims arising from disability or death due to service since March 4, 1861.

Who is Entitled to Invalid Pension.

Invalid pension, under the general law, is, by Section 4692, Revised Statutes, conferred on the following classes : "Section 4693. The persons entitled as beneficiaries under the preceding section are as follows : First. Any officer of the army, including regulars, volunteers, and militia, or any officer in the navy or marine corps, or any enlisted man, however employed, in the military or naval service of the United States, or in its marine corps, whether regularly mustered or not, disabled by reason of any wound or injury received, or disease contracted, while in the service of the United States and in the line of duty.

"Second. Any master serving on a gunboat, or any pilot, engineer, sailor, or other person not regularly mustered, serving upon any gunboat or war vessel of the United States, disabled by any wound or injury received, or otherwise incapacitated, while in the line of duty, for procuring his subsistence by manual labor.

*   *   *   *   *   *   *   *   *   *   *   *

"Fourth. Any acting assistant, or contract surgeon, disabled by any wound or injury received or disease contracted in the line of duty while actually performing the duties of assistant surgeon, or acting assistant surgeon, with any military force in the field, or in transitu, or in hospital."

*   *   *   *   *   *   *   *   *   *   *   *

That a man has property affording him a sufficient maintenance, or is able to follow successfully some profession, or to support himself and family at some light employment, does not debar him from the pension to which he is justly entitled under the law. It matters not what his business is, whether it be that of a farmer or physician, a day laborer, mechanic or lawyer ; invalid pensions are granted, nevertheless, having regard only to the person's incapacity for the performance of ordinary manual labor, as compared with a sound, able-bodied man.

What is Pensionable.

There is no particular class of wounds, injuries, or diseases, for which pensions are granted. It depends not so much upon the wound, injury, or disease itself as upon the disabled condition arising therefrom. It may be said that anything in the nature of a wound, injury, or disease which materially incapacitates him for the performance of manual labor entitles him to a pension under the law. The disability arising therefrom may be slight, and yet a rating of not less than $6 per month can be had.

The results of typhoid fever, malarial fever, and the like, are often serious and permanent in character, and many diseases grow out of other diseases or

COMPANY C ON THE ROAD TO CAMP MEADE, PA.

injuries; and whenever, in any case, the primary disease or injury was incurred in service, and in line of duty, the recognized results are pensionable.

Disability at Discharge.

It is not absolutely necessary to the securing of pension that a man be discharged with or on account of disability, nor that a hospital record of the disability exist. Such records are evidence, but not the only evidence. Consequently soldiers or sailors in the war with Spain, who, from carelessness or any other reason, made no claim of disability at discharge, or were not reported by the examining surgeons at discharge as disabled in any way, or whose discharges show there existed no objection to their reënlistment, are not thereby debarred from applying for and obtaining pension, if they are, in fact, affected by any wound, injury, or disease, or their results, incurred in the service and line of duty. The report of the surgeons at muster-out is not necessarily conclusive as to lack of title to pension.

Rates of Invalid Pension.

The rates of invalid pension under the general law are from $6 to $100 per month, according to the degree and character of the disability and the rank of the soldier or sailor at the time of the origin or incurrence of the same. For the ordinary disease, wound or injury there is no particular rating, because the disability may exist in a greater or less degree, and be different in degree in different men, some of whom would consequently be entitled to a higher rate than others. For certain disabilities, which cause substantially the same degree of disability in all men, rates are fixed, and are given in the following tables:

RATES FIXED BY LAW.

Loss of both hands	$100 00	Any disability equivalent to the loss of hand or foot	$24 00
Loss of both feet	72 00	Amputation at or above elbow or knee, or total disability of arm or leg	30 00
Total disability in both hands	72 00		
Total disability in both feet	31 25	Amputation at or near the hip joint	45 00
Loss of sight of both eyes	72 00	Amputation at or near the shoulder joint	45 00
Loss of the sight of an eye, the other lost before enlistment	72 00	Inability to perform any manual labor	30 00
		Disability requiring regular and constant aid and attendance of another person	72 00
Loss of one hand and one foot, or total disability of the same	36 00	Disability requiring frequent and periodical aid and attendance of another person,	40 00
Loss of a hand or a foot, or total disability of the same	30 00	Total deafness	30 00

RATES FIXED BY THE COMMISSIONER FOR CERTAIN DISABILITIES NOT SPECIFIED BY LAW.

Anchylosis of shoulder joint	$12 00	Loss of thumb, index and little fingers	$16 00
Anchylosis of elbow or kneejoint	10 00	Loss of index, middle and ring fingers	16 00
Anchylosis of ankle or wrist	8 00	Loss of middle, ring and little fingers	14 00
Loss of sight of one eye	12 00	Loss of thumb and index finger	12 00
Loss of one eye	17 00	Loss of thumb and metacarpal bone	12 00
Nearly total deafness of one ear	6 00	Loss of thumb and little finger	10 00
Total deafness of one ear	10 00	Loss of index and middle fingers	8 00
Slight deafness of both ears	6 00	Loss of middle and little fingers	8 00
Severe deafness of one ear, slight of other	10 00	Loss of any other two fingers	6 00
Nearly total deafness of one ear, slight of other	15 00	Loss of thumb	8 00
Severe deafness of both ears	22 00	Loss of any finger without complication,	6 00
Total deafness of one ear, slight of other	20 00	Loss of all the toes of one foot	10 00
Total deafness of one ear, severe of other	25 00	Loss of great, second and third toes	8 00
Deafness of both ears, nearly total,	27 00	Loss of great toe and metatarsal	8 00
Loss of palm and fingers of hand, the thumb remaining	17 00	Loss of any other toe and metatarsal	6 00
Loss of thumb, index, middle and ring fingers	17 00	Loss of great and second toes	8 00
		Loss of any toe	6 00
Loss of all the fingers, thumb and palm remaining	16 00	Femoral hernia	10 00
		Double inguinal hernia . . . $8, $12 and	14 00
Loss of thumb, index and middle fingers	16 00	Inguinal hernia . . . $6 and	10 00
		Varicocele	6 00

Widows and Minor Children.

The general pension law as to widows and children is embodied in Section 4702, Revised Statutes, which, as amended by the act of August 7, 1882, provides : "Section 4702. If any person embraced within the provisions of Section 4692 and 4693 has died since the 4th day of March, 1861, or hereafter dies, by reason of any wound, injury or disease which, under the conditions and limitations of such sections, would have entitled him to an invalid pension had he been disabled, his widow, or if there be no widow, or in case of her death without payment to her of any part of the pension hereinafter mentioned, his child, or children, under 16 years of age, shall be entitled to receive the same pension as the husband or father would have been entitled to had he been totally disabled, to commence from the death of the husband or father, to continue to the widow during her widowhood, and to his child or children until they severally attain the age of 16 years, and no longer ; and if the widow remarry, the child or children shall be entitled from the date of remarriage, except when such widow has continued to draw the pension money after her remarriage, in contravention of law, and such child or children have resided with and been supported by her, their pension will commence at the date to which the widow was last paid."

The rate of pension of widows and other heirs under the general law is determined by the rank of the soldier or sailor at the time of incurrence of disability resulting in his death. If below the grade of commissioned officer, the rate is $12 if the parties were married before March 19, 1886, or before or during the service ; 2d lieutenant $15 ; 1st lieutenant $17 ; captain, $20 ; major, $25 ; lieutenant-colonel and officers of higher rank, $30. Heirs of officers and men in the naval service of corresponding rank have similar ratings.

Section 4703, Revised Statutes, provides for the increase of widow's pension at the rate of $2 *additional* per month for each child of the soldier under 16. Children's pension has the benefit of the same additional rate in all cases.

Dependent Parents, Brothers and Sisters.

The general pension law as to heirs other than widows and children is embodied in Section 4707, Revised Statutes, which provides : "Section 4707. If any person embraced within the provisions of Sections 4692 and 4693 has died since the 4th day of March, 1861, or shall hereafter die, by reason of any wound, injury, casualty or disease, which, under the conditions and limitations of such sections, would have entitled him to invalid pension, and has not left or shall not leave a widow or legitimate child, but has left or shall leave other relative or relatives who were dependent upon him for support in whole or in part at the date of his death, such relative or relatives shall be entitled, in the following order of precedence, to receive the same pension as such person would have been entitled to had he been totally disabled, to commence from the death of such person, namely : First, the mother ; secondly, the father ; thirdly, orphan brothers and sisters under 16 years of age, who shall be pensioned jointly ; *Provided*, That where orphan children of the same parent have different guardians, or a portion of them only are under guardianship, the share of the joint pension to which each ward shall be entitled shall be paid to the guardian of such ward : *Provided,* That if in any case said person shall have left father and mother who are dependent upon him, then, on the death of the mother, the father shall become entitled to the pension, commencing from and after the death of the mother; and upon the death of the mother and father, or upon the death of the father and the remarriage of the mother, the dependent brothers and sisters under 16 years of age shall jointly become entitled to such pension until they attain the age of 16 years, respectively, commencing from the death or remarriage of the party who had the prior right to the pension: *Provided,* That a mother shall be assumed to have been dependent upon her son within the meaning of this section if, at the date of his death, she had no other adequate means of support than the ordinary proceeds of her own manual labor and the contributions of said son or of any other person not legally bound to aid her in support : and if, by actual contributions, or in any other way, the son had recognized his obligations to aid in the support of his mother, or was by law bound to such support, and that a father or a minor brother or sister shall, in like manner and under like conditions, be assumed to have been dependent except that the income which was derived or derivable from his actual or possible manual labor shall be taken into account in estimating

EFFECT OF BULLETS ON PALM TREE NEAR SAN JUAN.

a father's means of independent support: *Provided,* further, That the pension allowed to any person on account of his or her dependence, as hereinbefore provided, shall not be paid for any period during which it shall not be necessary as a means of adequate subsistence."

The act of June 27, 1890, Section 1, amends the law as to *dependent parents*, making it necessary to show only *present dependence*. The act provides: "Section 1. That in considering the pension claims of dependent parents, the fact of the soldier's death by reason of any wound, injury, casualty, or disease which, under the conditions and limitations of existing laws, would have entitled him to an invalid pension, and the fact that the soldier left no widow or minor children having been shown as required by law, it shall be necessary only to show by competent and sufficient evidence that such parent or parents are without other present means of support than their own manual labor or the contributions of others not legally bound for their support; *Provided*, That all pensions allowed to dependent parents under this act shall commence from the date of the filing of the application hereunder, and shall continue no longer than the existence of the dependence."

The rate of pension of dependent parents, brothers and sisters, under the general law, is the same as that of widows and children, without the $2 additional rate. If parents' claims be made under the act of June 27, 1890, Section 1, the rate is uniformly $12 per month, irrespective of the rank of the soldier or sailor.

Date of marriage is of no consideration in this class of cases.

Commencement of Pension.

Invalid pension and dependent parents', brothers' and sisters' pension commence from the date of filing of formal application therefor in the Pension Bureau at Washington.

Widows' and Minor Children's pension, under the general law, commences from the date of the soldier's or sailor's death, or, in case of children, if the widow was pensioned, from the date of her death or remarriage; children's pension terminates when they become 16. A widow may, after remarriage, claim pension, under the general law, for the period of her widowhood, and children may claim pension, under the general law, for the period of pensionable minority after they become 16.

Procedure to Secure Pension.

An application in proper legal form must be made in every instance. After the filing of an application for Invalid Pension, the claimant is ordered for examination before a Board of U. S. Pension Examining Surgeons, composed of civilian physicians, and which determines the existence of and recommends the rate for the alleged disabilities. Evidence submitted by the claimant is also admissible to show the character and degree of disability. Widows and other heirs are required to prove themselves the legal heirs of the soldier or sailor, in addition to showing his death to be due to the service and line of duty; and in cases of fathers, mothers, brothers and sisters, the financial circumstances of the claimants must be shown.

Early Settlement.

A special division has been formed in the Pension Bureau for the consideration and adjudication of Spanish war pension claims. It is generally believed that the delay so often encountered in claims arising from the war of the rebellion, largely due to difficulties in the securing and verifying of the mass of evidence usually required in such cases because of the lapse of time since the war, will not generally arise in the settlement of Spanish war cases.

Delay in Claiming.

Persons who are entitled to pension should, out of regard for their own interests and the interests of their families, present and prospective, promptly file their claims. Many survivors of the war of the rebellion, and their heirs, who delayed their applications for pension, have had cause to regret that they slept upon their rights. Delay begets difficulty and sometimes impossibility of securing the necessary proofs, and creates the doubt attaching to all claims long resting unasserted on an existing right. Especially is this true where the soldier or sailor was entitled but neglected to apply in his lifetime, and his heirs, being entitled, seek to obtain the pension due them on account of his death.

What is a Pension Worth?

Failure to apply for pension may arise from inattention to what a pension is worth. Its value may be learned by comparison with the cost of an annuity from a life insurance company. Pensions begin at date of application therefor, and ordinarily continue during life. The average value of each pension now being paid under the general law—which is the law applying to Spanish war soldiers—is nearly $14 per month; or exactly $163.21 per year (report of the Commissioner of Pensions, for fiscal year ending June 30, 1898). Taking twenty-one years as an average age of Spanish war soldiers, a man of that age, to buy a pension (annuity) of that amount per year for the rest of his life, would have to pay, according to the standard rates of life insurance companies, the sum of $3,270.73. Therefore, the average pension of an ex-soldier of twenty-one years of age is worth, in cash, $3,270.73. That is what it would cost him if he should buy it. On the same basis, a pension of $8 per month is worth $1,823.84; $12 per month, $2,884.76, and other rates in proportion. Of course, the above figures are based on insurable persons, but they give an idea to even those whose lives may be shortened through the hardships of service. Soldiers who are entitled to pension but neglect to claim it do not, perhaps, realize what they are losing.

Attorneys.

The need for persons who make a specialty of securing to claimants their just dues under the pension laws is as great as is the necessity for persons who make a specialty of securing justice in the courts. Some claimants succeed as their own attorneys; many more believe that they can, but it is believed that all will find it to their advantage to secure the services of a competent attorney when entering into the perplexities which are often attendant upon the prosecution of a claim against the Government, and which require experience to overcome.

There are competent attorneys and incompetent attorneys. The law governing attorneys' fee in pension cases makes no distinction between the two classes; so that the services of the one cost no more than the services of the other.

Fees in Pension Cases.

The fee generally in claims for invalid, widows', children's, parents', brothers' and sisters' pension, under the general law, is $25, the maximum limit prescribed by the fee law, act of July 4, 1884. In parents' and other pension claims under the act of June 27, 1890, the fee is $10, the maximum amount allowed in such cases.

As these fees are by law made *wholly dependent on success*, no matter how long delayed a favorable settlement may be, and as no fee may be lawfully claimed or accepted in unsuccessful claims, and in especially difficult claims *no extra fee* may be lawfully claimed or accepted, no attorney adhering to the fee law can afford to accept claims at less than the maximum fees.

Under an order of the Commissioner of Pensions, an attorney may receive not exceeding *50 cents* in any one case to cover the correspondence expense therein, aside from his fee and independent of the success of the claim.

Points of Information for Your Attorney.

Give the following information;

1. Your full name, and the company and regiment, or ship, in which you served, giving dates of enlistment, place and date of first illness and discharge, and cause of discharge.

2. The name or nature of all disabilities (wounds, injuries or diseases) incurred in the service and line of duty, from which your physical ability for performing the work of a sound, able-bodied man at manual labor is materially impaired.

3. State *when* and *where* and *how* each disability was incurred or contracted.

4. The name and location of each hospital in which you were treated.

5. The name or nature of the disabilities (wounds, injuries or diseases) found to exist by the surgeon who examined you at the time of your muster-out. *Give your full post office address.*

The First Afro-American Volunteers.

THE following letters to and from Lieutenant P. L. Carmouché are of great interest, and we reproduce them in the order they were written, in order to demonstrate the loyalty and patriotism of the men of Ascension Parish, Louisiana:

DONALDSONVILLE, LA., February 26, 1898.

HON. R. A. ALGER, ESQ.,
Secretary of War, Washington, D. C.

Dear Sir: After carefully considering the situation of these United States, and a possibility of a declaration of war between the United States and Spain, I deem it advisable to offer my services and those of 250 colored Americans, on short notice, in the defence of our country, at home or abroad.

Yours loyally,

P. L. CARMOUCHÉ

—

DONALDSONVILLE, LA., February 28, 1898.

M. J. FOSTER, ESQ., Governor of Louisiana.

Hon. Sir: After carefully considering the situation of these United States, and a possibility of a declaration of war between the United States and Spain, I deem it advisable to offer my services and those of 250 colored Louisianians, of Ascension Parish, on short notice, in defence of our country, at home or abroad.

Yours loyally,

P. L. CARMOUCHÉ.

— —

DONALDSONVILLE, LA., March 11, 1898.

HON. MURPHY J. FOSTER, Governor, State of Louisiana.

Hon. Sir: The position assumed by the United States on the Cuban question caused me, as a loyal son of Louisiana, on the 28th of February, to tender to the honorable Governor of our state, my services and those of 250 colored Louisianians. Failing to receive an answer, I am at a loss to know whether my letter reached you. Trusting to hear from you soon, I am,

Loyally yours,

P. L. CARMOUCHÉ.

- -

DONALDSONVILLE, LA., March 17, 1898.

HON. R. A. ALGER,
Secretary of War, Washington, D. C.

Hon. Sir: After carefully considering the position assumed by the United States on the Cuban question and the horrors of the battleship Maine, I, as a loyal son of these United States, on the 26th of February, tendered to the Secretary of War, the Hon. R. A. Alger, my services and those of 250 colored Americans from the State of Louisiana, Parish of Ascension, on short notice, in defence of our country, at home or abroad. Failing to hear from you, I am at a loss to know if my letter reached you. Trusting to hear from you soon, I am,

Loyally yours,   P. L. CARMOUCHE.

DONALDSONVILLE, LA., April 21, 1898.

HON. WILLIAM McKINLEY,
President of the United States, Washington, D. C.

Carefully considering the situation of the United States, and the advantage claimed for the colored troops to invade Cuba, caused me to offer to the President my services and those of 250 colored men from Ascension Parish.

Have written two letters to Hon. Alger on the situation, one dated February 26, and the other March 18. Failing to hear from him, I deem it advisable to write to you.

Permit me to congratulate you upon your judgment on the present question.   Yours truly,

P. L. CARMOUCHE.

EXECUTIVE MANSION, WASHINGTON, D. C., April 25, 1898.

MR. P. L. CARMOUCHE, Donaldsonville, La.

Dear Sir: I beg leave to acknowledge the receipt of your letter of the 21st instant, addressed to the President, tendering the services of yourself and 250 colored men, and to inform you that what you say in this connection has been noted.

By the President's direction, your communication has been forwarded to the Secretary of War for consideration and further reply.

Very truly yours,

JOHN ADDISON PORTER,
Secretary to the President.

DONALDSONVILLE, LA., May 16, 1898.

EDITOR *Picayune:*

Your article, "Immune Troops for the Tropics," in yesterday's *Picayune* has been read in these parts with much surprise. The colored patriots around here have been so anxious to get into the military service of the United States that, even without any kind of encouragement from the authorities, they have enlisted enough men for two companies from this parish alone. Neither the hot sun, dangerous contagious diseases of the tropics, nor the terrible and deadly bullets of the Spaniards, have been of any dread. They are as willing to make sacrifices for the honor of the American flag as any of the favored volunteers who have already been accepted. But "Sambo" is not permitted to take up his place in the front rank of those who are patriotic. He must wait, and he is waiting, anxiously waiting, to be bidden to step up and take his post of duty. There will never be any need to have draft made on them around here: they are volunteers. Please use the influence of the venerable *Picayune* to get the authorities to permit the colored patriots to serve the country in the war.

Very respectfully,   P. L. CARMOUCHE.

Words of Praise.

SINCE the publication of the first edition of the History of the Ninth Regiment U. S. V. I., the author has received many kind words and encouragement for his work. Below will be found a few of the many letters he has received:

WAR DEPARTMENT, WASHINGTON, D. C., June 26, 1899.

W. HILARY COSTON, B.D., Springfield, Ohio.

My Dear Sir: I find on my desk, upon returning to Washington today, the copy of the souvenir of the Ninth United States Volunteer Infantry, entitled "The Spanish-American War Volunteer," for which I desire to thank you. I shall endeavor to find time to look through its interesting pages.

Very truly yours,

R. A. ALGER.

_____

FINDLAY, OHIO, July 4, 1899.

REV. W. H. COSTON, Springfield, Ohio.

My Dear Sir: I have to thank you very much for your very neat and excellent book, sent me recently. I had lost sight of you for some time, and I did not know what had become of you. Let me hear something from you with regard to yourself.

With kind regards,

Yours, etc.,

H. P. CROUSE.

SPRINGFIELD, OHIO, July 17, 1899.

REV. W. H. COSTON,
      Chaplain Ninth U. S. V. I. Regt.

My Dear Brother: With great pleasure I have several times perused the pages of your most interesting work, "The Spanish-American War Volunteer," which you were so kind as to present me. The artistic work is of a high order, while the brief biographies will be of inestimable value to those who in future years desire to read the records of those who freely offered their services to our country in her hour of need. The views of scenes and places and incidents in that sunny island will be exceedingly entertaining to the youth, helping them to a better understanding of the country and its customs. You will please accept my thanks for the same, and at the same time my best wishes for your future success and prosperity in the work the Great Captain of souls has called you to engage in. With great respect, believe me,

Yours most respectfully,

V. F. BROWN,
Pastor Central Methodist Episcopal Church.

(220

SPRINGFIELD, Ohio, July 18, 1899.

"The Spanish-American War Volunteer," by Rev. W. Hilary Coston, B.D., Chaplain Ninth U. S. V. I, is a work of real merit. It is a model of the printer's art, and full of useful information, not only concerning the Ninth Regiment, but Cuba also. The Chaplain is a writer of high order, and by this book has given us a valuable contribution to the military history of our country. I am glad to add my help in any way to further the splendid progress being made by our Afro-American citizens in pushing along our American civilization. With love and regards I am,

Faithfully yours,

ALEXANDER C. McCABE,

Rector Christ's Protestant Episcopal Church.

LAW OFFICES OF DICK, DOYLE & BRYAN,

WASHINGTON, D. C., June 26, 1899.

REV. W. H. COSTON, Springfield, Ohio.

Dear Sir: I am in receipt of your card and souvenir volume of the Ninth U. S. V. I. The work is very tastefully prepared, and reflects great credit upon you and the organization to which you have the credit of belonging. I will take great pleasure in perusing the same carefully at my first opportunity. Thanking you for the courtesy of your remembrance of me, I remain,

Very truly yours,

CHAS. S. DICK.

WASHINGTON, D. C., May 10, 1899.

W. H. COSTON.

Reverend Sir: Your valuable service in the Ninth U. S. V. I. will never be forgotten.

Yours truly,

P. L. CARMOUCHE, Donaldsonville, La.

June 23, 1899.

REV. W. H. COSTON, Springfield, Ohio.

My Dear Sir: I thank you for the handsome little volume which you sent me a few days ago. With best wishes for you,

Very respectfully,

SETH W. BROWN.

COMMONWEALTH OF MASSACHUSETTS, EXECUTIVE DEPARTMENT,

BOSTON, July 26, 1899.

REV. W. H. COSTON, Springfield, Ohio.

My Dear Sir: I beg to acknowledge receipt of your letter of July 24th, and to say in reply that during the recent war, one of our Massachusetts regiments which saw active service in Porto Rico, namely, the 6th Massachusetts Infantry, contained, as it has done for many years, a colored company, commanded by colored officers. This company has always maintained a very high reputation for efficiency and good discipline, and ranking with the very best companies in our state militia. Its service during the war was fully worthy of its past reputation.

Very truly yours,

ROGER WOLCOTT.

———   .

HARRISBURG PA., July 25, 1899.

MR. W. H. COSTON.

Dear Sir: In reply to your favor of the 24th inst., would say the conduct of your regiment was very creditable.

Respectfully yours,

JOHN A. FRITCHEY, Mayor.

[The regiment had no provost guard at Camp Meade, and there was not a single member arrested by the civil authorities of either Middletown, Steelton or Harrisburg.— CHAPLAIN.]

— —

STATE OF OHIO, EXECUTIVE DEPARTMENT,
OFFICE OF THE GOVERNOR, COLUMBUS, July 29, 1899.

W. H. COSTON, CAPT., LATE CHAPLAIN, ETC.,
297 West Euclid Avenue, Springfield, Ohio.

Dear Sir: In reply to your favor of July 24th, which I found at the office awaiting my return, I beg leave to say that in my opinion the Ninth Ohio Volunteer Infantry in the Spanish-American War was the peer of any organization in the service. I know that officers and men conducted themselves well, and that their record was a splendid one in every particular.

Very truly yours,

ASA S. BUSHNELL, Governor.

INDEX.

ILLUSTRATIONS.

Illustrations.

www.ingramcontent.com/pod-product-compliance
Lightning Source LLC
Chambersburg PA
CBHW030127030726
47498CB00007B/2586